URBAN
FLIGHT

URBAN FLIGHT

A NOVEL

Jonathan Kirshner

2022
LEWIS COURT PRESS

ISBN 979-8-9854785-0-1

Published by
Lewis Court Press

For my family—past, present, and future

URBAN FLIGHT

ASON SIMS WOKE UP and stared at Richard Nixon. Nixon didn't look back—he was gazing off to the right, lost in his own thoughts. There was something about that cover of *Rolling Stone* that seemed to understand everything, and Jason had it framed and nailed it to the wall. The lighting, subtly uneven, revealed more lines on the right side of his face, but Nixon betrayed no emotion—and didn't even see what they were calling him: "The Quitter." After all those years taking shots at the president, the headline had a hint of bittersweetness—more sad than taunting, like they were pissed he threw in the towel just when they were going to knock him out. The subhead, "Our memories of a broken ruler," even suggested a touch of nostalgia.

It was 4:59. Jason always woke up before the alarm went off. He gave up on Nixon and stared at the ceiling, then looked around, stretching his neck. There wasn't much in the room, but somehow he managed to keep it a mess. The walls were bare, except for Nixon and another framed poster on the opposite wall, faded with age, that said: SUPPORT YOUR LOCAL PRINTER'S UNION. At five the clock radio came on, playing that staccato music every news station played, though each in its own way, kind of like how for a couple of years every band sounded like the Beatles.

"This is Ten-Ten W-I-N-S New York. You give us twenty-two minutes, we'll give you the world. The Traffic Commissioner is out, the Mets drop a pair, and the president says No. It's five A.M.

this Tuesday, September fourth, nineteen seventy-five—fifty-two degrees and cloudy, heading up to sixty-five this afternoon. In our top story, reports out of Washington that President Ford has closed the door on aid to New York City; economists predict that the Big Apple will declare bankruptcy by year's end. One man who won't draw a city paycheck either way is Traffic Commissioner Donald Sorley, fired yesterday by Mayor Cohen after surveys showed rush hour toll delays now exceed fifty minutes. A defiant Sorley told reporters that he was the fall guy for the Mayor's ill-advised expansion of road maintenance—"

Jason flicked off the radio. Why did they have the news every day? The city's broke, the Mets suck, and the Mayor fired someone because of the traffic. We knew that yesterday, and the day before. Next you'd get murder-fire-weather, or fire-murder-weather, if it was a really good fire.

Jason sat up in bed and pulled on a pair of jeans. He made his way to the dining area—a table off the living room—and fixed himself a bowl of Cap'n Crunch. The living room was as modestly and haphazardly appointed as the bedroom, but strewn with considerably more stuff: records, guitars, abandoned shirts, a smattering of books, stacks of reel-to-reel tapes. Jason read while he ate, a few pages of the new Muddy Waters biography. Five pages a day over breakfast, but he was making progress. Muddy had already left the plantation and was traveling to Chicago, and in just twenty more pages he would invent the Urban Blues.

It was cloudy out but not so dark that you had to turn the light on to read, and four pages later Jason reached into the box for a handful of cereal, put the book down, and walked over to the window. Opening it, he arranged the pieces in a small pile on the fire escape and stuck his head out to look down the alley. The City was already starting to come to life, and while Jason waited he could hear a police siren in the distance.

Finally a small gray squirrel appeared. Urban wildlife, they survived because they could adapt to anything. Leaping from the bending branch of a tree and landing expertly on the telephone lines just below, Oscar—he looked like an Oscar to Jason—scurried across them and jumped onto the fire escape. He sat up at the other end, near the stairs, and looked at Jason. Jason went back inside and closed the window as Oscar cautiously approached his breakfast. They had a pretty good relationship, but they also respected each other's space.

Jason left his apartment and headed down an open staircase. Five floors, but the elevator was pretty old, and at this time of the morning the milkman would sometimes prop the door open with his cart anyway. Outside there were already more than a handful of people on the street. A few were climbing onto a bus, which had a large airline advertisement on the side, FLY AWAY WITH BOB AND CAROL AND TED AND ALICE. Staring at the picture of a couple running on the beach, with a plane in the background over the ocean, Jason thought it was a good place for that ad, which disappeared behind a plume of black smoke every time the bus dragged itself away from a stop.

Next to the subway a short man in his sixties was setting up one of those small metallic booths that sold newspapers and magazines. He had a face that looked like it had seen some pretty tough times, and he wore a wedding ring, which Jason found reassuring. He didn't know the man's name and they never exchanged a word, but Jason saw him every day and was one of the only people who knew for sure that the guy had legs. Most people never saw him outside the booth, which was about six feet by three. But when the papers came in the morning he had to cut open the bundles and stack them in place. Then he'd go back inside, and watch the world pass by, a quarter at a time.

Jason liked the subway. Sure, it was gray and dirty, and the walls were covered with graffiti, and maybe it even smelled a little. But it felt good. When he was a kid his father worked in Manhattan, and sometimes on the weekend he would take Jason to the print shop, and they would take the train. Unless you've been there, you can't imagine how cool riding the subway to work is when you're eight years old.

"Never talk to anybody on the subway," his father told him once. "You can watch, but there's this space between you and everyone else. Like that guy in *Rear Window*. He watched his neighbors like a hawk, but there was this big courtyard between him and them. On the subway, every two inches is a courtyard."

Jason looked around. There were about a dozen people on the platform, also standing alone. He peered down the tracks to see if a train was coming, then up at the clock—5:25. A big sign over the clock read TO MANHATTAN AND BRONX, like anyone was going to the Bronx. A man with a loosened tie was reading the *New York Daily News*, and the sports headline DISMAL METS DROP DUO stared Jason in the face. The guy looked tired, and single, like he worked nights and was heading home to sleep. This time of day, everybody had a different story to tell. You needed a specific reason to be on the train at five in the morning. Even two o'clock made more sense. Rush hour had no stories to tell; it was just one big song played in a million keys.

Jason looked back down the track; two train headlights were visible in the distance. Turning again, he caught sight of a homeless man sleeping on a bench, then looked back to the guy reading the paper, who flipped it over, revealing the front page headline, FORD TO CITY: DROP DEAD. About ten feet away, sitting on the steps, a woman was working hard not to make eye contact with anyone. She had on just a little too much makeup and not quite enough clothing, and every now and then she rotated her ankles. Maybe an off-duty hooker, he thought, but it didn't seem like the right neighborhood. The rich and the poor, they went in for hookers. It wasn't really a working-class vice. There were probably more bookies than hookers in Queens, but she wasn't a bookie.

Jason gave up on the inbound crowd and looked across the tracks. An attractive woman, probably in her mid-twenties, was peering down the tunnel, waiting for a train going in the opposite direction. Smiling—Jason thought for a split second at him— she engaged in a lighthearted conversation with another person who was obscured by a pillar. Jason could hear the sound of her voice, but not what she was saying, and he drifted towards the edge of the platform, straining slightly to hear. She stepped forward as well, but only to embrace her companion, as Jason's "F" train rushed past suddenly and loudly, bringing him back to the moment.

Five stops, four blocks, and one elevator ride later Jason pushed through the large translucent doors marked WNYS-TV6, a television station newsroom. Making his way through a maze of cubicles already buzzing with activity, he approached a door marked SPOTLIGHT WITH ADAM SHAKER. Adam was the same age as Jason, thirty, and also had longish hair, but was more neatly dressed, a habit he had picked up only in the past couple of years. The office was cluttered with large stacks of paper taking up every available space: the sofa, the tables, the floor. The walls were decorated with framed album posters, 'sixties memorabilia, and a publicity still of a younger Adam, sporting a goofy handlebar moustache and much shaggier hair, standing next to his book, *This Machine Kills Fascists: Rock and Roll in the Age of Revolt*.

"Hey," Jason said, entering. It was their standard salutation.

Adam, dictating into a tape machine, didn't look up.

"…confused and nihilistic, the man whose anthems helped bring down a president is staggering through the mid-nineteen-seventies with no direction home in this—"

"Who's the victim?" Jason asked.

Adam waved him off and continued without breaking his concentration, "—his second drug-addled album in twelve months." Adam turned off the tape machine and looked up at Jason. "Neil Young. Shouldn't you be up in the air?" He asked, making a twirling gesture with his index finger.

"Not for eight minutes. Neil Young? Didn't you write in the *Village Voice* that *On the Beach* was, if I remember correctly, a 'brooding, post-apocalyptic masterpiece'?"

"It is," Adam said casually. He turned the machine back on. "Jackie, put this on cue cards for Thursday."

"Isn't that, you know, totally inconsistent?"

Adam started rummaging through his desk, opening drawers and sifting through papers, dividing his attention between the search and the conversation. The desk was winning.

"People who watch TV don't read the *Voice*," Adam explained without looking up, as if he were reciting a rule that Jason should have already committed to memory. "And people who read the *Voice* don't own TVs."

"You have a TV."

"Trust me, Jason, the schmucks who watch the local news show don't want to hear *On the Beach*."

"How do you live with yourself?"

"Look, I don't know how many times you want to have this conversation. We're not kids anymore. Things are complicated. I'm like a lawyer—"

"Sure sound like one," Jason interjected.

"I'd like to do legal aid work, but I can't live on what they'd pay me."

"Depends on what you call living."

"So I have this corporate job, see, and that pays the rent. If the suits are happy, I'm happy, everybody's happy. And the suits don't want to deal with—"

Harry Ross suddenly burst into the room, waving a photo.

"Shaker, are you responsible for this piece of crap I found on my car this morning?" He wasn't exactly shouting, but it was a much louder tone of voice than you would hear in normal conversation.

Harry was about fifty, and the news producer at the station. He didn't much like *The Mary Tyler Moore Show*, because he knew that people said he was like the Lou Grant character. Which wasn't really fair. Sure, Harry and Lou both fought in the big one, got their start in print journalism, and had that tough on the outside–loyal on the inside thing going, but Harry was different. First of all, he was thinner. More importantly, he wasn't in a TV comedy. Not that TV comedies weren't realistic, but they only show those bits of life that happen to be funny.

Adam barely looked up from his desk, trying to play it cool, but in truth he was quite pleased with himself.

"Your secretary won't let me in your office," he deadpanned.

Jason gestured at Harry. "This one of the happy suits?"

Harry turned, noticing Jason. "Shouldn't you be up in the air?"

"Not for six minutes." Jason turned back to Adam. "Lot of suits in that picture."

There were—about five. One of them looked like the Mayor. Probably was the Mayor, but the picture was a little fuzzy, washed out, and off-center. Whoever he was, he was having drinks with four other guys that Jason didn't recognize, though one of them might have looked familiar. Jason wondered if Adam bought the picture from some other nut, or whether he was actually spending his free time hiding in dumpsters, stalking the Mayor.

"Why can't you cut me some slack on this story?" Adam asked Harry, now with an edge in his voice.

"Because there is no story," Harry responded, enunciating the final three words with authority.

"No story? The Mayor and the Brooklyn Borough President are consorting with known criminals. Give me one good reason why that isn't—"

"I'll give you five good reasons," Harry interrupted, with the tone of a journalism professor handing back a failing paper, covered in red ink. "First, Mayor Cohen is allowed to eat dinner wherever he wants. Second, if the Mayor didn't socialize with a few white-collar criminals—"

"White-collar criminals!" Adam threw his hands up in protest.

"He'd be eating alone for the rest of his life. Third, this is TV news, and your non-story has no footage."

"Give me a camera and I'll get you the footage!"

"Fourth—"

Lou Bettleheim, who directed the show, stuck his head in the office. He wore a headset around his neck, and, as always, his hair was a little wild from the way he pulled the set on and off over the course of the day.

"Harry, what's the sequence?" he asked.

"Open with Ford, then go straight to traffic." Harry turned and stared at Jason. "That's what everyone in New York wants to know about."

"All right, all right," Jason said, leaving the room. As he walked down the hall he could still hear Harry rattling off the items on his list.

"Fourth, I don't fucking pay you to cover city politics!"

2

JASON WENT UP TO the roof. WNYS-TV owned the whole building, or at least Jeb Morgan did, and he wanted a helipad on the roof. Morgan was a self-made man and didn't like to be told what to do, so when he bought the station he re-did the roof. "An investment in autonomy," he had explained to Jason when he hired him a few years back. It was the first and only time Jason had seen Morgan in person.

Jason walked toward a small booth. Rising from a chair to greet him was Sammy, a black man with one of those faces that didn't easily betray his age. Jason figured he had to be at least fifty, but couldn't possibly be sixty. He wore a New York Mets cap, ear protectors around his neck, and carried a clipboard. Sammy wore the Mets cap a lot. Jason tried to figure it out once, convinced that there was a specific rhythm to it. It was either on days after they played, or only after they lost. But there was definitely a pattern.

Sammy's was always the first smile of the day Jason saw. Sammy had two smiles, and Jason usually got the good one. It was warm and sincere and reassuring, and it wasn't for everyone.

"Hey, Jay, how you doing this morning?"

"Pretty good, Sammy. Better than your Mets, that's for sure."

"You lose a few, makes the wins that much better."

"How would you know?"

Sammy smiled knowingly. "Listen to you—I bet you watched both games, that's what's got you."

Sammy and Jason walked toward the helicopter, which was already warming up, the rotors moving around just fast enough to keep going.

"I know you didn't have a gig last night."

"No. Tonight."

"Did I ever tell you what Mr. John Hurt told me about baseball?"

Jason stopped walking, and stared at Sammy. Sammy had seen a lot of things in his life, but he didn't talk about them in any regular sort of way. They just kind of popped up in conversation, like a five-dollar bill in an old coat pocket, and you got used to it. When Harry was handing out cigars after his grandson was born, Sammy said, "That reminds me of the time I worked as a cook on President Truman's train. Winston Churchill once came back to the kitchen and gave us all cigars." Apparently that was a cigar story, following connections that must have made perfect sense to Sammy.

But Mississippi John Hurt, this was news. Everybody sings the blues different, but nobody played the blues quite like John Hurt. He played slow, and gentle, and peaceful, but it was still the blues. It dripped with the blues. You'd think Sammy would have mentioned this before.

"Mississippi John Hurt?" Jason asked, with just enough in his voice to let Sammy know that he could take it back if he wanted to.

"Now you know that's where I'm from."

"I saw him at Newport in 'sixty-five."

"Should have seen him in Avalon in 'thirty-two."

Jason thought about what that meant, to have seen one of the great old bluesmen before he was "great," and before he was old, on some dark night in an obscure Mississippi town, with Herbert Hoover in the White House during the depths of the Great Depression. They started walking again.

"He said to me 'Son…' I was just a boy you know, he said, 'Son, you know why baseball's like nothing else?'" Sammy stopped talking and looked over at Jason.

"No clock?" Jason offered.

Sammy just stared back at him, but his eyes were smiling.

"The defense holds the ball?"

Now Sammy was smiling broadly. Jason grew increasingly desperate.

"The open field?"

"The space between the pitches."

"Between the pitches?"

"You know, after the last pitch, but before the next one."

Jason climbed into the pilot's seat of helicopter. He looked back at Sammy, asking to be put out of his misery.

"You got the whole world in front of you. What's the count? What's he gonna throw? What'd he throw last time? Who's on deck? You watch a baseball game, that's how you're spending your time. Between the pitches. Like floating on air. Two hundred times a game…anything can happen. Four hundred times in a double header. Only lost twice."

Jason stared outward and didn't say anything, and Sammy had to nudge him a bit with the clipboard. Jason took it, and regained his focus. He noted the gauges on the instrument panel, checked a few boxes on the chart attached to the clipboard, and then signed at the bottom and handed it back to Sammy. Jason then brought the idling helicopter to life, and the initial moan of the engine was slowly drowned out by the sound of the rotors.

As Sammy stepped back, Jason called out, "You taking good care of this tired old lady?"

"She's doing fine," Sammy shouted back. "'Bout the only way to get around the City today!"

"See you on the other side!"

Sammy stepped farther back, put his ear protectors on, and then pulled the stays away from the helicopter. Only now that the copter was ready to go did Dave Edwards emerge from the door of the roof. He came trotting over to the passenger side of the helicopter. Handsome and in his late twenties, he was the station's youngest on-air employee. He wore a suit and his tie blew from the wind of the rotors, but every hair was in place as he sat down next to Jason and put his seat belt on. He got right down to business.

"Let's take a sweep first: downtown, then up the East River, take a look at Connecticut, then over to Jersey."

"You got it."

Jason looked over to Sammy, who shook his raised fist, which was their "okay" sign. Sammy didn't cut an imposing figure, but it was hard not to be reminded of the raised fist salute from the 1968 Olympics in Mexico City. Sammy must have known this, though they had never even come close to having a political discussion. Which was just fine with Jason. He smiled, shook his fist back, and lifted off.

New York looked its best early in the morning, when Jason and Dave previewed the day's locations to plan the timing of their reports. From the height of the helicopter the City's scars faded into the background, and the skyscrapers stood together with the majesty of an old black-and-white photograph. Ribbons of concrete seemed to lead perfectly from the boroughs into the City, and the bridges, more than twenty and no two alike, stretched sinuously across the rivers.

Jason headed downtown, planning to use the Verrazano Narrows Bridge as a starting point, before hooking around and up the East River, where they would catch the Brooklyn, Manhattan, and Williamsburg Bridges in quick succession. The Statue of Liberty kept watch over the Verrazano, and Jason liked to check in with her before heading back uptown. She was pushing a hundred, and the rust on her face looked like teardrops.

Jason and Dave didn't have a lot to talk about. Dave didn't know much about music and Jason had never gotten a manicure in his life. But it was hard not to talk at all for four hours.

"When do they want the first one?" Jason asked.

"Seven-oh-seven."

"Closer to the top every day. Gonna make you a star."

"I'm going to ride this traffic right to the anchor's desk. This business is just like any other. The thing is you gotta know what story is going. Traffic isn't traffic. It's what it means to—"

"What's that?" Jason interrupted, or would have interrupted, had he been listening.

"Where?"

Jason changed the helicopter's direction sharply, and pointed at the road below. "There—on the BQE. Some maniac. He's going to end up wrapped around a pole."

Jason gestured at a large black four-door car driving wildly down a relatively empty highway. It was going fast and jerking suddenly across lanes.

"It's eastbound," Dave observed, "not our problem. The hell with it. What are you doing?"

"Just a sec." Jason started to follow the car, but it disappeared from view under a network of overpasses. He flew past them, brought the helicopter around, and hovered where he anticipated the car would emerge, but nothing showed.

"Where the hell is he?" Jason muttered, mostly to himself.

"I don't care where he is. I care where we are, which is not where—Hey!"

Jason pulled the helicopter down suddenly. He wanted to get a closer look, but he also figured if he went down fast enough, it would shut Dave up. He moved in lower and close to the overpass.

"There he is!" Jason called out, more triumphant than excited, like he'd won a game of hide-and-seek.

The black car was at rest on a patch of grass by the side of the highway. Jason couldn't tell if its engine was on or off. There was no sign of damage or movement, or anything for that matter, except that the rear passenger door was open. Jason held the copter in position and looked around. He spotted a man in a light-colored suit a few feet away from the car, standing with his back to the helicopter and his hands on his knees. The guy didn't turn to look up at the helicopter, which he must have heard hovering above, and Jason waited to see what he was going to do next. There was something about the scene that wasn't right, he thought. The pieces didn't quite fit together, and Jason was waiting for the clue that would make everything clear. The guy still had his hands on his knees, but he didn't seem to be throwing up. There was a bag at his feet.

Dave, looking a little white, broke the silence. "Are we through with this joyride? Because New York is waiting for me to tell them how long it will take to get to work."

Jason gave up and finally pulled away from the scene. "You think he's okay? What was he doing? I think he was alone. Why do you figure the back door was open?"

"Didn't see it. Maybe his girlfriend's husband got home a little early this morning. Out the window, down the fire escape, drove like hell, then pulled over to catch his breath when he thought it was safe."

"Is that the voice of experience?"

"No comment."

Less than an hour later, the morning rush was in full swing. From that point on, the gig was pretty straightforward. Fly from toll to toll, check for crashes, report on delays. For more than six months the story had been the same: traffic, delays, construction. Not that many accidents. A car has to build up some minimum speed to get into an accident that matters, and nobody was going anywhere fast near the City these days. So the main thing was to tell people where it was bad and where it was worse, so anybody who had a choice could cut their losses. Dave was good at his job, and he took it seriously. He had a little formula written on an index card and by tracking certain cars for just a few minutes he could calculate how long the delay would be at each place. Jason once thought about asking how it worked, but then decided better of it. They reported live, and his job was to hold the copter as still as possible during the reports. Dave spoke into a camera mounted behind Jason's seat.

"It's another nightmare out there on the roads today. We're sitting on top of the George Washington Bridge, and it looks like about an hour and a half wait.…The Lincoln Tunnel is a better bet, you can probably keep it under an hour. On the other side of town, two lanes closed for construction on the Triborough Bridge, and the FDR Drive is bumper to bumper. If you're coming in from the boroughs, the subway is still your best bet. The transit desk reports all trains running on or close to schedule. This is Dave Edwards reporting from Channel Six's eye in the sky; we'll be back in thirty with another update."

By ten to ten Jason was done for the day. He set the helicopter back down on the pad, and Dave jumped out almost before it landed. Last on, first off, like he lived on the second floor and still took the elevator. Sammy came over, and they went through the same routine: engine, stays, clipboard, but in reverse. Jason had come up with some good stuff during the ride, and he was looking for a way to ease back into that John Hurt discussion just by accident.

"Hey, Sam—"

Sammy cut him off abruptly. "Any problems today, Mister Sims?"

"Uhh…no."

"Don't forget to sign the bottom, Mister Sims."

Jason signed the clipboard without looking, trying to decipher the look on Sammy's face, which was blank. Not mad, not fooling around. Just gone. Sammy took the clipboard and walked away. Jason just stood there.

"Nothing like a rooftop on a late summer day."

The voice came from behind Jason, who turned as he spoke. "Mr. Morgan?"

It was Morgan, who looked pretty much the way Jason remembered. A little shorter, though still tall, and in his sixties. He had a hint of a southern accent.

"Ever sneak up on rooftops when you were a kid, Jason?"

Jason squinted a bit, trying to get a read of Morgan's expression. It was overcast, but still he managed to throw a bit of a shadow, and it was hard to get a sense of him. "Sure, I mean, didn't everyone?"

"I never got out of the habit. Lot of romance on a rooftop. Most people think it's the view, but it's much more than that. It's the hint of fear—more than just a hint, really—that makes it special. That primal fear of heights, of the possibility of falling, maybe even jumping. Makes a great view…majestic. Walk with me, Jason."

Morgan stepped forward but even in the light Jason couldn't tell what he was up to. He walked slowly to the edge of the roof with Jason a half-step behind, and they looked out at the City.

"This is my favorite roof in the City. I come here all the time. All alone up here, eight million people right down there."

"I don't remember seeing you here before."

Morgan turned slightly, the way a teacher would lift his eyes to quiet a whispered conversation. "If you did, I wouldn't be alone, now would I?"

"Hard to argue with that."

"I wouldn't try."

Morgan looked back out at the City with its long lines of traffic. On the avenues the traffic went back for miles, and across the streets cars pushed their way into the intersections. Everybody trying to get a few feet ahead just pushed the traffic back farther. One problem with Manhattan traffic was that most people didn't own the cars they were driving. Buses, taxis, trucks, and commercial vans, they wrote their own rules. With no place to pull over, they just stopped where they wanted, creating new pools of traffic in their wake.

Morgan kept talking, and Jason decided to counterpunch until he could figure out what the hell was going on.

"Boy, traffic's a bitch today. Guess I don't have to tell you about that."

"The subways are running pretty well."

Morgan smiled tightly, and Jason could tell he'd decided to skip the speech about how he used to walk six miles to school in bare feet.

"You still in law school?"

"No, I dropped out last September."

"Huh. Right after Nixon resigned?"

"I guess.... Listen, I don't see—"

"My wife left me about the same time. Must have been something in the air."

Jason stared blankly, and then turned and looked back out at the traffic. The gridlock was expanding, and more and more drivers were leaning on their horns to help pass the time.

Morgan continued. "Point is, once you finish the morning shift, you're a free man?"

It was windy on the roof. Jason was getting cold, and at that particular moment, he didn't feel very free. "Free man?" he asked back, lifting his gaze and inviting Morgan to rephrase his question.

"You don't have another job or something you do in the afternoon?"

"I play in a band at night, so sometimes I sleep in the afternoon."

"What kind?"

"Huh?"

"What kind of music do you play?"

"Nothing special. Mostly blues, a little rock, nothing you would have—"

"I can see nine of my buildings from here. Upper West Side, lower East Side. I can see 'em, but these days it's near impossible to get from one to the other. Two over in Jersey."

"Traffic's a bitch."

"That's what I wanted to talk to you about, really," Morgan offered, casually scuffing the rooftop with the tip of his right shoe. "Got a little proposition for you."

"Yeah?" Jason was not fond of the word "proposition."

"The traffic copter isn't used from ten to four. Six hours, it just sits there."

"Well, there's maintenance." Jason decided he wanted to make Morgan work a little harder. He wasn't buying the shoe trick, and doubted the old man ever made an unstudied move.

"Okay, five hours. Still seems like a waste."

"I guess."

"How would you like to spend that time doing a little flying, let my people get some work done, instead of sitting on their asses in traffic."

"I don't know, I mean—"

"I'll pay you half again what you get for the morning shift."

Jason stared ahead. He wasn't opposed to making money, it was just that there was only so much that he would do for it. He looked down. It was a long way down.

"Just one problem, though," Morgan continued, brushing some dust off his sleeve, "technically, we aren't allowed to use this copter for anything but the news. Bastards in City Hall have a permit for anything, and anything for a permit. Got to fill out three forms just to take a crap. No wonder people think this city is going down the drain."

"They say bureaucrats are the silent killers of every civilization."

"I could have my office get started on the paperwork, but it would be months before it came through proper." Morgan sounded confident. He was wrapping up.

"Uh-huh."

"Technically, then, we'd be in violation of city code. Not that you'd be doing anything wrong, mind you, or that wasn't allowed. It's just that we wouldn't have jumped through all the hoops and gotten all the rubber stamps that we need to make everything just so. But if I paid you in cash, and we kept this little arrangement between us, I can't see how there'd be a problem."

3

JASON GOT DOWNSTAIRS in time to watch the end of the newscast. Nothing looks as fake as a news set from the wings. It's not that it looks any less real, just less authentic, like watching a puppet show from backstage. The little news desks sit on an island in the middle of the room, bright, sharp, and perfect, but one foot to either side the place looks like a warehouse, strewn with cables, hand trucks, and half-eaten sandwiches. The newscasters are like astronauts sitting in the shiny lunar module having a little Tang, an oasis in the vast desert moonscape. Probably where the Chinese got the idea that the whole space program was a hoax.

Jason wasn't watching the news so much as he was watching Carol Chase, one of the anchors. Carol was a striking woman, if in a TV sort of way—pretty, blond, and busty. She wore glasses during the newscast, but they were part of the costume and came off with the blazer. The blazer was navy, and the shirt was always a light color, so the contrast and the V from the jacket showed off her chest. This worked, because between the blazer and the glasses the guys who ran the station could act like they were covering her up while they were showing her off.

The other anchor was Nathan Johnson, black and in his late forties. Most of the talent had an on-air voice and an off-air voice, but Nathan didn't. He spoke with the same clipped formality all the time, and was almost always working. He read the news in advance, did a little editing, and had quiet conversations with Lou about content. When Carol wanted something done, she would dispatch her assistant to communicate her instructions, and spoke directly only with Lou or Harry. Nathan didn't have a personal assistant, and didn't push people away, but he kept them at arms' length. He was always the anchor man. He could have a cup of coffee with you, but he'd still be the anchor man. Most people talked to him like he was an ambassador at a state dinner.

The show was in its final commercial break, which was visible on the monitors, and technicians and assistants hurried about. Adam, who had been walking by, eased over to where Jason was standing and whispered in his ear.

"Give it up. You're out of your league."

"Give what up?" Jason whispered back.

"That chick once went to Europe with Warren Beatty, then dumped him for some duke."

"So?"

"So you ain't no Warren Beatty."

"Neither is he."

Lou stepped out on the floor and the room became silent.

"Okay, we're back in five, four…"

Lou signaled the last three numbers with his fingers, and Adam continued down the hallway, waving playfully at Jason. Carol's face lit up suddenly as the cameras turned on.

"Reviewing our top stories, municipal bond prices fell sharply at the start of trading today, while the Ford White House issued a statement denying that it was, quote, 'out to get' New York City. And Mayor Cohen announced that to deal with the traffic crisis he was ordering increased road construction and maintenance at night. The overtime will be paid for by emergency surcharges at all city tolls, parking meters, and garages."

It was Nathan's turn. All this sharing was actually worked out by their agents in advance. The less formal it looked, the more precise the rules were.

"Be sure to join Cathy and Steve for the five-o'clock report, with updates on all our stories, Tommy Thompson with local sports, and our nightly feature on rush hour traffic tips."

"What are we going to do, Nate…? We're heading home right now!"

"I watch the night before, and try to plan ahead."

"I'll have to give that a try." Carol swiveled slightly in her chair to pick up the first camera. She went from a grin to a smile.

"Hope you have a great day. For Nathan Johnson and the rest of the Channel Six News Team, I'm Carol Chase. We'll see you bright and early with the morning report at six A.M. tomorrow."

Everybody froze for a second, till Lou cut in. "That's it people, we're out." He started to walk off the floor.

Carol took off her glasses and tossed them aside as she rose from her chair. She called after Lou, but he didn't hear her, and she chased him down.

"Lou, we're supposed to have forty-five seconds of head shots after the recap."

"Sorry honey, big news day. We ran long."

"My contract doesn't say anything about the *size* of the news. You need extra time, take it from somewhere else. You owe me thirty seconds."

"You want 'em right now?"

"Spread 'em out over the rest of the week. Ten a day, I don't care if the fucking mayor gets shot."

Carol turned and walked away, with Jason in pursuit.

"Good show today."

Carol didn't break stride, and the sound of her heels striking the floor marked her pace. "I didn't know you had a TV up there."

"I, uh, saw the beginning and the end." Jason had looked down for a moment, and now hurried to catch up. "So, what do you do now?"

"What do you mean?"

"Well, it's ten o'clock, and you're pretty much through for the day."

Carol stopped walking and stared, hard, and Jason scrambled to recover.

"I mean, on camera." Carol started walking again, and Jason

figured this was progress. "And I was kind of wondering, you know, how the rest of your day went."

"Why?"

"Just curious. Actually, I play in this band, and I thought—"

They reached Carol's dressing room, and she turned on her heel and stared again, silencing him once more. It was a hell of a stare. Jason wondered if she practiced it, or if it just worked because when a really good-looking woman stares you down, you stop talking.

"Not interested."

Jason decided to interpret this as a specific rejection rather than a global one. "So what do you do with your free time?"

"Apparently you haven't read the memo instructing staff not to bother the talent with personal matters."

"I've never been much of a memo person."

Carol looked Jason up and down. "No, no, I suppose not. You been wearing that same outfit for ten years?"

"What's that supposed to mean?"

"It means, though I doubt you've noticed, that I'm the only woman at this station who's not answering phones. It means that I'm looking forward. I'm not here to be patronized by the director or hit on by the staff."

Carol closed the door to her dressing room, sharply but without a slam, which was reserved for more important business. Jason waited for a moment and studied the name on her dressing room door. The two names ran together in gold letters with oversized C's: CarolChase. He slid a finger gently across them and then headed down the corridor, passing a slightly open door. The room was dark, and Jason, curious, peered into the room. Suddenly a giant picture of Dave Edwards appeared on the wall. It started talking.

"...and the Tappan Zee Bridge is piled up as far as the eye can see. More and more people reading their papers, not even bothering to look up at the...."

The film flickered off, and the lights came on. Dave was sitting at a small desk, taking notes.

"Last Thursday?" Jason offered.

"Uh-huh."

"A particularly memorable moment?"

"Nope. I watch every film we shoot. At least three times."

"Hmm. Making a compilation for your mother?"

"I told you. I'm going to anchor. You want to anchor, you have to connect with the camera. That's not like a person, something that comes naturally."

"More like a mirror." Jason wished Adam was there. That was a great line. And he nailed it, without missing a beat. But it just blew over Dave's head and out the window, gone.

Dave kept on talking while Jason thought this through. A really good line is only good once. You couldn't tell it as a story, it was an in-the-moment sort of a thing. He made a mental note to consider the meaning of this as a potentially important division of life's experiences into two distinct categories. Probably not.

"Like just then when I said 'people reading their *papers*,'" Dave's voice resurfaced. "That should have been '*people* reading their papers.'"

"Not 'people *reading* their papers'?"

This counterpunch finally got Dave's attention. "Don't look at me like that. Just 'cause a guy is trying to make something of himself. What's it to you?"

Dave set down his pad, dimmed the lights, and turned the projector back on. "At least I'm going somewhere," he called out as Jason left.

4

THERE ARE SOME SONGS that can only be sung by a really big black man. Of course, as with most good rules, there are exceptions. Stevie Winwood was a slim seventeen-year-old white kid when he sang "Gimme Some Lovin'," and somehow he managed to sound like a big black guy, but in general, the rule holds. Freddie King's "Going Down" is an example. Freddie was six-five, and when he sang "Going Down," you went down with him.

Oz McKinley wasn't six-five, but he was six-two, and he wore boots. Oz was the leader of One Mile Short. He sang and played lead guitar. Jason played rhythm, and there were two kids who played bass and drums. Oz and Jason had played together for years, mostly three nights a week at the Irish Cottage, a bar not far from Jason's apartment. Every now and then they opened for bigger acts, once at the Felt Forum next to Madison Square Garden. It wasn't much money, but it wasn't nothing. Oz made a pretty good living as a session man for a couple of the studios in the City, and he was able to turn down stuff he didn't want to play.

"Going Down" was one of their big closers, and Oz tore into it, giving up whatever he had left. Jason was a pretty good guitarist, but he always felt a little bit desperate when they played that song. Oz had astonishing concentration, and would lose himself in his solos, as if the world had been reduced to him and his guitar. This was not an ideal recipe for collaboration, and Jason had to watch his hands to keep up, while at the same time making sure not to trip over his wire when it was time to step forward and scream "down, down, down, down, down" into his mike. A decent second guitar gets out of the way of the lead. But a good rhythm guitarist doesn't just fill space, he creates a platform that allows the lead to shine, to explore new places to take his stuff. Jason put a lot of stock into being a good rhythm guitarist.

Oz was winding up, firing notes that seared through the room, and Jason felt good about how it was going. Oz leaned in to sing, and the bass player, a black kid with an afro that was more 1968 than 1975, dropped to his knees for the culminating round of "going downs." The move was a little too cute for Jason, but it worked for the song.

With one last crescendo they were out.

"Thank you!"

The louder Ozzie said thank you, the better he felt about the gig. Jason always listened like it was his report card.

A little while later, Jason sat at the bar, off to the corner, having a beer. Jason spent a lot of time at the Cottage, but didn't usually hang out at the bar on nights he played. The kind of small talk that people made with musicians was so boring you'd think Rod Serling had stopped by and turned the bar into a giant elevator. But by the far corner of the bar the racks of unwashed glasses provided a buffer, and Jason could talk to Pat, one of those bartenders who had a sharp eye for details, and with the confidence in his opinions that good bartenders needed. Pat had thick, small-fingered hands and a boxer's nose, and he wasn't afraid to keep order when necessary. But he was surprisingly well-read, though he more or less kept that to himself.

Jason looked around. "She here?"

"Uh-huh."

He looked more carefully. "Where?"

Pat gestured at an empty table in the corner, underneath a large TV set mounted on the wall.

"Went to the ladies' room." Pat paused to wipe down the bar. "She was looking your way, though."

Jason looked toward the restrooms, which were off the side of the soundboard, down a dimly-lit hallway. Sitting on the stage was a skinny white kid, who couldn't have been much over twenty, fiddling around with an acoustic guitar and chatting with several young women who had gathered at the foot of the stage. He was dressed for the part—tousled hair, studiously unshaven, black T-shirt, faded jeans, decent sneaks. Jason was familiar with the look.

"She alone?" he asked Pat, without turning his head.

"She will be till somebody has the balls to go over and talk to her."

Jason looked back toward the restrooms and then shifted his gaze back to the kid with the guitar, who had stepped to the front of the stage. The stage stood only about two feet off the ground, a raised black platform that went back about ten feet to the wall, not enough to discourage amateurs, and if you weren't booed off the stage they let people play after the band had quit. This kid stood close to the edge of the stage, which was a pro move for a bar singer because it made you look larger than life. He started to sing a plaintive version of the Pink Floyd song "Wish You Were Here."

Jason was impressed, and thought it was a good omen. If this was the night he was going to make his move, it was hard to beat "Wish You Were Here" for a soundtrack. Adam had raved about it in print, controversially declaring that its spare lyrics and understated arrangements "captured a quiet despair that was too often drowned out by generic, would-be cathartic arena-rock extravaganzas that pass for greatness in these vestigial times." Taking names, as it were, he added that the lines "Can you tell a green field/from a cold steel rail/A smile from a veil," had more to say "than the ten songs the

Rolling Stones sleepwalk through in *It's Only Rock 'n Roll.*" Jason thought that was a bit harsh, but when Adam got worked up he was hard to stop. There were a couple of decent songs on *Rock 'n Roll.* And while he thought the line "Did they get you to trade/your heroes for ghosts" from "Wish You Were Here" was incisive, and more than a little moving, he didn't share Adam's interpretation that it "was a deliberate slap in the face of audiences holding their hands out for recycled imitations of comfort-food classics."

Jason turned back to Pat. "Who's he?"

"Some college kid. Just started coming around."

"Not bad."

"The chicks dig it. Doesn't sell much beer." Pat half-raised his eyebrows.

"Heads up, Romeo."

Jason slowly swiveled his seat and watched as Alison Monroe emerged from the small corridor to the left of the stage. About thirty, she had dark hair and was casually but neatly dressed. There was something immediately intriguing about her. She had a kind of wholesome look but confident manners, the kind of daughter that June Cleaver would have had if James Bond had passed through town one weekend. The music filled the room, and you couldn't hear people talk, or their feet on the floor, and so from Jason's perspective she seemed to float across the room. He was right about the song, too. "Two lost souls swimming in a fish bowl/year after year," was great first date material, though Jason knew he was projecting—she didn't look lost.

Alison sat down to the applause in the background. In the movie in Jason's mind, it was as if they were applauding her entrance.

"Something wrong with your legs?" Right. It wasn't a movie. Pat was real. She was probably real, too.

Jason downed the last of his beer. "Okay, okay."

As Jason got up, Pat grabbed his arm. "Don't use any of that soulful shit. And don't look at the fucking floor. Be a man."

Jason negotiated his way across the room and made it to Alison's table. She was reading a newspaper that had been left at the table, or she was pretending to; he was never sure when it came to women. He waited for her to look up, but she didn't. "Excuse me, I couldn't help but notice you here the last three times we've played."

She lifted her head most of the way. "It could just be a coincidence."

"Twice is a coincidence. Three times is a story."

"A story?"

"I was almost a reporter once."

Pat arrived carrying two beers. He exchanged one for Alison's empty glass, and set the other down by the chair on the other side of the small round table.

"Your drinks, Mr. Sims." Obviously Pat didn't think Jason could make it into the chair on his own.

"Uh, thanks."

"Almost once?" She said it cheerfully, but she seemed to know how to get the most out of small talk.

Jason sat down. "I went to the Columbia School of Journalism. Never finished."

"How come?"

"I had this problem with deadlines."

"So now you're a musician? Don't they have to—"

Adam suddenly appeared. He plopped himself down at the table and started to talk to Jason.

"Jason, there is something very wrong going on in this city. Very wrong." He grabbed a handful of pretzels from the bowl sitting on the table, and stared at Jason, waiting for the obligatory "What do you mean by that?" response.

"That's Adam," Jason explained to Alison. "He finished Columbia, a real reporter now."

"Covering the same story?"

"Sometimes he misses the big ones by staring too hard at the little ones." He looked over at Adam. "Didn't you once tell me that there was a pact among men about coming over—"

"There's an escape clause. News first, women second."

"A close second?" Alison offered.

Adam finally acknowledged Alison, but didn't miss a beat. "Depends on the story."

"And the woman?" Jason suggested pointedly.

"Alison Monroe." She extended her hand to Adam, who shook it. "I hope there's nothing wrong with the City that can't be fixed. I don't want to lose my security deposit."

Adam resumed talking, essentially to himself. "The corruption in this city is thicker than the traffic. You can't tell the trustees from the teamsters...."

Adam kept on going, and Jason decided to tune out the monologue. Following her example, he shook Alison's hand and introduced himself. "I'm Jason. You just moving in? Everyone else is heading out."

"That's the best time to head in, don't you think?"

"Depends on what you're looking for."

Adam poked Jason with his finger, emphasizing his current point. "Nobody will touch the story. Not with a ten-foot pole. Forget about TV going anywhere near it. City *owns* them."

"You sure you guys are reporters?"

This managed to register with Adam. "Journalists," he replied, a little sharply.

"He is. I never finished, remember?"

"You don't look like a reporter."

She had definitely gotten Adam back into the room.

"What time is it?" he asked, with sudden inspiration.

"Eleven twenty-two."

"Matter of fact, I'm on TV right now. Hey Pat—put on Channel Six."

Pat looked at the stage, which was empty. The scruffy musician was now on the floor engrossed in conversation with several young women. Pat pulled a large remote control clicker from behind the bar and pointed it at the TV.

"Oh, a *television* reporter," Alison noted, as if classifying a species of some obscure insect. "I don't have one."

Jason thought about playing off the double entendre, but it seemed too risky. The TV image slowly came on, and Adam was already speaking, with a picture of an album cover behind him. In the bar, Adam lifted his chin and looked around with a hint of triumph in his eyes, like he could turn on a TV in a bar any time of day and poof, there he'd be.

"…turned away from protest toward an examination of the soul. The result is aching, almost painful at times, but without doubt a masterpiece. *Blood on the Tracks* is the Dylan album fans have been waiting almost a decade for. This is Spotlight with Adam Shaker."

"Is it really that good?" Alison asked.

"Uh-huh. *Rolling Stone* is going to run a special issue on it." He turned to Jason. "They called this afternoon—asked me to write something."

"Cool."

Alison seemed more impressed with the *Rolling Stone* bit than she was by the TV. "I saw him at Newport in 'sixty-five."

"So did I!" Jason exclaimed. "Didn't see you, though."

"I was wearing a different outfit."

"He wasn't." Adam was getting ready to reopen the great selling out versus arrested development debate, but now Alison was talking about seeing Dylan—you know, When-He-Was-God, and there was no time for small talk.

"When he plugged in…it was like…."

"I know what you mean." Jason nodded intently.

"Doors flew open."

"Wow…wow. I remember…."

"That he was booed off the stage? That the sound sucked?" Nothing bothered Adam more than nostalgia. And Dylan would have backed him up—don't look back—that was Dylan's line. Maybe Satchel Paige said it first, but Dylan put it to music. "She's got everything she needs/she's an artist/she don't look back." Get it? She doesn't look back. "I swear," he continued, "sometimes I think I'm the only one who can remember the 'sixties."

This didn't deter Jason, who was still blown away by "doors flew open." That's what Dylan meant. That's what it all meant. Great music was an invitation. You either got it or you didn't. Jason must have played Dylan tapes for seven hundred people. About half said they liked it. Maybe seven got it.

"So what do you do now?" he asked Alison.

"I teach history at NYU. Starting next week, that is. I just finished my Ph.D. at the University of Wisconsin."

"A woman professor?" Adam asked, half male-chauvinist, half revenge for Alison's reporter crack.

"I tried to be a man professor, but I could never learn to go to the bathroom standing up."

"That reminds me—I'll be right back." Adam bounded off toward the restrooms.

"I have to apologize for Adam. He can be a little—"

"New York? I like it." She looked a little harder at Jason, but he was looking up at the TV, distracted, and didn't pick up on it.

"Yeah, well, uh, not everybody is...."

"What?"

Jason stared intently at the TV, looking confused and a little concerned. "I've seen that car before."

Jason stood up in his chair and reached up to the TV, raising the volume manually. The TV showed footage of police milling around the large sedan that Jason had seen that morning on the side of the road. There were a lot of cops at the scene, and all kinds of flashing lights, like there had been some major pile-up instead of just one stopped car. An authoritative male voice added some voice-over to the pictures.

"Repeating tonight's top story, Brooklyn Borough President Sidney Maynes was found dead in his car late this afternoon, an apparent suicide. Associates of Maynes report that he had been despondent over his role in failing to contain the City's financial distress."

The TV footage showed a body being removed from the front of the car and placed on a stretcher. The body was covered, but the attendants were having a little trouble pushing it across the grass, and one of the arms, in a dark sleeve, slipped and dangled off the side. The camera unsteadily closed in on the body, but then the picture jerked to a wide shot, and Jason could imagine the director back at the station screaming at the hand-held for getting so close. He could see the car was in exactly the same spot as this morning, but now only the front driver's door was open. The cops were treating it like a crime scene, closing off the road near the car and putting up yellow tape. Jason leaned in closer to the screen, but the picture switched back to the studio, and he was startled by the bright life-size image of a female news anchor.

"Maynes's body was discovered slumped over the wheel of his car on the shoulder of the Brooklyn-Queens Expressway. Police were alerted to the vehicle by motorists idling in rush hour traffic. In other news, commenting on the City's finances...."

Jason lowered the volume and climbed down from the chair. He stared at the wall underneath the TV.

"Did you know him or something?" Alison was searching for context. It seemed unlikely he knew the Brooklyn Borough President, but she was reading that level of concern in his face.

"No. It's probably nothing." Jason said it, but he wasn't selling it. Adam landed back at the table with a thud that shook their beers.

"What I miss?"

Jason kept quiet, and guided a drop of beer back up the side of his glass.

"This Mayes guy killed himself," Alison said, watching as Jason continued to study his beer.

"Maynes," Adam corrected.

Jason looked up. "You knew?"

"I told you when I got here. You never listen to me."

"I hear you plenty. You didn't say anything."

"It was implied. You gotta listen right. Whatever's going on, he was in it up to his neck." Adam put his hand sharply under his chin.

"How do you know?"

"You keep waiting for the facts to catch up with what I know, by then it'll be too late. I'm telling you. I know things. A lot of things."

"Did you know that when I flew over Maynes's car this morning, the back door was open?" Jason rested the side of his face in his palm, trumping Adam's theatrics with Jack Benny understatement.

"Don't fuck with my head. You're fucking with my head."

"Have I ever fucked with your head?"

"What does it matter if the door was open?" Alison jumped in. She could tell that Adam and Jason were on the verge of switching over to some all-guy code.

"Back door," Adam said sharply.

"Could mean nothing," Jason said, collecting himself. What did it matter, anyway? "Could have been jarred loose when he went off the road."

"Or it could have been left open when someone took off in a hurry," Adam countered, leaning in on the table, challenging Jason to shoot him down.

Adam was just warming up and Jason decided to go the other way, and throw some meat into the cage. "And I could have sworn he was wearing a tan jacket."

"You saw him?"

"I saw somebody."

It was like watching a tennis match. "Shouldn't you tell the police?" Alison asked innocently, mostly to stay involved.

"No!" Adam and Jason spoke at the same time, and the combined effect was quite startling. They continued to talk over one another, elaborating their positions. "Not till I have more of the story." "Nothing much to tell."

Alison seemed unconvinced by the barrage, but got the clear impression that this was a crowd that did *not* go to the police, for one reason or another.

"Couple of hundred feet up in a moving helicopter," Jason mused. "I've got nothing to say to them that they don't know by now. Even New York cops can tell the difference between a murder and a suicide."

"I'm telling you," Adam said confidently, "this whole thing is about the money. If I could just get into the City's books, I'd blow this whole thing wide open."

5

IT WAS VERY LATE when they left the bar, and Jason walked Alison the long way back to her apartment building. The neighborhood looked good at night. The lighting took the edge off the streets, the way a tinted mirror didn't show the lines in your face. It was also good to get some time with Alison alone. He'd known Adam for so long that when they were together it was like he wasn't a single person.

"Adam's always digging at something," Jason explained. "He spent over six hours at the Hall of Records yesterday."

"What for?"

"You heard most of it. He's convinced that there are these dark secrets in the City's financial records. But he can't get his hands on the ones he wants, so he tries to put the pieces together by filling in all the information that's available to the public."

"What do you think?"

"About what?"

"*Are* there dark secrets in the City's financial records?"

"I don't know. There are dark secrets everywhere, if you're looking for them," he said, waving his hand at the scores of unlit windows looking down on them from the apartments that lined the street. That came out gloomier than he wanted. "Anyway, Adam's pretty excitable, is all I mean."

"Everybody should be excitable about something."

"I guess."

It was quiet, and Jason looked around. He loved walking the

streets after hours. Traffic lights dutifully performed their silent ritual, the changing of the guard in front of an empty palace—green lights would turn yellow and then red, and the opposing red would fall to green. With just a few lonely cars on the road, you could appreciate the majesty of how the lights turned green, one after the other, in precise rhythm down the boulevard as far as the eye could see. At the right speed you could probably make it all the way to the City without stopping.

He looked over at Alison, and wondered if she would ever think about traffic lights that way. Probably not, but then again, Adam probably didn't either, so he decided not to hold it against her.

"You never married?"

"No." She answered matter-of-factly, much to Jason's relief. He regretted asking as soon as the words left his mouth.

"And you?" she countered.

"I was engaged once," he offered, as if mentioning a summer camp he once briefly attended.

"Really?" She stopped walking for a half-step, but only just. "What happened?"

"Good question." Actually, he wasn't quite sure of the answer. "She, I, it was…I guess there was some disagreement about how long an engagement was supposed to last."

"I bet you didn't beat my record," she said with a smile.

"Engaged?"

"Two years."

"Impressive. Then what?"

"It was more of a trial separation than an engagement. We met in college. Then he headed off to the war, and I started grad school, partly to mark time. He thought I should quit when he got back. So did my mother. She worked for three years when my father was in the Pacific, quit the day he came home, and never looked back. But it was too late for me."

She stopped abruptly. The flashing DON'T WALK sign froze to an urgent red, and the light turned against them. It would be thirty seconds, or even a minute, before it would exhale and give way to that reassuring, solid, white "Walk." Jason looked left and then right—there wasn't a car in sight. He gave her a long look, but she wasn't biting.

"I think we can risk it," he said.

They turned down a quiet street and continued talking. It was dark, and the trees threw shadows from what light there was. You notice different things about people when you can't see their faces—how they walk, the way they hold their heads, when they decide it's just the right time to push the hair back from in front of their eyes. Jason thought the night was more honest than the day.

"You like being a professor?"

"I don't know. I just started. I love history."

"Which part?"

"The last part," she said, laughing. "Sorry, we historians have so few good jokes. Trust me, you don't want to know," she said with a smile that gave him credit for showing interest.

"Sure I do."

"Okay, then…my dissertation was called *The Social Roots of Economic Decline in Medieval Empire.*"

Jason took his best shot, but it was obvious he had nothing, so he went with repetition: "The social roots—"

"It won a prize," Alison interjected quickly. "Sorry. I shouldn't have said that. It's hard. I mean, on the one hand I'm really proud of it, but on the other, no normal person would ever, you know.…"

"So what's it about?"

"Well, it's really interesting, actually." Jason could see the whites in her eyes as they widened. "You see, nobody really understands why these empires declined—you know, usually there are good reasons why the rich just get richer. And these vast empires, they were stronger and richer than everyone around them…but they just kind of ran out of steam, and faded away."

"So it's a mystery story."

"That's what my advisor used to say, but not as nicely. I think history is big mystery story, when you really look at it. And I love a good mystery. But it drove him crazy. He used to call me Agatha."

"Agatha?"

"You know, like Agatha Christie."

"So, did the butler do it?"

"Nobody knows for sure. I said it was suicide. It sure wasn't murder. There wasn't some foreign force that conquered them. They just…kind of died inside. Once they reached the height of their power, they lost their sense of purpose."

She glanced over quickly before continuing, to make sure his eyes hadn't glazed over. "It was as if after spending all that energy to get to the top, once they got there, they had nowhere else to go. They understood the challenge but didn't know what to do with the achievement."

"Sounds interesting," he said after a pause, referring more to the timbre of her voice when she talked about it.

"Uh-huh." She gave him a skeptical smile.

"No, really."

Even by Jason's route, they had finally reached Alison's apartment building. It was older, and small for the neighborhood, four stories high with a half-flight of brick stairs leading to the entryway. Alison fumbled for her keys.

"So," Jason offered tentatively, trying to rise to the occasion, "the last three times I've played at the Cottage you've been there. This raises an interesting question. It's going to be three, maybe four days till we—"

Alison silenced him with a kiss, which lasted more than a moment.

"Maybe we should plan something sooner," she offered, walking up the steps.

"How about dinner?"

She reached for the door. "Sure, call me."

"I don't have your number!" he said hurriedly, as she had one foot in the door.

She barely looked back. "Get it from Adam. He asked for it when you were in the bathroom."

JASON'S FIRST DAY OF extra-curricular flying made it obvious why Mr. Morgan was in the market for a helicopter. He had already been to the Bronx and was now cruising towards Staten Island. The trip would have taken hours under the best of circumstances, and these days, it was just not a practical possibility. Even off-peak, the FDR Drive looked like a parking lot.

Jason looked over at his unnamed passenger, who earlier in the day had greeted him with a rather monotone "Mr. Morgan said you'd be expecting me." His own uncharacteristically warm "Hi, I'm Jason" had been met with a slight nod and firm shake of the hand. The guy looked to be about Jason's age, athletic, with sharp dark features that held his initial impenetrably stoic expression longer than you would have thought was possible. He wore a suit and tie—a nice suit that fit well—but he had the hands of a bricklayer. Jason passed the time guessing about his background. Second generation, maybe third. Southern European, big family, probably from Brooklyn. And for some reason Jason convinced himself that his father was a butcher.

"What did you say your name was?"

"I didn't."

"Oh." Some people are intimidated by awkward silences, but Jason wasn't one of them. He looked over, wide-eyed, feigning innocence.

"You can call me Bill," he offered, making no effort to avoid the distinct impression that his name was anything but Bill. But it was better than nothing.

"Okay, Bill, where exactly in Staten Island are we going? It's a big-ass island."

"I'll point it out when we get closer."

"Listen, I don't care where you want to go, I just gotta make sure we're clear to land."

"That won't ever be a problem."

"Still, it would help if—"

"Look, I'll tell you everything you need to know, okay?" He stretched out the word *need*, and it effectively ended the conversation. They rode on in silence. Bill had two attaché cases at his feet, and he occasionally tapped one of them with his fingertips, as if he was keeping time.

As they approached the Queensboro Bridge Jason subtly swung around a bit to get a better view. There were a few things in the City that really mattered, things that you anticipated seeing again no matter how many times you'd seen them before. The Statue of Liberty, the Chrysler Building, the Fifty-ninth Street Bridge, for sure. Even with the Simon and Garfunkel song, the Fifty-ninth Street Bridge was under-appreciated. Most people wouldn't put it in the top three, maybe even top five. But most people hadn't driven across the Queens-bound lower roadway at night, veered off at Northern Boulevard, and then thought to look out the back window. The bridge was spectacular from below and the darkness of the river framed the lights of the City all the way downtown.

They passed the bridge and cruised effortlessly down the East River, leaving Manhattan behind. When they reached Staten Island, Bill directed Jason to an isolated spot on the northeastern part of the borough.

"Over there," Bill gestured, pointing at a large industrial park in the distance. Even from the air, it looked big, and as they got closer it also looked very empty. The factories were idle, shut down, maybe even abandoned; it didn't look like the grounds were being maintained. But there were a few cars around and some scattered lights were illuminated.

"There's a good spot behind those tanks," Bill directed. "Set it down on the far side, across from that warehouse."

Jason did as he was instructed, and as they were landing, Bill turned to him.

"Leave it running. I'll be right back," he said, and quickly hopped out while the rotors were still spinning. He took one of the briefcases with him, leaving the other on the floor. Jason was looking down at it when Bill suddenly reappeared.

"Hey!" he shouted over the blades.

"What?"

"I forgot to tell you." A hint of warmth slipped into his voice, though his eyes stayed firm. "If you're ever not sure what to do… if anything happens when I'm away from the copter, just take off. Don't worry about it, don't think about it, just go. Got it?"

Jason nodded. He watched as Bill walked briskly, and then broke into a trot towards a limousine that was idling near the warehouse about one hundred yards away. As he approached the driver got out and opened the back door, and a middle-aged man emerged. The gray streaks in his dark, slicked-backed hair had advanced beyond his temples. Well-dressed and heavy-set, he wasn't really fat, but big in a way that suggested a certain toughness. He turned for a moment toward the driver, who walked toward the warehouse and entered through a large, rusted metal door.

The heavy-set man waited for the door to close, and then began talking to Bill. He quickly became animated, gesturing and shouting, with Bill nodding and apparently acknowledging. At one point he looked suddenly at the helicopter, and Jason studied the instrument panel intently. He counted to five and then stole a quick glance over—the chewing out, or whatever it was, had resumed and continued angrily for a few more minutes. Bill stayed cool—Morgan must have hired this guy for his stoicism—and eventually the older man had said his piece. He reached back into the limo and pulled out an oversized manila envelope, which he handed to

Bill in exchange for the black briefcase. He then jabbed a thick finger at Bill's chest, as if to emphasize a final point. Bill nodded again and then trotted back to the helicopter and climbed in.

"Let's go!"

Jason pulled the helicopter up into the air. Looking back, he saw the heavy-set man walk into the warehouse. As they lifted higher, another car could be seen winding its way slowly across the empty industrial compound, which in its day must have been inhabited by hundreds of workers. He turned back to Bill.

"Where to?"

"Upper West Side." Hints of warmth were no longer on offer.

Jason held his gaze.

"I'll point it out when we get closer."

The two men flew in silence for a while. Jason didn't concern himself much with other people's business, but the day was getting long and there was something about the heavy-set man that was sticking with him.

"I feel like I've seen that guy before."

"Everybody looks like someone," Bill said, looking out the window.

"He looked pretty pissed."

"Nah, just a little frustrated."

"Rich guy like that?" Jason questioned, fishing a bit.

"Yeah, his driver is getting on his nerves. Keeps asking him too many questions."

It wasn't an unfair analogy, but Jason didn't like being called a driver. "Maybe he likes to know where he's going."

"Maybe he's better off not knowing."

"Yeah, well—Hey! Look down there!"

There seemed to be some sort of scuffle going on in the street below. Jason eased in to get a better view, and hovered in place. It looked like a fistfight, with four men surrounding an obscure figure. Actually, it looked rougher than a fight, which was usually plodding, and over quickly. Whatever was going on down there was more frantic.

"Tough city." Bill was not impressed.

"Maybe we should do something."

"Plenty of cops around," Bill said, utterly uninterested. He pointed at a building about three blocks from the struggle. "That's the Twenty-seventh Precinct."

Jason snapped his head. "You a cop?"

Bill smiled for the first time. "I grew up there. Years ago it wasn't a half-bad neighborhood."

Jason hesitated and turned for one last look. One of the attackers was kicked violently backwards, revealing that the victim was a woman. Jason stared over at Bill, who didn't flinch. He held up his arm, displaying his watch.

"Let's go," he said firmly, tapping it with his index finger. "In two minutes the place will be crawling with cops. They don't like to see that sort of thing near the station. Too close to home—it's bad for business."

"No there aren't! That may be the Twenty-seventh, but there are no cops anywhere! No cops, no cars!"

Jason looked around. There were long lines of gridlocked traffic, and lots of buses and taxis, but there were no police cars to be seen, not even near the stationhouse.

"Where the hell are they? I better radio for help!"

Bill grabbed Jason's arm. "You can't do that!" His voice was full of emotion, and that surprised Jason even more than the fact that he grabbed him.

"What do you mean?" Jason shot back.

"It wouldn't do much good, would it?" The calm returned to his voice.

On the street below the woman had broken free from the group and was making a run for it. Her dress was torn and she tripped as she ran, with the men in pursuit. Jason abruptly veered the helicopter downward.

"What the fuck are you doing!"

The woman ran into and across a vacant lot, and then fell again. Jason brought the helicopter straight down the side street, interposing the copter between the woman and her attackers. The wind from the rotors threw newspapers and debris into the air. Jason moved directly at the attackers. Two of them fell to the ground for cover, but one stared up defiantly. Tilting the helicopter, Jason menaced him with the blades, forcing him to retreat as well. But the maneuver threw up even more dirt, and Jason was having trouble maintaining control. The copter was spinning, and the sound of shouting and honking horns pierced through the dust storm, sending all of the men scrambling from the scene.

"All right," Bill shouted, "let's get out of here!"

"Can't do it! I can't see—too much dirt. There are buildings on three sides of us, and I don't know which three! I'm gonna try and find the ground!"

The helicopter hit the ground hard, unevenly, and everything fell to the left. Jason was thrown against the side on the cabin, and Bill fell on top of him. Jason hit his head hard, and when he reached up with his hand he felt blood. Bill climbed off Jason and pulled himself back into his seat. He grabbed the second briefcase, set it on his lap and opened it. It was full of cash, stacks of twenties neatly bound with bankers' wrapping. He grabbed a set of twenties and stuffed them inside Jason's jacket pocket.

"I was never here!" Bill shouted, and, hoisting himself out the passenger side, disappeared into the dust. Jason wasn't sure what happened after that.

7

ADAM HAD SPENT THE early part of that morning making a few calls about the freshly departed Sid Maynes. It turned out all those flowery obituaries were swimming upstream against a pretty nasty undercurrent of ill will—he couldn't find one person who didn't use the word "asshole" at some point in the conversation. Looked like dying was as good a career move for politicians as it was for rock stars. And he still didn't buy the suicide thing—nobody that vain and ambitious would punch his own ticket without a really good reason, and even then he would have done it in a more dignified way. Pills, probably. Image management is crucial, especially the last image. That definitely ruled out guns, to say nothing of slitting your wrists on the shoulder of the BQE. It wasn't even an A-list road.

In between calls he was able to revisit most of the cuts from the new Led Zeppelin album, *Physical Graffiti*. He was going to trash it in the *Voice*, as soon as he could come up with a good synonym for "spent force," a phrase he burned in his review of the Stones' *It's Only Rock 'n Roll*. Actually, neither album sucked, but the drop-off was painful.

He still managed to get to the Hall of Records precisely one hour after it opened, exactly as he had planned. City workers were so dolefully predictable; they would make great cult members. They watched the clock religiously, never starting a minute before nine or lingering a second after five, and they followed the rules without ever bothering to question them, or even really thinking much about them. At the DMV they'd renew Hitler's license if his papers were in order. Assuming he passed the eye test.

The key to a successful Hall of Records visit was not attracting any kind of attention, and Adam thought through every detail, even putting on a suit for the occasion. There was always a long line waiting to get in when they opened, and it took about forty-five minutes for the first wave to clear. After that it was pretty much a steady trickle. Most of the clerks took a coffee break at ten-fifteen, so at ten o'clock they were settling down as the pressure of the morning crush waned, and looking to avoid any complications that might interfere with that upcoming doughnut.

Good timing or not, the suit, polite smile, and *Village Voice* ID was enough to get him over the first set of hurdles, and he was able to submit his requests and secure a table in one of the reading rooms. You had to know how much to ask for, and how to ask for it. Otherwise the system would crash, and they'd want you to explain the purpose of your visit, or worse, claim that the stuff you wanted was being held at "central archives," a mythical institution and/or black hole that was often spoken about but quite possibly didn't exist.

Adam had asked for all the campaign contribution records, everything, for all candidates in the 1968 mayoral election. He really cared only about the contributions to the Cohen campaign, and was more interested in the last election, but '72 was too recent and singling out the Mayor would have raised red flags. The camouflage worked, and it was not long before Adam found himself surrounded by boxes filled with binder notebooks.

They were classified by donor, not by candidate, which was a setback, but Adam was still happy to have it all in front of him. He knew exactly what he was fishing for—evidence that the Mayor was involved in some sort of unspecified corruption, most likely involving organized crime in some way. Unfortunately, the mob wasn't listed as one of the categories of contributors, so Adam started with the Union book for any entries related to dock workers, restaurant and hotel employees, and the teamsters—three organizations whose donations might be used for the same purpose. But there was nothing there, at least as far as he could tell.

Three hours later he had scanned every promising binder, with nothing to show for it but tired eyes. Cohen's financing looked just like everybody else's, except, oddly, there was a lot less of it across the board. That didn't make sense; usually everybody loved a winner, and a guy with Cohen's connections should have been swimming in cash. Big business usually hedged their bets and coughed up some tribute to both sides, even if they had to hold their noses to do it. But there was almost nothing from the high rollers—at least no contributions big enough to report. No wonder Cohen seemed so casual about the City's finances—he was used to getting something for nothing.

It was probably another dry well. Maybe Cohen spent a little more time with reputed gangsters than he should have, but Adam didn't find anything close to a smoking gun; he wasn't even sure he'd seen any smoke. He leaned back in his chair, rubbed his eyes, and stared at the ceiling, which was vaulted, double height, and the remnants of a mural were still visible. The room must have been something in its time. Large oil paintings, begging for restoration, adorned the walls. Shafts of light exposed particles glittering in the air. Adam slipped out of his chair and quietly left the room by the back door in search of a water fountain, breaking two rules in the process. You weren't supposed to leave until you were done, and you had to use the main door. But Adam wasn't sure he was finished and didn't want to get into a debate with that scary looking clerk in the red dress.

Cruising the hallways to stretch his legs, Adam gave himself a little unauthorized tour in the process. Turning one corner and then another, he noticed a door marked NEW DOCUMENT PROCESSING, adorned by a newer sign posted below that said AUTHORIZED PERSONNEL ONLY. He kept walking but stopped about two doors down, resting his hand against an old steel ladder. The New Document room was calling; he had a vision of fresh, unedited documents showering the room like a geyser from a just-struck oil well. He slipped back down the hallway and gently tried the knob—locked. A glance up revealed that the lights were not on in the room. And that the transom was ajar.

Adam went back to the ladder, which was probably left by someone servicing the open light fixture hanging above. No one else was in sight; a check of the time supported the theory that the maintenance man had probably taken a late lunch. Acting quickly, Adam took off his jacket and tie, mussed his hair and rolled up his sleeves. He checked the coast before quietly carrying the ladder down the hallway, only scraping the ground once, and set it up near the New Documents room. Estimating there would be almost a half-hour before the real maintenance man got back, he climbed up the ladder and tried to remove the light fixture. Failing that effort after a short struggle, he poked one of the ceiling squares out of place and pushed it into the crawl space above. Ducking back down and using a dime as a screwdriver, he tried to coax the transom open the rest of the way. It took a few minutes, but he was able to get it open enough to try to crawl through.

Leaning in, he poked his torso into the room, trying to figure out how to slip the rest of the way though the transom without landing on his head, which at that moment seemed like the most likely—and possibly inevitable—outcome. Fate intervened in the form of a firm tapping on his leg, still dangling in the outer hallway. He froze. There was no chance to stick his head in the crawl space and pretend to be working on the wires. "I'll be with you as soon as I finish fixing this," he said gruffly. "Wait for me at the office."

Another tap. "You're finished now," said a voice, even gruffer than his. He lowered his head and looked down to find a man in a dark green outfit, presumably the maintenance man, along with two large uniformed security guards and, perhaps most frightening of all, the clerk with the red dress. Her arms were folded angrily across her chest and with her small black glasses pulled up over her forehead, from Adam's angle she looked a little like Catwoman on a very bad day.

LESS than a mile away, Alison was trying, with mixed results, to get her office into shape. "Temporary" was the key word in her life, and she was getting sick of it. She'd managed to move from the temporary office she'd been in for several weeks, but everything else was still in transition; a temporary sign instead of a name plate, a lamp until they fixed the overhead light, and a phone that didn't have a number written on it, but at least it worked.

She spent the morning trying to figure out the best configuration for the office. She much preferred the warmth of desk-chair-chair to the conventional chair-desk-chair format, but realized that the standard style was so ingrained that any change might freak out the students, and decided reluctantly to go with tradition. Nobody wanted to turn on the "Tonight Show" to find that Johnny had moved the desk. On the other hand, she wasn't going to back off the whole plant thing, at least not completely. She hadn't seen a single plant in any of the offices she'd visited, or in any of her profs' offices in grad school for that matter, but she was going to draw the line at plants. There was nothing gendered about plants; they even reproduced asexually.

She grabbed two yellow pads—one so overworked and disheveled it looked like it might have been dropped in the bathtub and dried out, the other tight and neat—and clipped her way downstairs to the department's main office. Three secretaries were typing away busily, and Alison stood for a while, waiting for one of them to notice her. They didn't look up.

"Excuse me…Miss Steinlitch?" she said, sounding out the nameplate of the woman who appeared to be in charge. She was older than the other two, had a phone crowded with extension buttons like campaign ribbons on a general's chest, and her desk implied the authority of a command post. It was a larger, old-school wooden affair, the kind you would see at an interwar law firm, and it contrasted with the uniform green-gray metal desks seen everywhere else.

Steinlitch glanced up at her, peeking over her reading glasses, still typing. "Yes?" she asked impatiently.

"I need to have my syllabus typed and mimeographed," Alison said, holding out the neater of her two pads.

"Don't you know how to type?" she responded, without removing the cigarette from her mouth.

"Yes, I do." Alison waited for a response, but didn't get one. "Do the professors type their own syllabi?"

Steinlitch stopped typing and took the cigarette from her lips, hesitating for an almost imperceptible moment. "Put it in the workbox on Cindy's desk," she said, waving across the room with the two fingers that held her smoke.

"Thanks. By the way, do you know if there's a ladies room on the fourth floor? I need some water for my plants."

"There's one just down the hall, to your left. I don't know about any of the other floors," she said, just audible over the sound of the keys.

Alison got back to her office and dug out her dissertation award, and decided to hang it up after all, even though she'd given her folks enormous grief when they'd had it framed. She liked the way it said "A. Monroe," the name she insisted on using when it was submitted to the awards committee. She didn't care what people thought. One third of her department would have hired her even if her work wasn't that good, and another third wouldn't take her seriously if she walked on water. But it was nice to know that according to the American Historical Association, A. Monroe had written the best dissertation in 1974.

She sat behind her desk and looked around; things were slowly falling into place, and she celebrated by reading *The New York Times*. There it was on page one: MAYNES DEATH TO BE RULED SUICIDE, but it was the subhead that caught her eye: "Questions remain about motive, money." She scrunched her nose and stared at the ceiling, wondering what she might be able find out with a few phone calls.

8

JASON WOKE UP IN THE HOSPITAL. He was okay, nothing broken, but he had this big white bandage on his head that made him look like an extra from "M*A*S*H," and they wanted him to stay overnight for observation, since he probably had a concussion. Alone in a semi-private room, a TV, a telephone, and a call button were his only links to the outside world. He'd missed dinner, and he learned when he tried to call Adam that the phone wouldn't let you make outgoing calls. So that left the TV—a big black-and-white job mounted to the wall. The Mets were off, which meant Channel Nine would probably show an old movie.

There was a knock at the door, and Harry walked in.

"You all right, kid?"

"Yeah, it looks worse than it is."

"Good, 'cause you look like shit,"

"How did you know I was here?" Jason asked.

"The helicopter. Those big WNYS-TV letters on the side were a dead giveaway," he added. "And they didn't know who else to call."

"How is it doing?"

"The helicopter? Better than you—it's already back on the roof, good to go."

There was another knock at the door, and a nurse entered. She was young and pretty, with brownish red hair and a nice figure. Jason was disappointed she wasn't wearing one of those little white hats nurses wore in World War II movies, and wondered if she had the overnight shift.

"Excuse me, gentlemen, but, I think the Mayor is here to see Mr. Sims."

"Me? Are you sure?" Jason pushed back against the raised bed. He had appreciated the incline, but now it seemed confining. You couldn't roll out of a hospital bed.

"Yes, I think so, definitely."

Jason stared blankly, and the silence filled the room.

"Well, ask him in," Harry blurted out.

The nurse left and Jason and Harry waited for the door to open again. Jason scanned the room as if double-checking for an emergency exit. Harry looked at his hands, and tugged at his left shirt-sleeve so that it peeked out from his jacket, matching the right. It took longer than they thought for the Mayor to appear. And Alfred Cohen was more than the Mayor of New York. He *was* New York. First as a day laborer, then as a pipe-fitter, Al Cohen had worked his way up through the union ranks during the Depression and became the youngest President of a major city chapter. He resigned in 'forty-one to volunteer for the Army, fought in the some of the fiercest battles of the Italian campaign, and came back with two medals that he never talked about. After the war he swiftly rose to the top of the City's Democratic Party, and for more than fifteen years, he ran the Party, and the City, as its chairman. Mayors, council speakers, even congressmen would come and go, but Cohen was always there, both king-maker and king. National leaders sought his private counsel, and they liked to be seen in public with him too. Then in 1964 the impossible happened—a charismatic Republican was able to parlay low turnout, a sluggish economy, and tired-looking incumbent into the mayoralty. Cohen took it personally, and on top of that he didn't like being out in the cold. So he finally gave in and put himself before the people for a vote, and won the next two Mayor's races, the first by a landslide, the second by almost as much.

He came into the room without knocking. Jason knew from

experience that all rock stars looked smaller in person. But Cohen filled the room, with big strides and broad shoulders that seemed to block out the light as he walked over to the bed and extended his hand.

"How you doing, Jason?" he asked in a way that made you feel a little better just by the tone of his voice.

"Just fine, sir."

"More than just fine, I'd say." He smiled warmly, then looked over and took notice of Harry, and squinted. "Harry Ross? Used to cover the city desk for *The Herald*?"

Harry was surprised and impressed.

"Yes sir. That was some time ago."

"Was a hell of a paper, though. That stuff you guys did on the housing authority in 'fifty-nine — without *The Herald* there wouldn't ever have been a Franks Commission."

Harry shuffled his feet, which Jason had never seen him do before. "I don't recall that you were much fond of the Franks Commission at the time."

The Mayor, who had been mostly looking at Jason, turned to Harry. "I thought you boys in the trade understood that sometimes a person like me has to say one thing in public, even if he knows something else."

"Of course." Harry didn't so much concede the point as he chose not to debate it with the Mayor.

"There was a time when the papers made this town," the Mayor said, talking again at Jason. "Used to be there were seven papers and three TV stations."

"Now it's just the opposite," Harry offered in agreement. "I don't know how they fill all that air."

Jason watched in silence, and had no interest in throwing in his two cents. He was glad Harry was there.

"I wonder, Harry, could you give me a moment with Jason? Couple of things I want to ask him."

"Of course. An honor to see you, sir." Harry shook the Mayor's hand and left. As the door closed, Cohen sat down at the foot of the bed and leaned in a bit, like they knew each other pretty well.

"Sorry to bust in on you like this, son, but I'm just doing my job—if that's okay with you."

"Sir?"

"Taking care of the City."

Jason wasn't quite following. And for whatever reason, being that close to Cohen was making him uncomfortable. He stole a glance at the call button resting about four inches from his right hand and wondered if his fingers could slip over unnoticed and ring for the nurse.

The mayor stared right at him, with penetrating, alert eyes. "You know the most important thing about taking care of this city? New York City?"

"Crime?" Jason offered. It was the first thing that popped into his mind, and in retrospect seemed like a good answer.

"Nope. It's not crime, or taxes, and it sure as hell isn't traffic." He paused for effect. "It's making sure people get up in the morning and say 'I live in New York, goddamit! Capital of the world! What I do matters.'" He held up his hands when he said it, and looked triumphantly at Jason, like he'd pulled off the sheet and revealed a brand new car to a game show contestant.

"What does that have to do with me?"

"Last couple of years, been kind of tough on the City. Hell, I don't have to tell you that. There's a lot of people heading out, lot of people giving up. Most of 'em nowadays see a crime, they turn away, maybe even count themselves lucky. You...you didn't turn away."

"I guess not."

"No," he said with a smile, "you dove right in. A genuine New York hero." He said *he-ro* like it was two words. "Just like your father."

"You knew my father?"

"I didn't know him so much as know of him. You know, them printers and us old pipe fitters, our paths didn't cross that much.

But we both worked our way up the union ladder, and this City ain't nearly as big as people think."

There was a knock at the door, and an aide to the Mayor poked his head in.

"Excuse me sir, but everybody's here. Are we ready?"

"Give us another minute, Paul."

Paul disappeared, and the Mayor stood up.

"Which would bring us to the main reason for my little visit. After all, what's the point of having a genuine New York hero...." He paused again. Jason wondered if he practiced the pauses or if they came naturally. "...if nobody knows about him."

Jason didn't like the sound of that, and quickly realized who "everybody" was. He'd noticed from working at the station that people reacted to TV cameras in one of two ways. Most people, for reasons he never understood, jumped up and down and waved at the camera. The rest turned away. He was definitely in the latter group.

The room seemed too small for cameras, very small, and Jason felt the dull ache of his injuries more now than before. His elbow was bruised worse than he had realized.

"Listen, I can't imagine that people really want to—"

"Of course they do!" The Mayor interjected. "This is exactly what they want to see."

Jason glanced around the room, sensing the inevitable. His eyes rested on the window, and he had a vision of tying bed sheets together and rappelling safely down the side of the building to the ground below. He looked back at the phone—932—probably not enough sheets.

"What's more important, a few minutes of peace and quiet or making eight million people feel good about themselves?"

Jason didn't answer.

"If you'll just press that little nurse button right there, we can get this over with in no time."

Moments later the room was packed with reporters and photographers. The Mayor stood alongside the bed, and for some reason the nurse was positioned next to him. A silver lining to this circus act was that she was bound to be impressed by all the attention. Paul and two other aides stood by the wall, creating a space between the foot of the bed and the reporters and cameramen that seemed to be understood as a buffer zone. The mayor orchestrated.

"Everybody set? Thanks for coming. I've come here this evening to present the City's Badge of Valor to Jason Sims. On a routine maintenance flight of his traffic helicopter, he showed how New Yorkers can rise to any occasion."

There was some laughter from the crowd, and photos were taken as the Mayor shook hands and handed a small medallion to Jason. The reporters began to call out questions, and, especially with the lights that now filled the room, it was hard to tell who was asking what.

"How's your head, Jason?"

"They say it's okay."

"What were you thinking about when you came down so low?"

"I don't know. Not crashing, I guess."

Jason wasn't trying to be funny, but the answer brought laughter and the room buzzed with chatter. There was a brief gap in the questioning.

"Mr. Mayor, can you possibly avoid declaring bankruptcy now that the President has abandoned the City?"

A silence fell over the room. Paul stepped forward. "Gus, you know this isn't the appropriate time for —"

"That's all right, Paul," the Mayor interceded. "Normally, I wouldn't take a political question in a hospital room," he said, effortlessly seizing the high ground while inhibiting aggressive questions that might have followed, "but I know some of you younger fellows are a little eager."

Everyone's attention was redirected and several microphones were placed more prominently.

"Let me tell you something about this City. Forty-four years ago I stood on the steps of the Capitol, Washington, D.C. Union reps from all the big cities were staging a sit-in. We camped out, swapped stories — I still remember this one rep, skinny kid like me —"

This generated some laughter from the reporters.

"Oh, believe me, I was skinny as a rail back then. So was this other kid, he was with the printers." He gave Jason a knowing look as he said it. "Musta looked like a good wind would blow us both away. Anyway, after a few days, I guess the President had seen enough. Ordered federal marshals to clear the steps. Things got pretty ugly, six men were killed. Good men. Family men. Unarmed, asking for nothing more than the chance to work hard, with dignity. Looking to have their voices heard."

The Mayor held the room, and he again paused, and pointed his finger.

"So let me tell you something. I've been told to drop dead by the feds before, by guys way tougher than Ford. But we're still here. We'll see how long this fella is around."

There was another round of laughter that faded to chatter as the Mayor leaned back with satisfaction, while more photos were taken.

"I guarantee you this city will not go bankrupt while I am mayor."

9

ADAM PICKED JASON UP at the hospital the next day, and they took the subway downtown. The train rocked rhythmically and the lights blinked on and off, but it was relatively clean and making good time. They stood, even though there were a few seats available. Adam didn't hold onto anything, as if it was a point of honor. Jason had a big manila envelope full of his hospital paperwork under one arm and leaned against a door with the other for support.

"She didn't say why?" Adam asked.

"No. She just insisted that I bring you down. She was very mysterious," Jason said, with just enough inflection in his voice to amuse himself.

"Really. You get over on her?"

"Jeez, no. I just saw her Tuesday night. She's from Wisconsin, for Christ sake." Looking out, he set his gaze on the rhythmic pattern of girders, lights, and recessed shelters in the tunnel as they whooshed by. The train was an express, and rushed through the Fiftieth Street station, changing the lighting in the car. It lurched a bit and Adam stuck his hand against the door for a moment to steady himself.

"What's the matter with you? What do you think they do in Wisconsin? It's nothing but beer and cheese. No woman can resist that combination."

"Well, I'm just a simple city boy, okay?"

"A simple city chicken," Adam said without missing a beat. "You know, it's a good idea to try and get laid at least once a President."

"Yeah, well, at least I didn't wait till you went to the bathroom to get her number."

"You were on a roll, I didn't want to interrupt you—"

"Fuck you," Jason said with a smile, and turned slightly, towards the interior of the car.

"Fuck me?" Adam responded, with exaggerated innocence.

Jason's smile slipped slowly from his face. "Oh, man," he whispered, gesturing with his head towards the middle of the car, where an older man in a tweed jacket and dark fedora hat was reading the *New York Daily News*. The headline HELICOPTER HERO commanded the front page, which featured a stock footage photo of some random helicopter. Jason bolted and walked to the end of the car, opened the door and headed for the next car. Adam followed and grabbed Jason's arm. Between the cars, the lights flashed more violently. The noise was deafening, and the chains on either side of them danced frantically up and down.

"What do you think?" Adam shouted over the noise. "They don't have papers in that one?"

Jason pushed his way through into the relative quiet and looked around. The coast looked clear, and he found a good spot to lean and looked out the window. They rode silently for a minute.

Adam looked around, scanning the passengers. He nudged Jason with his shoulder.

"You know that guy over there—glasses, tan coat, gold watch, manicured nails?"

Jason looked toward the window, which mirrored the car against the darkness of the tunnel, and carefully checked the guy out in the reflection.

"No."

"Me neither."

Jason turned slowly away from the door. "This makes me regret that we never drove cross-country like we always talked about."

Adam smiled, pleased with himself.

"You really think he knew your old man?"

"I don't know," Jason said, thinking it through. "He could have. But you think my dad would've mentioned it at some point."

"What about that other stuff—that Washington rap, steps of the Capitol," Adam said derisively. "You think that really happened?"

"Oh yeah, that happened. My uncle told me about it. My dad only mentioned it once, when we were having this huge fight about LBJ. Gave me this big speech about how he protested when it mattered, not because it was fun. He didn't mention Cohen, though. I remember it really well—it was in 'sixty-seven, right before he stopped talking to me."

"I thought you guys stopped talking in 'sixty-eight."

"Yeah, I stopped talking to him in 'sixty-eight. But he stopped talking to me in 'sixty-seven, you know, except for regular talking."

"Well, I don't care if he did the right thing a million years ago. I say Cohen is a crooked bum."

"Maybe," Jason said, even though he had little doubt that all politicians were crooks, one way or another. "But he definitely had a…presence."

The train slowed and then came to a stop. The doors shuffled open without incident, although Jason ritually ignored the PLEASE KEEP HANDS OFF THE DOORS admonition. If you knew where you were, you could have deciphered the conductor's announcement: "West Fourth Street, New York University." Adam took the stairs two at a time with Jason following, and they cut through Washington Square Park on their way to the NYU Library. Jason was going back over everything with Bill, still trying to make sense of it all.

"I don't know, he had much more on his mind than someone who didn't want to get caught in violation of city air-traffic code."

"You don't like cops much either. Never did report that time you were mugged after the Knicks game, did you?"

Jason walked a step ahead of Adam. "Take a good look around, will you—those two guys over there, got to be selling drugs, hard drugs. Those three over there, hookers for sure. And that guy on the bench—I don't even want to know what he's doing."

Adam didn't argue with the survey, and Jason continued, still with a bounce in his step.

"Eleanor Roosevelt saved this park—they wanted to let Fifth Avenue run right through it. But if she lived here today, she'd be afraid to set foot in this dump." He paused, realizing he'd drifted off topic. "My point being—some chick gets raped couple of blocks from a police station, and you want me to ask them to get my twenty bucks back?"

"Man, three blocks!" Adam still found it hard to believe. "There weren't any cops around at all?"

They climbed the steps of the library, and entered through the revolving doors. The large entry room was buzzing with people, but they continued their conversation in hushed tones.

"And the money. It sure looked like a lot."

"How much did he give you?"

"Must be a thousand dollars." Jason opened his coat slightly with his left hand and Adam could see the tips of the bills sticking out of the pocket. "Look at that," he hissed. "That's my blood. Blood money!"

He started to get angry. "A thousand dollars. Like I was going to say something. I can take a lot of bullshit, but—"

"Hey. Isn't that Alison?" Adam asked with a nudge of his elbow, squinting like he was trying to tell if the left fielder had been replaced.

It was Alison. She was waving at them from across the large room, and Adam waved back, wiggling his fingers in a way that Jason found suspiciously uncharacteristic.

"My aunt Dora used to wave like that."

"Wave like what? Like Alison? She just wanted to get our attention."

"No. Whatever. Forget it."

"Forget what?"

Alison was on the far side of a little black booth that marked the entryway to the book stacks. You needed an ID to get in, and on the way out, they checked your bags.

They reached the desk and she smiled brightly.

"It's okay, they're with me," she said to the work-study student manning the booth, and he waved them through.

"Okay, here he is," Jason said, with a slight emphasis on "he."

"What's the big mystery?"

"You'll see."

They followed her down several flights of stairs and through a myriad of book-lined passageways. Alison walked a few steps ahead, with tighter strides than when she walked on the street. The echoes from her shoes striking the hard floor stoked Adam's paranoia.

"Where are we going?" Adam hissed to Jason. "I don't like the way she's smiling. I don't know what you guys are up to—"

"You know everything I know" Jason whispered back.

"Is that supposed to be reassuring?"

"Look, pretend you're Woodward, heading down to meet Deep Throat at the bottom of some creepy garage."

"You be Woodward. I'll be Bernstein."

"Quiet down, guys, it's a library," Alison said without breaking stride or looking back.

They continued through another endless series of book stacks until they reached a door marked GOVERNMENT DOCUMENTS. Entering, they found a large and largely empty study room lined with perfectly matching reference books and annual reports. The air was stale from poor circulation and the lingering traces of cigarette smoke that mocked a faded, browning NO SMOKING sign. A clerk, who looked more like a doorman than a librarian, sat inattentively at a desk on the other side of the room reading the *New York Post*. He had small eyes and a red face that suggested more than a passing familiarity with hard liquor. Stuffed into a navy blue NYU blazer, he had a full head of dark hair that should have been gray. Alison walked confidently across the room, pushed her way right past a little brown half-height swinging door and approached another door, but found it locked.

"Sorry, honey. Faculty and staff only." His eyes never moved from the *Post*.

"Thanks. I'm Professor Monroe, and these are my research associates. Would you let us in please?"

"Professor?" He looked at her skeptically. "What department?"

"History."

"You look a little young for the history department," he offered, without a hint of humor. "Got your ID?"

Jason wondered how long it would take Alison to explode, but she just dug into her purse and pulled out a small piece of paper. She handed it to the clerk.

"This is temporary. You're supposed to have a picture. I can't use it."

"Why don't you call the department office? I'm sure they can confirm that—"

"Makin' calls ain't part of my job."

Adam walked up to the desk and pressed an open hand on the newspaper. Bending slightly, he leaned up and in from below. "Look buddy, you seem like a smart guy. Why don't you improvise a little, okay?"

"It's extension fifteen twenty-two," Alison added, in a voice that smoothed over Adam's rough edge.

The clerk looked at the three of them and figured he'd wasted enough of his time. He dialed the extension and listened.

"Yeah. This is Phil Gates at documents. You got a young lady professor over there, name of…" he studied the temporary ID card "Marone? Yeah? Monroe? What she look like?" His eyes scanned her up and down. "Yeah?" Then he smiled. "Yeah. I guess. Go figure. Okay, thanks."

He handed her a key attached to a long, worn rectangular block, pushed a clipboard across the table, and then returned to reading his paper. "You gotta sign for the key. You gotta return the key directly to me, and sign out. No food in the room, no books out. No writing on the books, no Xerox copies. All reference services close at four-thirty."

Alison led them into the room and turned on the lights. It was the size of a large office, and looked to be the hub of a suite of rooms, a self-contained complex that had its own small card catalogue and a set of stacks that went back into the darkness. There were file cabinets of various sizes, some designed to hold maps and microforms. Rows of matching bound books lined the walls.

Alison spun on her heels and turned swiftly, and smiled like she had gotten them inside the Batcave.

"So? How about that!" she said.

"How about what?" Adam responded. The same sentence had popped into Jason's head, but he kept it to himself.

"Don't you know where we are?"

"The library," Jason chimed in.

"Not the library, *the* library," she said triumphantly, and quickly became impatient with their cultivated blank stares. "NYU is a government depository. Copies of federal, state, and local government documents are sent and stored here automatically. This is the City Room."

Adam looked around, amazed. "You mean that—"

"Every piece of paper produced by the City of New York, from nineteen nineteen to nineteen seventy-three, is supposed to be somewhere in this room."

"What about 'seventy-four and 'seventy-five?" Jason asked.

"It's too soon. And certainly those numbers will be a little different. But the patterns and trends, they can't change much from year to year."

Jason looked over at Adam, who was silently taking an inventory of the room. "But there's so much. I mean, where would you start?"

Alison grabbed a book. "How about the budget? Where the City spends its money."

Adam came to life. "No. My mother could get you a copy of the budget. Let me tell you about cities. They're like guitar players. Rock stars all spend their money on the same stuff. Chicks, cars, and dope. Same thing with cities, except its cops, garbage, and teachers."

"Okay, so, what are we looking for?" she asked.

"You want to know about someone, find out who pays them. That means revenue."

"That's probably on film," Alison offered.

Adam bounded off behind some cabinets. Jason was not going to spend the day figuring out the City's finances, and he began to wonder why he was even there. Besides, he had other business to attend to.

"Is there a pay phone around here?"

"Back through the stacks, the way we came, to the left."

"Listen, I'm going to take off. Are you staying here all day, or are you walking back to your office...?" his voice trailed off, unconvincingly.

"I should stay here. I've spent half my adult life in rooms like this. I think Adam gets most of his data from peeking through windows."

"That's not the half of it," Jason responded quickly. He started for the door, but Alison tugged on the sleeve of his jacket.

"The color's back in your face."

"Yeah, well, I'm feeling a lot better."

"Then, you're still going to be able to change my life tonight?"

"Huh?"

"You know, dinner, your place? We had a date. If you're still up to it, I mean. You said I'd never understand New York until I had genuine Chinese take-out. You promised I'd 'never go back.'"

"You won't," he said, doubling down on his word. "Eight o'clock? 108-16, off Queens Boulevard."

"Apartment 506," she said sweetly.

"Yeah. Come straight up. Don't bother with the intercom. The downstairs buzzer is broken."

"You mean the entryway is just unlocked?"

"You can't really tell unless you know," Jason said. "It's either that or calling up from the streets. Besides, anybody who wants to rob the place will probably hit the first floor."

"I'll try and keep that in mind."

Adam called from the other room. "I can't get this tape in the machine."

"Go ahead. I should make this call." Jason left the room feeling much better than when he went in. Not good enough to forget that Alison was going to spend the entire day with Adam, but pretty good in any event.

Phil the clerk stopped him as he tried to leave. "Hey. Let's see that envelope."

"They're just some medical forms."

"Look pal, this ain't the honor system. No papers leave the room, and I gotta check every bag."

Phil looked carefully through the records. He pulled out an x-ray. "This come from in there?"

"No." Jason pointed at his head. "Up here."

Phil stared at Jason and returned to the papers, checking each one individually before letting him go. Jason headed back through the library stacks, trying to retrace his steps. Each turn led to another maze of identical corridors and endless rows of dark stacks. After a few more minutes of wandering it was clear that he was in uncharted territory, and he toyed with the idea that being lost in the library had some cosmic meaning.

With the steel gray of the stacks and the uneven lighting, it was like wandering around below decks of an abandoned freighter. Jason heard a slight humming sound and navigated towards it. As he suspected, it led to an elevator. Level "D," four floors below the main lobby. He pressed the button, but gave up after two minutes and headed for the nearby staircase.

There was more action three levels up. Students were working at individual desk carrels, some studying intently, others quietly socializing across open books. They looked young, more like high school students, and it dawned on him that a few months ago some of them probably were. The realization was off-putting. College seemed very close to Jason, but high school felt like it was a lifetime away.

Jason followed a sign toward the restrooms, anticipating that was where a phone booth would be, and once again his instincts were right, encouraging him to fantasize about teaching the course "Navigating the Library 101." Entering the booth he closed the fold-

ing door and pulled out the business card Morgan had given him. It
was blank except for the phone number written on one side.

He dialed the number, and a male voice answered.

"Morgan Enterprises, Mr. Morgan's office. This is Mr. Stearns
speaking. How may I assist you?"

"Mr. Morgan please."

"Who may I tell him is calling?"

Jason had known this guy all of two sentences and already he
didn't like him.

"Jason Sims. And tell him it's important."

"Hold please."

There was a click and elevator music came on the line. Jason
waited, then dropped the phone to his shoulder so that he wouldn't
be subjected to the music but would be able to tell when it stopped.
He studied the graffiti carved into the wooden walls of the booth,
none of which was very imaginative: "bite me," "draft this!" "NYU
girls R-E-Z," and the inevitable "Impeach Nixon." A shopworn telephone book dangled from a small chain.

"Hello?" Stearns was back on the line, and Jason pulled the
phone back up.

"Yes?"

"I'm afraid Mr. Morgan is unavailable. But perhaps Mr. Barings, his personal—"

"When will Mr. Morgan be available?" Jason interrupted, and
thought about telling this guy that he didn't sound all that afraid.

Stearns waited before responding, as if to provide a lesson in
manners. "Mr. Morgan rarely speaks on the telephone, sir. Perhaps
I could take a message—"

"Will he be in at any time today?"

"As I said, Mr. Morgan doesn't usually speak on the—"

"I meant in person."

"Oh I don't think that would be possible," Stearns responded
immediately. "Mr. Morgan—"

Jason hung up, irritated. Flipping through the phone book he
found the address for Morgan Enterprises: 1221 Sixth Avenue.

10

AFTER A QUICK SUBWAY RIDE uptown, Jason found himself on the corner of Sixth Avenue and Forty-Seventh Street. It was a part of town Jason had a certain fondness for. The long line of stocky skyscrapers that marched uptown weren't very imaginatively designed, but he found them reassuring. Each one took up a city block, so solid they looked like they'd give Godzilla a run for his money if he showed up. And the streets always buzzed with a positive energy, teeming with pedestrians, hot dog and pretzel stands, three-card Monte dealers, gypsy vendors, guys pushing hand carts; for whatever reason all the sounds mixed together harmoniously. It looked chaotic in the moment, but if you stood and watched for a while you could recognize an unspoken logic that everybody seemed to understand.

Jason shaded his eyes, which were still adjusting from the subway, and tried to get his bearings. He walked along the avenue but the only address he could find didn't tell him anything except that he was on the wrong side of the street. He looked around and saw a taxi idling in gridlocked traffic.

"Hey," he shouted to the cabbie. "Is Twelve-twenty-one Sixth uptown or downtown from here?"

"What am I, the fucking tourist bureau?"

"I'd hate to walk to Forty-eighth and find out I went the wrong way."

"Yeah, it'd be a fuckin' shame." The cabbie looked up at the flashing DON'T WALK sign off to his left and contrasted it with the green light ahead of him. Only two cars from the intersection, but he knew the light was about to turn against him, and he pounded on the horn. Many of his gridlocked neighbors had already introduced this particular tactic to limited effect, but it served as an expression of anger and frustration. "Come on, let's move it!" he shouted at no one in particular. "Green means go!"

Jason found the right building. Characteristically massive, it was one of those modern steel and glass statements that were built by trading zoning exemptions for public space, and so it had a huge atrium two, maybe three floors high, with fountains, a couple of newsstands and even a café. The city was desperate to attract new construction and to compete with all the office space popping up in Jersey, so they cut all the deals they could to keep the contractors happy. Jason worked his way through the crowd and studied a large directory mounted on the wall. The entire thing was framed with the title MORGAN ENTERPRISES above, but there was no Morgan listed under "M." But Stearns was there, and so was Barings, the assistant to Morgan that Stearns had mentioned. Both were on the forty-eighth floor.

Jason headed toward the elevator banks. There were two sets of six—one group served floors three to thirty-three; the second covered thirty-four to fifty-two. A uniformed guard stood at a podium between the two aisles, noticeably closer to the second set, but it was hard to tell if he was stopping people. Jason gathered his courage and walked directly past the guard toward the elevators. The guard never looked up, which was a relief but also somewhat surprising, at least until Jason noticed that there were cameras mounted above the far wall of the elevator alcove. He spun around to avoid the camera so fast that he faked a sneeze to cover the action, which left him feeling quite ridiculous and painfully aware that he would never be mistaken for James Bond.

Rallying, he peered casually into smoked mirrors below the camera, and was able to see the back of the guard monitoring TV consoles built into his podium. Shifting his posture slightly he limited his exposure to the camera and tapped the elevator button. Two young businessmen approached the elevator and also pressed the button, which was already lit up because of Jason's previous touch. People did that everywhere, and he always took it personally. Jason never went for the button if it was lit, especially if he had seen someone else press it. Otherwise you're telling that person that their effort wasn't good enough—or didn't count.

The businessmen talked just a bit louder than they needed to, as if an audience would appreciate their conversation. They were contemporaries, but a subtle pecking order was noticeable. The shorter one carried an air of superiority, while his companion had a hint of baby fat in his cheeks and a slightly too-small vest that left him with a "not-quite-ready-for-prime-time" quality.

"I still say the old man has lost his touch," the shorter man said.

"Well, maybe. But I wouldn't bet against him."

The elevator arrived, and two more people joined them—an older businessman who stood quietly at the rear of the car, and a redheaded woman who had the nervous energy of a secretary getting back late from lunch. Jason hit forty-eight, using the opportunity to turn away from the camera mounted in the upper right corner. The button didn't move, it just lit up from the heat of his finger, which was pretty cool, but somehow unfulfilling, and also left the impression that you were being fingerprinted. One of the businessmen pressed thirty-nine, and Jason noticed that one push seemed to be enough. They continued talking.

"I was talking to James Young today."

"James Young?"

"Yes, he handles all my accounts."

"Really."

"Oh, I've been with him for years. Anyway, according to Jim, two of the old-timers tried to form a syndicate, to back up a loan for the City. Their pitch was that we did it for President Cleveland in eighteen ninety-five, and he was a Democrat too! The joke on the floor was that these were the same two guys!"

They shared an exaggerated laugh as the elevator stopped and

the redhead rushed out. The men watched her depart and exchanged knowing glances.

"Anyway, there wasn't a single firm on the street that would
touch it. Jim told me that if this keeps up I should move all my...."

He stopped talking as the elevator finally reached thirty-nine,
and Jason restrained himself from shoving the two of them out the
door, much as he wanted to.

The elevator continued its ascent, and Jason became aware of
the older gentleman still in the car. He hadn't moved or spoken. A
glance of the buttons revealed no other illuminated numbers. Were
they heading for the same place? Who was this guy? Why was he so
unnaturally still, and silent? Why was it taking so long to get from
thirty-nine to forty-eight? "Knock it off," he grunted, unintention-
ally aloud. The old man didn't flinch.

Forty-eight finally arrived, and Jason froze for a moment, but
he was closer to the doors, and etiquette dictated that he get off first.
He stepped out slowly, hoping to encourage the other fellow to slip
ahead of him, but the air was still as the elevator doors hissed to a
close.

Jason turned to confirm that he was alone in the hallway. Looking around, he realized it wasn't really a hallway. Unlike most office buildings he had been in, there was no dark, industrial gray
elevator alcove from which you emerged to search the corridors for
the office of your choice. In this building, or on this floor, at least,
once out of the elevator you were already on the inside. It was well
lit and the floor was carpeted—green, not thin but not too thick
either. Deciding he would never solve "the mystery of the silent old
man," Jason lectured himself that odd, harmless things happen all
the time without having any larger meaning, and started to walk
through the wood-paneled corridor, following the room numbers.
The walls and the doors were strangely unmarked—no nametags,
no company logos.

Number 4819 was the entrance to a large suite of offices, and
seemed to be the right place. A receptionist sat near the entryway
commanding a circular mahogany desk; much farther back but still

stationed in the exterior of the suite was a male secretary, though based on the seriousness of his look it was a good guess his business card read "Executive Assistant."

The receptionist was attractive, in a serious sort of way, and conservatively dressed. She looked right through him.

"Deliveries should go to 4805," she said.

"I'm here to see Mr. Morgan."

This had an even more dramatic effect than Jason had been rooting for after she called him a delivery boy.

"You'll, uh, have to, uh, I mean people don't just...."

Jason watched her struggle and didn't notice the male secretary approach until he was at his side. The fellow was much larger up close than he had looked in the distance, and when he spoke, Jason recognized his voice as Stearns, whom he had been rude to on the phone. He hoped Stearns wasn't holding a grudge.

"Mr. Sims? I'll be with you in a moment. Would you have a seat, please."

So much for the element of surprise. Jason stood and watched as Stearns returned to his desk and made a phone call. Too few dials for an outside line. He strained to hear, but the desk was too far away, and Jason's lip-reading skills were limited to catching Stearns's final "okay." He put down the phone and walked back over.

"Right this way, please." This guy only had one tone of voice, and Jason wasn't crazy about it. Still, he was surprised to have made it this far without getting kicked out, and he began mentally rehearsing the speech to Morgan that he'd been working on. Stearns led Jason past his desk, which was equipped with TV monitors that showed the lobby, the elevators, and two other places Jason hadn't seen. They reached a large office, and Stearns guided Jason in, but did not follow. Jason wasn't easily impressed with things, but this was some office. Thick, brown carpeting, dark wood everywhere — a large desk, a couple of tables, built-in bookcases, also a couch and sitting area. No overhead lights, just ornate lamps that threw shadows at odd angles. The far right corner of the large room featured floor-to-ceiling windows that offered views of the City to the north and the east that you could charge admission to see. Windows that were so big you couldn't look at them without hoping they were reinforced. Just being in the room probably gave Morgan the upper hand in who knows how many deals. He stood with his back to Jason, looking out at the City—Central Park not too far in the distance, Rockefeller Center just off to his right. "Don't talk to the suit, talk to the man," his father once told him. It was advice that had stuck with Jason over the years.

"See any of your buildings from here?" It wasn't part of Jason's original script, but he thought the ad lib would put him on the offensive.

He stepped out of the glare and turned to face Jason. It wasn't Mr. Morgan.

"Who the hell are you?"

"Mr. Barings," he said, extending his hand. "Mr. Morgan's personal secretary." Barings was slim, probably in his forties, and impeccably dressed. He spoke with a modest clipped British accent that seemed genuine.

"I'm here to see Mr. Morgan," Jason responded firmly, and let the handshake go unrequited.

"Nobody sees Mr. Morgan. He sees them."

"Mr. Morgan told me personally that I was to discuss this matter only with him."

Barings was smooth and reassuring. "Of course. But let me assure you, when you're talking to me, you're talking to Mr. Morgan."

"That may well be. But how do I know for sure that you aren't just—"

Barings interrupted, and read from a file that was already open on the desk in front of him.

"Jason Sims, born October sixteen, nineteen forty-five. Father Manny, twice decorated for valor during World War Two, later printer and secretary-treasurer of union local four-oh-seven. Graduated Columbia University with honors nineteen sixty-six, arrested twice, once in nineteen sixty-seven for assaulting a police officer."

"That's bullshit!" Jason exploded, but Barings continued without missing a beat.

"Case subsequently dismissed. One year at Harvard Law, three semesters Columbia School of Journalism—"

"Let me know when you get to what I had for lunch," Jason snapped, still angry but cooling off a bit.

"We appreciate your discretion, Jason, especially after yesterday. If this is about money, we can certainly—"

"It is about money," Jason interjected. "I get paid"—he pulled the stack of twenties from his coat and tossed them on the desk—"not paid off."

He'd practiced that line all the way over on the subway, and he'd nailed it. Barings looked at the cash, but didn't make a move toward it.

"I see. And this is from Mr. Morgan himself?"

"Well, no, but—"

"Then he ordered someone to give it to you?"

"No," Jason said defensively, "there wouldn't have been time for that."

"Then I would suggest that whatever problem you have…it lies elsewhere."

Jason wasn't buying it. "I don't like this one bit. Maybe we should—"

"Has Mr. Morgan violated the terms of his agreement with you?" Barings queried, with the confidence of a man who knew the answer to his own questions.

"No. It just seems that—"

"Have you been forced to engage in any activities, unspecified in the original agreement, that you find unacceptable?"

"Not exactly…." Jason could feel himself losing the argument, and Barings kept his rhythm steady.

"Then your presence here is largely the result of action taken by a subordinate in a moment of extreme stress?"

"I guess." Jason felt the thickness of the carpet under his feet, and adjusted them slightly.

Barings waved his hand at the money on the table with a small flourish that renounced it. "Perhaps, then, this is a matter for you and him to resolve between yourselves."

Jason stood silently. Barings had won the debate. He was good—he punched like a lawyer and counterpunched like a therapist. But Jason wasn't going to be talked into a corner.

"Look, whatever brought me here, I'm still here. Maybe I was wrong from the start. And that doesn't explain your dossier, either."

"Dossier?"

"On me." Jason felt the heat rising in the back of his neck. "I thought that sort of thing was out of fashion, you know, last couple of years?"

"Mr. Sims, Mr. Morgan is quite particular about the men with whom he chooses to associate." Barings slid two fingers across the dustless desk as he spoke, as if to accentuate the perfect order of Morgan's universe. "That goes for his doorman as well as his accountant."

"That still doesn't—"

"He insisted on meeting with you personally, Jason, something, I think you can now gather, that was a rather exceptional gesture on his part. He seemed to think that was important. If you could just see this through to the end of the week—"

"You mean tomorrow, Friday?"

"—we might be able to rethink, maybe even speak to Mr. Morgan on Monday."

"Okay. I'll do it tomorrow. But that's it, I'm out," he said theatrically, realizing that he didn't really know just what he was in. He headed toward the door. "If Morgan wants to talk about it, I'm sure he'll be able to find me."

JASON AND ALISON SAT ON the living room floor in Jason's apartment. Open boxes of Chinese food were set out on the coffee table next to them. A small black and white TV on a stand off to the side was tuned to a Mets game. When Alison arrived Jason had walked over and turned town the volume, but, to her slight amusement, he left the set on. She was dressed more like she had been in the bar, not the library, and Jason liked it better. One bump down to jeans and a T-shirt and she would have been devastating.

"So how long did he stay there?" Jason asked.

"All afternoon. He said he only scratched the surface."

"Were you there the whole time?" Jason was ignoring the voice that told him to move on.

"Uh-huh," she said, swallowing. "He needed my help with some of the sources. But mostly I was working on a paper." She pointed at one of the cartons with her fork. "What's this one?"

"Shrimp with black bean sauce." He offered a tour of the other dishes. "Szechuan chicken, garlic braised Chinese greens…that one is the house special fried rice. Best fried rice in town." He said it like he was showing someone the Mona Lisa for the first time.

Alison picked up a chopstick and probed the fried rice like an archeologist, but Jason took the carton and shook some out on her plate. "You're supposed take it as it comes, not just pick out the bits you like."

"That's deep. You talking about the food or life?" she asked mischievously.

"Hey, we don't joke about Chinese food around here."

She tried some of the rice. "That is good. It tastes different, though. You know, this is the one thing I've had before. They used to have fried rice at Dave's."

"Dave's?" That didn't sound promising.

"Dave's Asian Garden. It was the greatest. Back in Kenosha. Chinese, Japanese, Korean, Indian."

"Indian?" he asked, against his better judgment.

"Yeah. The Chinese section had egg rolls, fried rice, and spare ribs. The fried rice went great with naan."

Within two seconds Jason sifted through twenty responses and rejected them all. "So…what's this paper you're writing?"

"Oh God. It's called 'Tax Farming and Imperial Decline.' You want to hear more about Dave's?"

Jason did not want to hear more about Dave's. "What's that? How they taxed their farmers?"

"No, no, tax farming, not taxing farmers."

"Uh…right," Jason offered, not getting it. He stole a quick glance at the TV.

Alison usually segued into different material in these situations, but she didn't this time. She wasn't going to back off, but spoke without lecturing.

"When a government gets so weak that it can't even collect taxes, it raises revenue by selling the right to collect taxes—you know, like subcontracting. Basically to local thugs, who then go out and shake people down."

"So there are no actual farms involved," he said with a smile.

"No, it's farming like 'farming out.' It becomes prominent when things are really starting to fall apart."

"So where was this taking place?" he asked, genuinely interested.

"Well, that's the really cool part—at least for a historian. It happens everywhere." Her eyes danced when she talked. "At least, everywhere an empire was falling apart. The late Roman Empire, the Song Dynasty in twelfth-century China…. Did you know the

Chinese issued paper currency hundreds of years before it was introduced in Europe?"

"No!" Jason widened his eyes in mock amazement.

"Laugh now, copter-boy, but it's the same thing that happened here. In the eleven-sixties the Song dynasty was at war with the Jurchen regime, and they were running out of money to pay for it. First they issued an edict that everyone had to surrender their copper objects to the government, so they could be melted down for coins. Then after those were all spent on the war they issued paper money. From eleven sixty-seven to eleven sixty-eight the inflation rate *doubled*."

Alison became self-conscious of the fact that the she was talking quickly and maybe had gotten a little too excited about twelfth-century inflation rates. She paused for a moment, but Jason seemed to be waiting for more, so she continued.

"Anyway," she said more matter-of-factly, "like I said, it's the same thing now. We went off the gold standard in 'seventy-one, and then the inflation—"

"We went off the gold standard?" He said it straight, but his eyes gave him away.

"Shut up!" she said with a smile.

Jason stood up. "You want another beer?"

"No thanks."

Jason walked to the kitchen and came back with a fresh beer. Alison was poking through some of the cartons with a fork, exploring. He sat down next to her, in the same spot as before but a little bit closer.

"How can someone who knows so much about China know so little about Chinese food?"

"I'm not sure that people from other places realize just how important Chinese food can be."

"Oh, there are few things that are more important," he explained. "When I was very young, we lived in Manhattan, pretty far downtown. Every Sunday night my father would take us out to dinner in Chinatown. For a kid, it was like…like walking into a magic closet. The streets would come to life, English would disappear from the storefronts and street signs. Inside, there were never any menus, he would always order for us. Later on, after we moved out here, I was a delivery boy."

"Did you have your own car?"

"No, this was when I was fourteen or so. But bikes were faster anyway. You know the neighborhood—crowded streets, lots of apartment buildings—we didn't go more than maybe three-quarters of a mile in any direction. I did it for three years. I once calculated that I probably brought Chinese food to over five thousand people. And it was a real learning experience, too. When you're young, you're exposed to a slightly sanitized version of humanity. But people don't tidy the house, or even stop arguing with each other, just because some kid shows up with the Chinese food."

Alison stole a quick glace over at the cartons, arrayed like a small sculpture garden, her eyes catching the light sliding off the thin silver handles.

"And you never knew who was going to open that door," Jason continued. "Little old ladies, young singles, rich and poor, families, everybody orders Chinese food. They were so different. I used to think about how they were all connected by this common thread."

A hissing sound radiated from the TV set. Jason tumbled over and turned up the volume, and the hiss turned into the roar of the crowd. A player was shown trotting around the bases, and an excited announcer described the action.

"A two-out pinch-hit home run for Kranepool wins the game for the Mets in the bottom of the ninth. It stops the losing streak at five, and makes a winner out of pitcher Tug McGraw. The Mets are streaming onto the field and mobbing him at the plate like they just won the World Series! We'll be back with the happy recap in just a minute."

Jason reached out to turn off the TV, but paused at the appearance of two news anchors, a black man and a white woman, the current coupling of choice for almost every station. The man spoke first, in a deadly serious voice.

"Gangland style execution murders on the West Side leave four men dead. And on the eve of his funeral, new questions emerge about money found in the trunk of Sid Maynes's car."

Then the female anchor lit up with a big smile. "All that and traffic, sports, and weather, and a cat who plays ping-pong, coming your way right after the game!"

Jason clicked off the set, then leaned back and turned on the reel-to-reel tape machine. It was soft blues music—some rare acoustic recordings of Ma Rainey from 1924, ideal for the occasion. He had selected it with Alison in mind—they were some of the oldest recordings he had, and a female artist to boot. Alison liked history, and she was a woman. Ma was also bisexual, normally a winning conversation topic, but Jason wasn't sure they discussed such things in the Midwest and planned to keep that tidbit to himself.

Jason looked to evaluate Alison's reaction to the music, which was always a pivotal moment for him. But she was still staring at the now-lifeless TV.

"Isn't that the same guy from the other day, that Maynes person?"

"Yeah."

"Did you see any of that money?"

"No. The trunk was closed when we were there. Maybe we interrupted something, I don't know."

Jason really didn't want to talk about it, but she seemed more interested in the whole affair than she was the other night. Probably just being near Adam. He could rub off on people. He decided to take it head on.

"Did Adam say whether he'd found anything?"

"He didn't say, but I'm sure he did. He was trying not to let on, but he seemed very excited to me. He told me to tell you he wants to see you in his office tomorrow. Did I mention that? I don't think he wanted to talk about it in the library."

"No. He can only talk in a *secure environment*," Jason said, trying for just the right amount of ridicule.

"He also told me that if the police ever questioned me, I shouldn't mention that I knew him or took him to the library." It was hard to tell if she was rolling her eyes or just looking up.

"You just have to get used to him," Jason said, trying to gauge the whole Adam situation.

"No, I didn't mean…he was just the opposite. It was really sweet. He had microfilm going in three separate machines, and kept running back and forth between like a kid at an arcade. He must have filled up two pads with notes. It was very…cute."

"Yeah, he's very popular with women."

"I didn't mean cute cute, I meant cute." Alison had forgotten that she was talking to another guy. "I like him and all, but he's not really my type."

"Really. What is your type?"

"Why do you ask?" Her voice regained the more viscous quality it had before Ed Kranepool had killed the mood with his home run.

"Just idle curiosity. Women are so mysterious."

Alison arched an eyebrow.

"Maybe that's not the right word. All I mean is…uh…you know…what do you look for in a guy?"

"Well," she said quietly. "I'll let you in on a little secret. You know how women always talk about men's eyes, going on and on about them?" She leaned forward a bit more. "That's not exactly right, at least not for me. It's actually the space around the eyes." She said the word "around" beautifully. "Take you for example. You don't have many lines on your face. But a couple here, right near your eyes, and they go up and down, instead of across."

She reached over and traced a line near his eye. "Not that long, but deep. It's where you carry your past. And that frames your eyes."

She took his hand and looked at his eyes before kissing him, about four minutes ahead of when he had planned to kiss her. Her kisses quickly became passionate and it took Jason a moment to catch up. She was uninhibited and uncalculating, but he had the fleeting thought that if they ever went ballroom dancing, she would insist on leading. And maybe she should—as they were, she seemed a step ahead of him at every thought. Not that he was complaining, but it was an unfamiliar experience and with that part of his mind not lost in the moment he started to calculate his next move, and whether they were better off where they were or if he should risk trying to move to another room.

His hand was on her right hip when she sat up. "Listen, I have to go."

Jason was taken aback, and very confused. Had he been too slow? Had he been too fast? Did he make a mistake?

"Really? Go? You have to?" He decided to wait until he could compose complete sentences. "I mean, I thought, you know, we would, you could…I mean, did I do something—"

Alison kissed him again. It was a robust, reassuring kiss, not with the same fire as before, but it got her point across.

"Tomorrow is my first class. I need to get a good night's sleep. I had a wonderful time."

They walked along the streets back to Alison's apartment building. Jason had put himself back together and was starting to assess the evening in a very positive light. It had been an uncharacteristically long time since he'd been with a woman, especially one that he was interested in. Technically, he hadn't really "been with" Alison, but it felt a little like he had.

"I can't believe that your family ate out once a week. We ate out exactly once a year—my mother's birthday."

They took the main streets this time, because Jason knew she wanted to get back. He listened to the rhythm of her walk while she reminisced—a skill he was quickly refining. Alison's walk changed depending on the context, like a mood ring. This was a good walk. "We'd make her breakfast in bed—my brother and I—and clean the house. There was never school, as we always observed this occasion on the first Saturday after her birthday—our own version of a federal holiday. There would be gifts and treats, of course, and at the end of the day we'd dress up and drive into town…and then— what's wrong?"

They were barely touching, just shoulder to shoulder, but Alison could feel his entire body tighten.

"What's the matter?"

"Nothing." He said it casually, but kind of steered them towards the edge of the sidewalk, closer to the street.

Alison looked ahead and saw two figures slowly approaching. She had a momentary panic that Jason's city smarts were anticipating trouble, but it was just two foot patrolmen walking down the block. They walked in silence as the cops got closer, and Jason stared straight ahead the whole time. Not at them, not at her, not at anything, apparently, but the horizon, though Alison speculated that he was focused on monitoring their progress. She tilted her head subtly as they passed, but the cops weren't looking for any eye contact either. They walked about twenty more paces before Jason spoke.

"Listen. Adam's a little paranoid about reporters. He thinks everybody's out to scoop him. But if he told you not to talk to the cops, he wasn't just kidding around."

"What do you mean?"

"Cops are like anyone else. Just people trying to make ends meet, maybe do the best they can along the way. In some cases, maybe not. But either way, they work for the City."

She looked at him, not sure of the point.

"Adam thinks he's in the cage-rattling business. Okay, that's his choice. But the cops are dogs guarding those cages. Who do you think writes their checks?"

It was quiet again, and in a few more blocks they reached the steps of Alison's building. She still seemed a little unsettled.

"There's more to it than that, isn't there?" she said. "About the police, I mean. More than just Adam talking."

"Maybe." He shrugged, like a kid refusing to confess but unwilling to lie. "But it's enough for now. Just steer clear of 'em, that's all. Don't worry—nothing's going to happen."

He reached out and pushed the hair back from her face. "Hey," he smiled, "big day tomorrow. What time is class?"

"Ten-ten."

"I'll call you after."

She kissed him again, walked up the steps, and disappeared into the building.

12

IT WAS CLOSE TO THREE-THIRTY in the morning, and Adam was alone in his office, and stuck three times over. It had been about two hours since he finally hit the wall with the big investigation, so he decided to try to work on his new book for a while. Adam didn't believe in stopping, just in changing lanes. But he couldn't move with the new book—in fact it was a disaster—he couldn't even bear to look at it, so he switched over to the Dylan essay he was supposed to write for *Rolling Stone*, which was due in just a few days. That wasn't going anywhere either.

Until then it had been a very productive night. He'd been on a roll, integrating all the NYU material in with the various fragments he'd previously accumulated. He worked on it for four solid hours without a break, and everything seemed to be falling into place, like it was a giant paint-by-numbers scheme and he'd just gotten a bunch of new colors. After he worked his way through the new stuff he stopped, had some Chinese food, then crashed on the couch for a couple of hours. But when he woke up around one-thirty he didn't have it anymore, and the last couple of hours had been frustrating. He started to panic, wondering if he'd confused motion for progress. Maybe integrating all those documents was just so much busy-work. Maybe there wasn't anything to find. Maybe...no. He cut those ideas off with the discipline of a surgeon, and forced himself to focus on productive thoughts. He had learned a lot, he reminded himself, but it was all about what wasn't happening, and maybe that's the way this one had to go, more a war of attrition than a treasure hunt. He was now convinced, for example, that there was nothing to be found in the school system. Class sizes were creeping up and minority test scores were falling, but that was nothing new. The whole garbage situation was a little more puzzling—not because they were spending more, but because they were leaving money on the table. Switching from three- to two-man trucks would have saved a bundle—they could cut 3,000 uniforms from the sanitation department and still haul the same twenty-five thousand tons of trash a day. It seemed like an obvious move for a city teetering on the edge of bankruptcy, but he was in the market for corruption, not stupidity, so he let it go.

"Follow the money," he said out loud, admonishing himself. It worked for Woodward and Bernstein and he knew that the money had to be even more important here. It wasn't the loose thread that would lead to the devil's lair, it was the entire tapestry—the money was the story. He closed his eyes and tried to envision how public funds circulated through the City, like blood through a body, but gave up and went for something more concrete—and arranged the piles of papers in the form of a map of the New York area: Manhattan, the Bronx, Queens and Brooklyn, Long Island, Westchester, Southern Connecticut, North Jersey. There wasn't a stack for Staten Island, but it didn't seem to matter. He climbed around the office, looking for different perspectives on the flows of dollars and people. There was something going on with cops and crime. Crime was, in general, way up, but unevenly so and in a noticeable geographic pattern. And the overall problem looked to be more from falling revenues than rising spending, though spending was up, apparently. Apparently—that was the word that was killing him— there seemed to be more money spent than could be accounted for. Staring at the paper model of the City, Adam hoped the answer would come to him. It didn't.

He decided to take another crack at the book, his third. He made his reputation on the first, six years ago, with *This Machine Kills Fascists*. It was one of the first books published on rock-and-roll, and it was damn good, he reminded himself, trying to psych himself up into writing mode. Initially the publishers just asked him to put together a bunch of his columns, with an intro and a conclusion, but Jason told him if he did that he'd be a "fucking whore, selling second-hand columns like they were used cars," and at the time, it was hard to argue with him.

Besides, he did that with his second book, *Come Together: Why Rock and Roll Can Still Change the World*," which was quickly published eighteen months later, to take advantage of the paperback release of *This Machine*. It had been a while since he'd tried to write a real book, and he was remembering why. But he knew what he wanted to say, and had the title set: *This is the End: Why Rock and Roll Will Never See 30*. It started from a bar rap he'd developed years ago about dead rock stars (chicks love talking about dead rock stars—there's nothing sexier than being young, talented, troubled, and dead) and why they all seemed to die when they were twenty-seven years old: Jimi, Janis, and Jim.

He'd come up with this theory that rock stars faced a crisis when they hit twenty-five. It's possible that he was initially inspired by the calculation that his target audience had just reached that age, but over the years he started to buy into his own logic. When you're twenty-five, you're an adult, there's just no way around it. If you got arrested for robbing a bank, when it was shown on TV they'd say "a twenty-five-year-old *man* was arrested today." Not a boy or a youth or even a young man; they'd just call you a man. But rock is about being young. So when rockers hit twenty-five, they freak out. After two years of freaking out, they either die or come out the other side.

About a year ago Adam started thinking that this was true not just for individual rockers but for rock-and-roll in general. Rock was growing up, and that presented it with an identity crisis, a struggle for the very essence of its soul. It was born in 1955, the year Chuck Berry invented the sound, Little Richard gave it a voice, and Elvis made it white. The first cycle ended with Elvis in the Army, Little Richard in Bible school, and Chuck Berry hounded by The

Man, and the Mann Act. But it was like the bomb—you could try to ban it, but you couldn't un-invent it. And the next seven years, pretty much tracking with the Beatles' recording career, 1962 to 1969, showed what rock could do—it *did* change the world. Since then, the third generation has had a tough time living up. If the pattern holds, 1976 would be the end of another seven-year cycle; rock would be twenty-one, and staring adulthood in the face. Worse, it wasn't just old, but had become a business, Big Business; and the phrase Rock and Roll business was an oxymoron—something would have to give. A few years ago, maybe he would have bet on rock, but now Adam was putting his money on business.

He picked up the microphone from his tape recorder and started talking. "Twenty-five is bad news for a rocker—that's how old Dylan was when he flipped over the handlebars of his motorcycle and disappeared. John Lennon was the same age when the Beatles quit touring for good; Brian Jones met the same challenge with three emergency hospitalizations, the start of a downhill slide from the top of the world that ended with him kicked out of his band and then dead at the bottom of a swimming pool. Dylan, the Beatles, and the Stones—the Mount Rushmore of Rock shook when it hit the quarter-century mark—what chance do mortals have?"

Well, that sucked. He rewound the tape, erasing it. He got up and tiptoed through the stacks of the paper city without disturbing them. Where was the money coming from? Saying it out loud three times didn't help, so Adam picked up the Nerf basketball that had been sitting on his desk, and shot it at the basket across the room. "Yes!" he cried, and continued talking out loud, retrieving the ball and roaming around the room. He started to sink one basket after another, deftly cutting through the accumulated clutter. "Clyde's got it, top of the circle, he looks left, moves right, head fake, puts it up.... Yes, and it counts!" Adam called it out in his best Marv Albert voice. Man, he was good. If there was a pro Nerf basketball league, he'd be the white Walt Frazier. He wouldn't just be great, he'd make his teammates great. And he'd look good doing it.

After twenty minutes of shooting around it was time to get back to business, and Adam went to the newsroom to put up another pot of coffee. With only a couple of hours left until people started to show up at the station, he needed to make the best of them. He slipped down the hall to use the bathroom while the coffee was brewing—feats accomplished without turning on the lights—a little game he'd invented that had only once led to disaster. But it was essential survivalist training: you never knew when you were going to have to use the bathroom without being seen.

He was walking back down the dark hallway when he thought he heard something. He stopped and listened. There was definitely something going on, back near the main office. Backing up, Adam circled around to his office in the darkness and retrieved his trusty stick-ball bat, the closest thing he had to a weapon. He hoped he wouldn't have to use it; it was probably the only thing he'd saved from his childhood.

Adam crept back towards the coffee machine, flexing his hands on the soft black tape that he'd wrapped around the bottom of the bat twenty years ago. He was able to make out two figures in the darkness—or maybe it was one figure and a plant. Crouching behind a row of desks, he slid along the floor until he was just near enough. He waited for the right moment, flipped on the lights suddenly and swung with all his might.

"Take it easy man, I'm just the janitor," Sammy said, good and loud, but without shouting.

Adam recognized him, and pulled the bat up at the last moment, taking out an overhead light in the process.

"Sammy, what hell are you doing?" Adam shouted while covering his head with his arms from the raining debris. His heart was pounding.

"Gettin' some of this coffee," Sammy said, with more than a hint of irritation. "What the hell did you *think* I was doing?"

Adam didn't really have a good answer for that. "What were you talking about? You're not the janitor."

"I know I'm not the janitor, but anybody who knows me, they ain't gonna shoot me. And anybody who doesn't know me, they won't know I ain't the janitor. And ain't nobody going to shoot the janitor, wouldn't waste their time."

Adam thought about it for a second, and it made sense. He got down on his hands and knees and started to collect the broken bits of the light fixture. Sammy got down next to him.

"Hey, I busted it, you don't have to do that."

"I don't mind. I kind of wanted to talk to you, anyway."

"How did you know I'd be here?" Adam asked casually, never more than two steps away from a conspiracy.

"I didn't. Sometimes I come in a few hours early. It's nice at night. Quiet, good TVs if you want to watch, but usually I'll sit on the roof and read a bit—sometimes just by the lights of the City, maybe a candle or two. Of course, not so much in the winter."

"Huh." Adam barely knew Sammy, but he could see why Jason took him so seriously. There seemed to be a lot going on under the surface of his words, if you were looking for it.

"So, what did you want to talk to me about?"

"How much you know about these suits your buddy Jay's been making time with?"

"You've seen them?" Adam asked, surprised that Sammy had used the plural.

"Course I have. They want to use the copter, they have to talk to me, at least a little."

"Not much. I can't imagine it could happen if Morgan didn't want it to happen," Adam indicated cautiously, "and guys like him want what they want. Why do you ask?"

"I don't know, some of these people, I don't know about them," Sammy said.

"How do you figure?"

"I see things people like you don't see," Sammy said, picking up a piece of glass near Adam's knee.

Adam didn't like the sound of that, and shot Sammy a quick look.

"It's not 'cause of you, it's 'cause of them," Sammy continued. "They don't change who they are just 'cause I'm there, like they would for you. And some of these people, well, I'm not so sure about them."

"I wouldn't worry too much about it," Adam said, "Times are different. At the end of the day, Morgan's a businessman. Just 'cause a guy breaks the law, doesn't make him a crook."

"Just 'cause a guy follows the rules, doesn't make him honest," Sammy countered.

Adam surveyed the ceiling, wondering what needed to be fixed and what wouldn't get noticed.

"You listen to an old man for a second," Sammy said quietly, forcing Adam's eyes back in his direction. "Laws change. People don't. Ain't no right or wrong in the law. It's just the law. People are good or bad. Well, parts of both, really, but more one than the other, and that's what matters. Don't be telling me about the law. Tell me about the man."

Adam held up his hands. "I don't know what to say, Sammy. Picking out the saints from the sinners isn't my strong suit. They all look the same to me."

"Just watch your friend's back, is all I'm saying. Not much more important in this world than that."

"I know."

Adam went back to his office, still looking for a spark. He tried the TV, a true sign of desperation. Didn't matter, it was just a bunch of dead air—all the stations seemed to have signed off for the night. Channel Nine was still on, and when it came back from commercial Adam realized that they were showing his favorite Stanley Kubrick movie, *The Killing*. *2001* might have been an important film, but *The Killing* was a great movie, and he'd watch a great movie over an important film any day.

It was near the end, and Sterling Hayden's perfect caper was in the final stages of its inevitable collapse. There he was, at the airport, watching the cops, and watching his bag, bulging with cash, sitting on the baggage cart bouncing along to the plane. Then out onto the impossibly dark runway, it rocks a little more, a little bad luck gives one final push, and it falls and bursts open. Money everywhere, millions of dollars, blown in the wind by the propellers. The cops approach, slowly. "Run, Johnny!" his girlfriend urges. But he just stands there. "What's the difference?" he says it flat—not scared, not bitter, just reporting the facts.

"Right on, Stanley!" Adam cheered to himself, "What's the difference! You tell 'em!"

He turned off the set and bounded over to his typewriter and typed quickly, not stopping to think.

Great albums are made by uncertain artists, struggling lost and half-blind to articulate the right question. Great movies are made by commanding craftsmen, masters of purpose and execution, who tell you the answer. That's why music, when it matters, is a universal prayer that draws you closer, while film's implicit certainty, even in the hands of an awe-inspiring genius like Bergman or Welles, must, to some extent, stand apart, just out of reach. And it is why, my friends, when people one hundred years from now play Blood on the Tracks *for the first time, it will still blow them away.*

He finished the Dylan essay in an hour, and then threw himself back into the City's finances. Closing his eyes he saw the money from Sterling Hayden's briefcase flying all across Manhattan.

13

JASON FINISHED THE MORNING traffic flight. He was getting a little bored with the traffic and a lot bored with Dave, neither of which changed much from day to day. Unbelievable backups invariably spilled endlessly into the distance from all the major crossings, and Dave spent even more time fixing his hair and makeup between reports, something that you wouldn't have thought possible. When he wasn't primping he would rehearse out loud, trying to punch up his material, occasionally tossing out new synonyms for "delay," which he expected Jason to critically evaluate.

Back at the station Jason was killing time. It would be more than two and a half hours before his next—and probably last—flight with Bill. He stood off to the side of the set, as was his habit, mostly watching Carol. Adam thought he understood Jason's fascination with Carol, since she was so self-evidently attractive and captured the attention of most of the men at the station. But Jason liked to think that he found her intriguing in spite of that, or, more accurately, not because she was so attractive but because she constantly had to deal with the consequences of that fact. Not that she wasn't nice to look at.

It was a commercial break, and various technicians and assistants were wandering around the set, including Lou Bettleheim, who somehow managed to range all over the station as he directed the show. Harry, who was in the enclosed control room just behind the cameras, tapped on the glass and motioned for Jason to come inside. Harry was having several conversations at once when Jason entered, and the whole room was buzzing with activity. Jason sat on a stool and watched a commercial on a small monitor in the corner.

"We're back in five," Lou's voice called out from somewhere, and a hush quickly came over the room. Jason looked over at Harry, who motioned for him to wait for the last part of the show to finish. Nathan suddenly appeared everywhere, and Jason compared the versions—on the cluster of big monitors in front of the control room, on Jason's little monitor, and looking through the glass onto the set. He looked best on the little monitor.

"Repeating our top stories," Nathan began in his confident, inimitable staccato, "four men dead in a West Side shootout… apparently.…"

One of the large control room monitors displayed mug shots of four young black men. Jason was startled, as he was almost certain that he recognized one of them as the glaring would-be rapist from his exploits of the other day.

"Apparently…" Nathan repeated, hesitating.

"He's off the cards" an assistant director alerted the room, with only a modest sense of urgency in his voice.

Nathan coughed, and then continued, "excuse me…apparently the victims of a turf war between rival gangs…though details are still coming in."

"He's still off," reported the AD, somewhat more urgently but still in measured tones, "I don't know where he—"

"New toll and parking surcharges go into effect tomorrow," Nate continued.

"Okay, he's back on."

"…and a large crowd is expected at the funeral of Sid Maynes, to be held later today in Brooklyn."

The monitors all switched to Carol, who lit up for the camera. "Be sure to join Cathy and Steve for the five o'clock report, with updates on all our stories, Tommy Thompson with local sports, and our nightly feature on rush-hour traffic tips."

She turned sideways and both anchors appeared together in a two-shot.

"Any big plans for the weekend, Nate?" she asked with an exaggerated smile.

"Not really. Actually, Carol, I'm going to be about the station tomorrow."

Carol's smile froze a bit at this piece of unscripted business, but she held it and kept with him.

"Look out! Last time you said that on Monday we had a new set and two new writers. I thought I came to the wrong station!"

"That was just a coincidence!" He was back to full staccato Natespeak, and the tension eased in the room.

"Well, just to be sure, Nate, call me on Sunday night if we're changing the format!"

"I sure will, Carol; you know what I say, better safe than sorry." He turned away and was alone on the screen.

"For Carol Chase and the rest of the Channel Six News Team, I'm Nathan Johnson. We'll see you Monday with the rising sun at six. Have a good weekend."

"And that's it, we're out," reported Lou, who had been in the control room but was out on the set before he finished his sentence.

Jason watched Nate rise slowly from his seat, pushing down on the desk with closed fists for leverage. He didn't remember having ever seen Nate angry before, or for that matter expressing any untethered emotion, and was curious about what was going on. But Harry came over and interrupted his train of thought.

"Listen kid, I need to talk to you."

Jason kind of liked Harry, as far as it went. He imagined him in his younger days as one of those committed New-Dealers who kept in touch with his army buddies and got into fistfights about McCarthyism. But they rarely spoke, and when they did it was usually about some rule that Jason hadn't been aware of or wasn't following.

"Look, if it's about that memo, I never got it."

"Memo? Which one?"

"Any of 'em. Fact is, I'm not sure if I have a mailbox. So I don't see how I could know—"

"What? Look, I just wanted—"

"Phone, Harry," the Assistant Director interrupted.

"Sorry, kid. Gimme a minute."

Harry walked over to the phone. Jason looked out from the booth and saw Nathan engaged in a hushed but very sharp conversation with Lou. Glancing down, he noticed that they were also visible on the little monitor next to him. Discretely surveying the control room to confirm, as expected, that nobody was paying him any attention, Jason casually turned the volume knob, not sure that it would do anything. It did, and the conversation was so clearly audible that he lowered it a bit.

"That's outrageous. I went off the cards because the story is bullshit! We've been over this before."

"Quadruple murder is bullshit?" Lou responded. "That's news, even in this town."

"I saw the notes on this—those kids were shot in the head. No shootout, no drugs. Four white kids shot in the back of the head, we'd run the story different. We *ran* the story different at eight, till you colored it in."

Lou took all this with an atypical patience—Jason had seen him ditch whining talent faster than a mother passing off a screaming toddler to the sitter. But Nate took a "contributing editor" credit, which Carol didn't, and Lou gave him his time.

"We got an update," he explained. "They weren't shot in the head. None of that stuff."

"Not shot in the head? Where the hell did you get that from? I read the copy. Hell, I *wrote* that copy."

"Cops messengered it over during the broadcast. We had to change it."

"*During the broadcast?*" Some inner version of Nate was climbing closer to the surface. "What do they do, watch the morning news, and correct every story they don't like? What's the matter with you people? You think every time the cops—"

"Sorry, kid. How's the head?"

It was Harry, back from his phone call. Jason slipped off the stool and tried to subtly turn the volume down on the monitor at the same time.

"All right, I guess," he answered, sitting down.

"Thinking of becoming a reporter?" Harry said, looking over at the monitor.

"No. Just violating a little privacy, I guess."

"Same difference, huh?"

"Nowadays." Jason was kicking himself for snooping, and felt like he'd been caught buying a dirty magazine.

"Jeez, loosen up. I'm supposed to be the tight-ass around here."

"That's what it says on the bathroom wall."

Harry let that one pass without even acknowledging it. He steered Jason towards the back of the booth, where they sat across from each other in a couple of small black director's chairs.

"Listen, this is serious," he said, leaning in. "I got a call from the guys upstairs—they'd like to see you in front of the camera. You know, helicopter hero and all that. Good for ratings."

"Huh?"

"They want to hire you as a reporter for the station."

"They want to make me be a reporter because I crashed my helicopter? I don't get it. Whose brilliant idea was this? It's a good thing I don't work at a hospital—they'd want to make me a surgeon."

Jason was riffing, something he rarely did with outsiders, and they were talking past each other.

"Don't worry, we'd keep you in the air," Harry said reassuringly. "But you could do the traffic, too."

"Traffic? Traffic reporter?" He repeated it as if it was a contradiction in terms. There was a job that had been invented by television. Could the conversation take a worse turn? If it had been anybody other than Harry he would have ripped into a long lecture on the subject. He was irritated by the very suggestion. He was irritated that he was irritated. He tried to adjust his posture, but you really couldn't move around in those damn director's chairs. Why did such chairs exist? Oh right, because they were light and mobile, so you could move them from set to set during a movie shoot. Why they had them at the station remained a mystery.

"I don't think so," he said more politely. It was time to get out and move on. "Besides, what about Dave?"

"Fuck 'im. I'll give him the afternoon rush. Pretty soon he's gonna figure out we're not going to put him behind a desk, he'll quit anyway."

Harry redeemed himself a bit with this unanticipated dumping on Dave. Jason was confident that Dave was exactly the sort of person who had a bright future in TV, but he appreciated Harry's assessment just the same.

"C'mon, Harry, you can't be serious. TV reporter? I couldn't cash that check."

Harry sat back in his chair. He didn't seem shocked, and Jason wondered if he had expected this, but had to ask.

"How about an interview? It would really help us. We're getting killed by Channel Eight."

"Interview?" This was a curveball, and Jason hadn't seen it coming. He flinched, and took a weak swing. "Look, I know Andy Warhol says TV is something to be on, not something to watch, but he's wrong. In fact, he's been wrong about everything except the Velvet Underground. And I haven't done *anything* that—"

Harry looked at Jason like he wasn't speaking English, and then cut him off before he could reach a definitive "no."

"You could do it with Carol. Just hang around for a while, we could shoot it today."

"I don't know, you know, I have a lot to do. I mean, how long would it take?"

"Half-hour, tops. Five minutes of makeup, ten minutes of questions, fifteen just standing around. Boom-boom-boom, it'll be over almost as soon as it starts."

"Look, this is crazy. But if it would really help, I'll try and meet you halfway. But that's it, right? One interview…with Carol." He shot a confirming look at Harry, who didn't contradict him. "I can give you half an hour. And no use of the phrase 'helicopter hero.'"

Harry leaned over with an open hand and tapped him on the knee three times.

"Great, kid, great. I'll set it up."

14

"HEY." JASON ARRIVED AT Adam's office. Remarkably, it was in more disarray than usual—Adam wasn't even visible behind the stacks of books and papers.

"Hey." The voice came from behind him, as Adam entered. He looked expectantly at Jason. "So?"

"So, what?"

"How was the big date?" Adam said, sounding like a gleeful prosecutor.

"Good. Very good."

"Did you—"

"I don't want to talk about it."

Adam grinned triumphantly. "Pussy."

"Don't call me pussy, asshole."

"Pussy."

"She talked about you a lot," Jason said, deftly outflanking him.

"Really," Adam said, eager to hear more. "Like what?"

"Nothing, just about how you were all jazzed about what you'd found. And she said you were cute."

"I am cute," Adam, said, beaming, and let Jason sit with that for a few beats. "She called you timeless."

"Timeless? What the fuck does that mean?"

"I don't know, but trust me, for a Ph.D. it's better than cute." Adam adjusted the orientation of a set of folders on his desk as if they were ever so slightly out of place. "Chick digs you, man. Try not to fuck this one up."

"Thanks, I'll try to fall back on that sage advice at the right time." Jason scanned the stacks of paper cluttering the room, which looked like they'd been rearranged. "So, you got something for me or not?"

"Not here. You're going on one of your top-secret missions again today, right? How much time before you fly?"

"Not till twelve-thirty. But I have to be here before. We can go out, but not far."

"How come?"

"Mail!" They were interrupted by a tall young black man pushing a cart. He handed Adam a bundle of letters wrapped together by a thick rubber band.

"Thanks, Jimmy."

"You got anything going out?" Jimmy asked.

"You know I don't mail anything from here."

"Yeah, but I'm supposed to ask."

As he started to leave Jason called out. "Hey, you got anything for Sims?"

"Sims?" Jimmy asked. The name wasn't ringing a bell. "What department?"

"I don't know, traffic?"

"That ain't a department. We got administration, custodial, editorial, executive, legal, personnel, staff, talent, and technical. Which one are you?" He gave Jason a long look. "Probably not executive, legal, or talent," he concluded, poking through the mail with his fingers. "No offense."

"He ain't any of 'em, Jimmy," said Adam, sorting through his letters. "He just wants some mail."

Jimmy took this as his cue to leave. "Well, you know what they say," he offered over his shoulder, "you gotta write 'em to get 'em."

Adam stared at Jason, waiting for him to speak. "Do we have individual mailboxes somewhere," Jason asked, "or do you have to have an office that they come and bring your mail to?"

"You must be under the mistaken impression that you're not speaking with the finest investigative journalist of our time," Adam said, who had set down his letters and was now deftly balancing the Nerf ball on his fingertip.

"Oh, I would never forget that—you remind me too often."

"In any event, this little mail rap of yours—it's not going to throw me off the track. I ask you again, Senator, why do you have to get back here before your flight?"

"Oh, that…it's nothing, really," Jason said. He pretended to absent-mindedly sift through some albums splayed on the far side of Adam's desk. "I agreed to do an interview for the station. This the new Dylan album? Nice cover."

Adam stood stone-faced, and casually tossed the ball across the room before shaking his head, lifting his hands and moving them back and forth, and letting out a big rasp, "A star! You're gonna be a big star!" It was in the neighborhood of a Jimmy Durante impression.

"Shut the fuck up. I really don't want to do it. An interview? On TV? Jeez, if Harry himself hadn't asked—"

"And Carol wasn't the interviewer?" Adam interjected.

"—I'd have never agreed. TV? That camera in your face? I don't know what I was thinking. Maybe I should—Hey, how did you know it was Carol? You talk to Harry about this?"

"I don't know Harry, I know you. You're not as complicated as you think." He sent the Nerf ball across the room and returned to sorting through his mail, wedging a few letters under his arm while tearing in half and tossing out most of the others unread.

"I am too, complicated," Jason insisted. It was the most ridiculous thing he'd ever said, even to Adam. "You're right, I shouldn't be doing this. I'm going to go up there and pull out."

"You know," Adam said solemnly, tossing a few final letters in the trash, "one of her tits is bigger than the other."

"What do you mean?"

"I mean one of them is bigger. A lot bigger."

"Which one?"

"Which one? What are you, blind? Whatever you do, don't look at 'em. She's very sensitive about it." Adam tore open one of the four letters that had survived his purge, leaving Jason with his thoughts. "Holy shit, will you look at this?"

He waved the letter back and forth, then read aloud, "Dear Mr. Shaker: Thank you for your inquiry. The information you requested can only be viewed at the Hall of Records. If we can be of any further assistance...blah blah blah." Stuffing the letter back in its envelope, he tossed it towards the second shelf of a nearby bookcase and considered it filed. "You know what they told me at Records? That the stuff had been sent to be archived and could only be requested through the mail! Well fuck 'em. I got most of what I need. Come on, let's go somewhere we can talk."

They left the building and weaved their way through the stopped traffic on Third Avenue. Navigating single file through the cramped spaces between cars, Adam was so caught up in what he was saying that he backed into a truck. He bounced off and kept talking.

"That reminds me—you know the one positive piece of data I've come across? Pedestrian traffic fatalities. They're down forty-two percent. Forty-two percent! Traffic can't move fast enough to hurt anybody. If this city wasn't in such bad shape, I'd be dead right now."

They turned down the corner, and headed east. The sun was out, but the shadows from the buildings formed a tunnel that narrowed all the way to the river.

"Speaking of dead bodies in traffic," Adam continued in a quieter voice. "You know why Sid Maynes was murdered?"

"I didn't know he was murdered," Jason said innocently. He'd been down this road before.

"No doubt about it."

"Last year you had no doubt about where Patty Hearst was hiding."

"You didn't see her in a tan suit, did you?"

"What's that supposed to mean?"

"It means that you didn't see Maynes that day. You saw one of the guys that killed him."

"You're out of your mind. Who knows what I saw?"

"You know how they say he killed himself? Slit his wrists."

"It's a proven method—as long as you go vertical. Horizontal is a cry for help. At least that's what my abnormal psychology professor said. I always wondered, what if you didn't know?"

"Are you getting any of this?" Adam asked impatiently.

"Yeah, he slit his wrists. Which way did he do it—vertical or horizontal?"

"That's not the point!" Adam yelled at Jason without raising his voice much. Jason waited for the punch line.

"The method doesn't match the venue," Adam continued. "What do you think, he goes for a car ride, gets out, takes a deep breath, gets back in, and slits his wrists? I don't think so."

They arrived at the Coffee-Café, one of Adam's favorite hangouts. It was nearby but out of the way, and nobody went there. They were greeted by a pretty young waitress, who smiled at Adam. Her light brown hair was pulled back from her face. She had delicate features, with innocent eyes for a waitress.

"Two for the counter?" It wasn't really a question.

"Got anything in a booth?" Adam asked.

"My boss has a rule about coffee drinkers in the booths," she said sweetly.

"My boss has a rule about giving away free concert tickets. It's a pity, really. I hear Elton John is going to play the Garden for Thanksgiving."

Jason checked the place out, not sure how long Adam would be flirting with the waitress. He hadn't been there in a long time. The food wasn't great but it wasn't bad, and the service was okay. There were a lot of regulars, mostly older folks who sometimes read while they ate. It was never more than half full, probably because it was too far from the subway to attract a commuter crowd. He couldn't see how they stayed in business. Maybe they were supposed to lose money. "You want that booth in the back corner you love so much?" the waitress finally asked Adam.

He was already walking past her. "I thought you'd never ask."

He barked out orders as went. "And two coffees! Ja-son! We're back here!"

Jason scrambled to catch up, and Adam was already sitting down when he got to the booth. An abandoned *Daily News* sat underneath a lipstick-stained glass on the next table. Adam leaned forward in his seat.

"Look. Here's what I've got," he said in hushed tones. "I know it's just bits and pieces. But it's the tip of an iceberg. I'm not just saying that, I can see it in the spaces between what I know for sure."

He stopped to see if Jason was still on board. "This isn't like the Patty Hearst thing," he insisted.

"Or the Jimmy Hoffa thing?" Jason added.

"No. This is different. Those were guesses. These are facts. And the facts are this: bottom line, by any conceivable account, the City should already be bankrupt. But it isn't. And that's why Maynes was killed."

"Because the City isn't bankrupt," Jason offered, suggesting Adam's logic was less than air tight.

"No. Because it should be!"

The waitress set down their coffees. "I brought a couple of menus just in case you see something you like."

"I'll have what I had last week," Adam said, without looking at the menu.

"I think we may be out of that," she responded.

Jason hypothesized that she was not from the City, and still relatively new in town. He also suspected that Adam might be a while, and retrieved the *Daily News* from the other table. Its headline shouted GANG WAR, and beneath that it featured shots of the same four men from the morning news. Studying the pictures, Jason was increasingly certain that the one on the top left was the rapist who got right in his face the other day. One less person to worry about running into, he guessed. He flipped through the pages, as "complete coverage inside" was promised. Pages two and three were reserved for the BABY BORN IN RUSH HOUR TRAFFIC and CHANNEL 2 HONCHOS MULL BANKRUPTCY FILE. Not until page four did he get FOUR MEN SHOT DEAD ON WEST SIDE. Adam was still fooling around with the waitress.

"Really? All out?" He said skeptically. "Are you sure there's none in the back? It was quite good."

"Quite good?"

"Excellent even. I was looking forward to having it again. Do you think any more will be coming in?"

"Not for a couple of days. Maybe you should check back. You never know, someone else might snap it up."

"You can count on it."

She turned to Jason. "How about you?"

Jason was reading the paper and lost in his own world. He learned a lot more from the paper than he had from watching TV, and none of it was good. First off, for those keeping score, between the four killed on the West Side and two unrelated murders in the Bronx, the City was on track to break last year's record-setting homicide tally. But he'd kind of assumed that was the case. More surprising was the *News*'s reporting that it was in fact a gangland-style execution, complete not just with shots to the head, but hands tied behind the back as well. Apparently it was harder to change something in print than on TV. Either way, it was impossible for both versions of the story to be true, and Jason was betting on the one that had circulated before the cops corrected it. The puzzle remained as to why they felt the need to.

"Jason!" It was the third time Adam said his name.

"Huh?"

"Anything to eat?" the waitress asked. She tilted her head to the side slightly.

"You getting anything?" he asked Adam.

"Not me."

"Nothing, thanks," Jason said softly. They both watched her walk away.

"So listen." Adam jumped right back into his exposition. "According to the figures at the library, this city's income tax revenues have fallen by over twenty percent over the past five years...."

Jason always shut down whenever Adam started throwing numbers at him. His eyes drifted towards the young waitress, who was taking an order a few tables down. She had very smooth legs, which got longer when she shifted her weight to her toes to confirm the order of a low-talking customer.

"How well do you know her?" he asked, mostly to himself, not putting a dent in Adam's monologue.

"…but according to the Hall of Records—and this is in the public domain, Jason—laws have to be passed and money actually spent, outlays have actually gone up by over six percent in the same period. These are facts, I can't just be making this up."

That got Jason's attention. Adam usually spent most of his tale-spinning explaining why he had to be right in spite of the obvious facts.

"What do you mean?"

"Let me try to explain this visually," he said slowly, "since you've never been a good aural learner."

Adam grabbed a small plastic container holding packets of sugar. "Essentially, here's what's happened. This box," he said, holding it up, "is the city tax revenue. If this box isn't full, then we can't pay our policemen, our firemen, our teachers, or our garbage men. Now, over the last five years, one out of every five of these packs has left town." He started to toss the sugar packets in various directions around the table. "Some to Jersey, a few out to the Island… even a couple over to Connecticut. But somehow…." He opened two packets of sugar and dramatically spilled them into his coffee. "…the City still has enough sugar for the same amount of coffee—in fact, even a bit more than before." He took a long sip of his coffee and smiled to illustrate that there was enough sugar to meet his needs.

"You should save some of that sugar for the waitress. She must be nineteen years old."

Adam smiled broadly. "Ever see the way Muddy Waters smiles when he sings that song?" He started chanting, "She's *nineteeeen* years old!"

"I thought you were serious about that switchboard operator."

"I'm serious about all of 'em." He said it like it was important to him, and that Jason should have understood that. "Look, I didn't bring you here to talk about women. I'm telling you—these numbers just don't add up. There's some inescapable math here. Revenues are down twenty percent, outlays are up six."

Adam could tell he was doing well, so he pushed on, well aware that he was still paddling upstream against Jason's inherent distaste for conspiracy theories. Just the phrase "second gunman" could drive him out of a room. Years ago Adam had done it on purpose when they were both hitting on this first-year law student at a party. She was good, too.

"Except for tolls, meters, and parking taxes, the only thing that's gone up is licensing fees. That's a laugh, by the way, cause we're paying for it. And I don't mean the royal we—I mean you and me."

"How so?" Jason asked pointedly. He'd been looking for a chink in the armor. He didn't have a car. Let them triple the tolls, for all he cared.

"TV licensing," Adam said to Jason's surprise. "I don't know what Morgan did to piss off the Mayor, but every station in this city has to pay triple what it used to just to keep their licenses to operate. You know part of that's gotta be coming out of our salaries." Adam felt like he was on a roll. A few cheap hits like that didn't change the score much, but they kept the momentum going.

"Morgan's got plenty of money," Jason said, dismissively. He wasn't buying the licensing stuff.

"Still, it's a business," Adam insisted. "I hear from my source at City Hall that two of the stations are up for sale—one of them network! Man, even the TV is leaving this town."

"Ah, somebody will buy 'em. Or they'll just have to lower the fees again. TV is inevitable. Like a plague."

"Maybe. But that's exactly the point. The City can't raise taxes, because if they do, then even more people will leave. But they need more revenue, cause they don't have enough money now to pay for what they need to do. I don't know how they're pulling it off—it's like Cohen has levitated the City's finances with the wave of his hand. It's a magic trick."

"But what does that have to do with Maynes?" Jason had started to get caught up in Adam's web and forgot that this whole thing started with the murder-suicide theory.

"Magic only works when no one knows the secret," Adam answered. "That money in Maynes's car—this is about the money, for sure. City doesn't have any, but he sure did."

"Even if everything you say is true, he still could have killed himself." Jason wasn't sure he believed that, but he wanted to get in one good shot. After all, technically, that's the only point they were arguing about.

"Maybe," Adam slowly. "Conceivably. But I doubt it. Everything points to murder. And he was at the center of something, something big." Adam could feel it in his bones. "I'm gonna go to the funeral today. You should come with me."

"You know I don't even go to funerals of people I like."

"Okay, but you're making a big mistake. We're looking at a Major Funeral here. Outstanding theatre—it's going to have it all. Staging, lighting, emotion, oratory, colorful characters—and all of the stars will be there."

"Sounds like a Bowie show. You should cover it for the *Voice*."

"I just might."

15

JASON GOT BACK TO THE STUDIO and reported to Lou, who walked him through how everything would go. There was a separate interview set, which Jason hadn't expected, and when Lou showed it to him he felt even more nervous. He thought he'd be sitting behind the news desk, which would serve as a security blanket, and a buffer between him and the camera. The interview set looked more like an operating room theater—two black chairs facing each other, surrounded by a circle of lights and with a camera just off to the side of each chair. Carol was still in her dressing room, getting what someone called her "pre-makeup" put on, whatever that meant. Camera operators, electricians, and assistants were buzzing urgently about, making Jason dizzy.

"Lou, I don't know if I'm going to be able to do this," he said, hoping he had turned such a convincing shade of green that Lou would pull the plug right there.

"Relax—it's just TV. It all goes by so fast." He lowered his voice, letting Jason in on a secret. "Nobody really knows what you say, anyway, they just know the way you say it. So no matter what, just keep going. If you screw up, don't go back and try and correct yourself. Sit up straight. Talk like you believe what you're saying. Half the time we'll cut to Carol smiling and nodding. It's a walk in the park."

"Okay." At another time, he would have enjoyed the irony that he wasn't reassured by what Lou said, but just by the way that he spoke to him.

"Oh, and another thing—don't screw up."

Jason's face fell.

"Take it easy, fella, it's an old joke." Lou tugged at his headset and plugged a dangling line into the pack on his hip. "Now, we're going to go mock live. You know what that means?"

"No." Jason felt like he was listening to his dentist as he was getting ready to drill.

"Okay. It just means that even though we're filming this for later, we pretend like it's a live interview. So that's what I want you to do, I want you to act like it's going out live."

"Why?" Jason said suspiciously. It sounded like a scam, and he wasn't going to be a party to such dishonesty.

"Trust me, if we didn't do it this way, it would take forever. Also it helps us time it out. When we show it, they know it's not live."

Okay, maybe it wasn't a scam.

As always, Lou walked as he talked, checking things out. "Now, we're going to have to put a little makeup on—"

"I'm not wearing makeup."

"Look, sweetheart, every guy in TV wears makeup. Doesn't mean they're wearing loafers behind the desk."

"That's not it. I just want to be myself."

"Yourself," Lou said with declining patience, "does not walk around with thousand watt bulbs stuck in his face. It's just a little powder. Don't put it on, you look like Nixon in the first Kennedy debate."

"Fine." Jason said. He hated TV.

"Also," Lou continued, sticking his hand out to gauge the lighting, "you got another shirt? That one's too dark."

Jason opened his mouth, but Lou spoke before he got a word in. "You gotta question everything I tell you to do? See that backdrop? Wear that shirt and you'll look like a fucking floating head."

A few minutes later, Jason was sitting in his chair, wearing a borrowed white button-down shirt that was irritating the back of his neck. A makeup girl had powdered his face, and he felt like a clown. Where the hell was Carol? He couldn't wait to get it over with. Harry walked over.

"Lookin' good, kid," he said with a smile. He was full of shit, but Jason was glad to see him. "I'll be in the booth the whole time." He stopped and thought for a second. "But don't look over." He started and stopped again. "Don't worry, you'll be fine," and left before he could do any more damage.

Carol finally arrived, with her assistant and a more professional makeup woman in tow.

"Hi, Jason," she said warmly, and sat in her chair. As she did, the room seemed to close in—the lights, cameras, overhead mikes all drew in tighter and lower and you could feel the heat. Jason's stomach chose this moment to tell him he might be claustrophobic. No one else seemed to notice. The A-list makeup woman studied the lights before putting the finishing touches on Carol's face.

"Could you lean back, please?" she said to Carol.

Carol arched her back and tilted her head. This accentuated her chest which rose into view like the morning sun. Jason, with Adam's words still ringing in his ears, was desperate to look anywhere else. Reluctant to disturb his posture, he shifted his head to the left, where two of the lighting technicians were staring at Carol and muttering to each other. To the right he could see Harry in the control room, standing next to a couple of unfamiliar suits, who reminded him of the team of accountants who show up in the middle of the Oscars to explain how the votes were counted.

"You all right?" Carol asked him.

Jason turned his head carefully and locked his gaze on Carol's face. It turned out she had hazel eyes. For some reason he had always assumed they were blue.

"Yeah, just a little nervous, I guess. I've never been on TV before."

"Just relax. It's one of those things in life, once you've done it for the first time you realize it's not as big a deal as you thought." Her eyes sparkled when she said it, but it might have just been the lights.

"Just sit back and focus on what I'm saying. Don't let the cameras and the lights distract you. Just pretend we're having a conversation, and when in doubt, keep talking."

"Okay, thanks. Do I look at you, or do I look at the camera?"

"You can look at me, or you can look at an invisible cat sitting just above my right shoulder. But don't look at the camera, and don't look at the lights, and don't look around, like at the booth or at Lou. Oh, and, if you hear a noise, don't look towards that either. Just pretend you didn't hear it." Turned out Carol had a lot of different voices—one for the news, one to shut you up in the hallway—and this one, which wrapped around you like a blanket.

"Got it," Jason said with a smile only half-forced, and managed to squeeze off a joke. "Does it have to be a cat, or can it be anything I want?"

She smiled brightly, and Jason quickly ran down the list in his head. Don't look at the booth, don't look at the lights, don't look at the camera, don't look at her tits. He held his entire body perfectly still. He was ready.

"Everybody set?" Lou called out from somewhere. "Okay, people, let's do it."

A perfect silence filled the studio, and after a few more beats than Jason expected, Carol suddenly lit up and started talking. "New Yorkers are known for their gruff exteriors, for not getting involved. Well, today we're talking with our very own Jason Sims, the helicopter hero. Two days ago Jason flew his helicopter down into the middle of a crime scene, possibly saving the life of a young woman. We thought we'd find out a little more about the story and about the hero right under our own noses. Glad to have you with us, Jason."

Jason's ears burned from that "helicopter hero" crack, which he thought they had an agreement about, but he followed Lou's advice and plowed ahead.

"Thanks, glad to be here." It seemed fitting that his TV career would start with a big lie.

"Everyone knows the story, but could you tell us in your own words exactly what happened?"

She looked right at him for the answer, and it gave him confidence, so he reciprocated by talking directly to her instead of to the invisible Nixon floating in the space above her shoulder.

"Well, it was just like you said, you know. I was in the air, and I looked down and saw something funny. Then when I saw what was happening, and that she had broken free, well, I thought I could get in between her and them."

Carol jumped in. "You make it sound so simple."

The camera behind Carol rolled towards him, and he felt his eyes widen. "Well, it-uh, seemed simple at the time." He kicked himself for letting go of that "uh."

"You nearly crashed into the side of a building!"

"That was after. I didn't think about how much dirt would be thrown up. I guess that part wasn't simple at all."

Inside the control room, Harry was pleased. "I told you the kid would be a natural," he said to no one in particular.

"The sound is clean, too" added the assistant director. The Price-Waterhouse gang watched from the back of the booth.

"Why didn't you just call the police?" she asked.

"We, uh, I thought about it, but you get a pretty good look at the City from up there. I could see a precinct house just a few blocks away, but no police cars. Anyway, there wasn't much time."

This line ruffled some feathers in the back of the booth, and Harry talked over his shoulder to reassure them.

"We talked about this. We can work around it." He picked up a headset off the console and spoke into the mouthpiece. "Lou, remember, we're going to cut any cop talk." Harry set the headset down. "We're not out to embarrass anybody."

Lou was on the set. He gave an "okay" sign to Carol, but it was directed at the booth.

Carol rolled her finger in a circle at Jason, letting him know they were about to wrap up.

"Jason, you're a native New Yorker. You hear a lot of talk about the City and its future. What does it look like from up there in your helicopter?"

"From up there, it's the same old New York it's always been. You can see the trains rolling, and the waves of people walking on the street. Sure, there's more traffic. But regular people know how to get around in this town."

"Thanks so much for giving us a few minutes of your time. Before we let you go, let me ask you, how does it feel to be a hero?"

"I don't know. I sure don't think of myself as a hero."

"Really? What do you think of yourself as?"

"Just a regular guy. I mean, anyone who saw a woman being attacked, they wouldn't just stand there. I just happened to have a helicopter."

Carol flashed her best smile. It could even have been real. "Just a regular guy with a helicopter—I'm not sure everyone would agree. But there you have it, another New York Story. Back to you, Nate."

Lou stepped forward. "Okay, we're out."

Jason looked at Carol. "Was that okay?" He felt good about it, and was really glad it was over, but worried about how it might look on TV.

"Sure, great," she said, still smiling, "You're a natural."

"Really?"

"Yeah. Are you going to take the traffic job?"

Jason wondered why she knew about that. He also noticed Carol had introduced a voice Jason decided to catalogue as "friendly-professional."

"I don't know—"

"A job like that opens a lot of doors."

Carol stood up as her assistant arrived and the two of them talked quietly.

Jason walked away from the set, changing course to intercept Lou, who was walking in the opposite direction. He was looking for a little more debriefing. "You know, I was a little worried about—"

"Don't worry about anything, it was great. And anything that wasn't great, they'll clean up in editing. Those guys are magicians."

Lou never broke stride, continuing towards the control room. The man was in constant motion.

Jason turned back toward the set, but it was already being taken apart. Carol and her assistant were gone.

16

JASON GOT TO THE roof early. Still a little pumped up from the interview, he walked around a bit, cooling off in the breeze. Usually he looked south, finding the Woolworth Building and tracking the great interwar skyscrapers farther downtown. But it was an especially clear day, and he looked east, first to the horizon and then coming back across Queens in a failed attempt to pick out the apartment building he grew up in, which was less than eight miles away.

"Good to see you out there this morning." It was Sammy, which took Jason by surprise. Sammy rarely drifted far from the booth. "I like to see you right back on that horse."

Jason smiled. "I figure as long as I keep it off the streets, it won't happen again."

They started to walk in the general direction of the helicopter.

"You never know," Sammy said after a moment. His voice was flat when he said it, missing the usual lift that hinted he could transition from talking to singing without missing a beat, even though it was impossible to imagine Sammy singing.

Jason stopped walking and looked at Sammy. "What do you mean by that?" Sammy didn't meet Jason's eyes, and he kept walking. "Accidents, they don't happen just by accident. They need a little help," he said, his voice almost back to normal.

"Not the piano story again, please," Jason called out to Sammy, who was getting a bit ahead of him.

"You broke your fool arm doing that, didn't you? You go around calling that an accident too, just cause you didn't mean to do it."

"This was different," Jason protested.

"I know." Sammy moved his feet a little more slowly, his head turned toward the Chrysler Building. Then he stopped and looked squarely at Jason. "Did I ever tell you how Robert Johnson died?"

"You did *not* know Robert Johnson," Jason insisted. Sammy's stories often placed him within the proximity of legendary figures, and Jason considered him to be a deeply honest man. But he had to draw the line somewhere.

"Now what makes you so dead certain I never made the acquaintance of Mr. Robert Johnson?"

"He was from central Mississippi, and you were all the way down south," Jason said keenly, boxing Sammy in and showing off his command of geography at the same time. "And you told me the first train you ever saw was the one that took you to Detroit."

"Very true, very true.... 'Course, that was where he was born. Died in Greenwood."

"Yeah? Where's that?" Jason asked reluctantly, knowing that Sammy must have had something good up his sleeve, and that he'd never heard of Greenwood.

"'Bout twelve miles south of my mama's backyard.... But no, I never met the man." His voice got serious again. "You know I'd never tell you anything that wasn't true."

"I know," Jason said quietly. He felt guilty, but wasn't sure why.

"I did have a friend worked at the Three Forks, though. You know, where he played his last gig. Saw the whole thing."

"He was stabbed, right?"

"Poisoned. Mr. Son House was there. I know you've seen him—you told me you shook his hand once at the bus station outside of Newport—well there you were, one handshake from the night Robert Johnson died. You couldn't tell it nowadays, but Mr. Son House was a giant back then, bigger than them all, and maybe seven, ten years older.

"Anyways, that night they play a little bit and dance a little bit and drink a little bit, and Robert, well, he had a wandering eye, kind of like that friend of yours you talk about. After a while someone passed Robert an open bottle of whiskey—no seal. Robert goes to drink, and Son House knocks it out of his hand. He says, boy, don't ever take whiskey from the bottle unless you break the seal yourself. You break the seal, you know where your spirits are coming from. Well now, Robert was a young man, twenty-seven years, and didn't like being talked to. Before you know it another open bottle is in his hand. Son doesn't move this time, just stares at Robert, and Robert looks him right in the face, lifts the bottle, takes a long drink. Couple of minutes later, he falls, crawls outside, and dies."

"They say he made a deal with the devil," Jason added.

"Well, they're wrong," Sammy said flatly, using the same tone Jason used with people who talked about UFOs. "Jealous husband did it. And he didn't howl at the moon, neither, just crawled outside and died in the dirt. Wasn't nothing special about it. Only mystery is why it didn't happen sooner."

Sammy started walking again, this time straight for the helicopter. Bill was already there, leaning against the door from the stairs holding two attaché cases. When Bill saw them he went over to the helicopter and got in on the passenger side.

Jason and Sammy reached the helicopter, and Jason started the engine. He left the door open as it started to warm up.

"So what's the lesson?" Jason said to Sammy over the increasing noise of the blades.

"Ain't no lesson," Sammy yelled back. "Just a story about accidents!"

The copter was good to go. Sammy stepped back, put his ear protectors on, and pulled the stays away. He stepped farther back from the helicopter, and looked at Jason, the wind rippling his light blue jacket.

"Let's go, already," Bill said to him.

Jason was about to lift off but stopped and turned his head to the side, as if trying to remember a forgotten name.

"Wait a sec," he finally offered.

Bill watched while Jason hesitated, then unhooked his safety belts and trotted over to Sammy. Sammy pulled down his ear protectors, and Jason leaned over and shouted into Sammy's ear. It was more than a couple of words, and Bill set down one of his cases, looked at his watch, and scanned the instrument panel. If there was a horn, he planned to honk it. Looking back over he saw that Sammy was nodding vigorously—a good sign, they were probably done. Jason trotted back to the copter and strapped himself in. Out on the roof Sammy was shaking his fist, the okay sign. Jason shook his fist back, and the helicopter lifted off.

A silence fell between Bill and Jason—and not their usual silence—this one wasn't empty. Jason didn't want to talk first, but unless he was willing to force the issue by flying in circles, he'd have to be the one to crack.

"Where to?" he finally asked.

"Queens. The parking lot behind Shea Stadium."

"I think the Mets are out of town."

"Could be, I don't know. The way they draw, you'd never know the difference."

They stopped talking again. It was tense, at least it seemed so to Jason. He took the stack of twenties from his inside jacket pocket and handed it to Bill.

"I think you dropped this. Sorry about the blood."

Bill didn't touch it. This was money nobody wanted, and with the economy the way it was, Jason figured that was a very bad sign.

"Keep it," Bill said gruffly. "You earned it."

"I don't keep quiet for a living," Jason responded, maintaining his cool in a way he once wouldn't have.

"No?" There was an edge in Bill's voice.

"No. I keep quiet when I have nothing to say."

Bill exhaled, and his shoulders rolled back a bit. It had never occurred to Jason that Bill was worried he'd go running to the cops or something.

"Listen…I don't know…." Bill's tone was apologetic. "We went down pretty fast. The people I work for, these people, let's just say they're pretty serious about their privacy."

"Aren't we all?"

Jason looked out the window. He didn't have anything against Bill, really, but he knew he couldn't keep going like this. He didn't care what Morgan was up to, but he was getting paid to be a part of it, and that wouldn't fly. He had to be all the way in or not in at all.

They flew over a huge cemetery, and Jason surveyed the congested highways below. The traffic was crawling on the Grand Central Parkway and the Long Island Expressway, but cars were actually moving on the Van Wyck, and Jason had this ridiculous urge to call Dave Edwards with the good news.

"Look at that," Jason said, pointing at the cemetery. "When I was a little kid, we only came out to the boroughs for a reason. I thought it was just the place they buried people from the City."

"The parkway looks like one long funeral procession today," Bill observed.

"The city will never have the money to fix these roads properly." Jason decided to float his only remaining political position past Bill. "I think they should just ban all the cars from Manhattan," he said nonchalantly. The theory was actually more sophisticated than that, with provisions for buses and taxis, and maybe permits for resident owners. But he didn't want to confuse the issue.

"It's got nothing to do with the City," Bill countered.

"What do you mean? The City's broke, so it can't afford to fix the roads once and for all. So they just keep patching them up—running to stand still. Politicians, they can only think about getting by in the short run, even if they're screwing the future."

"It's not money, it's politics," Bill explained. "Highway money is federal. The Feds fucking hate New York. Over there—set down over there. Not the main lot, but the smaller one inside that gated area."

Jason brought the helicopter right over Shea Stadium. He thought about getting down really low—low enough to see the grass move, but it was just a thought. He landed gently in an empty parking lot behind center field. There was no one in sight, and probably no one around; the Mets were at the beginning of a long road trip.

As usual, Bill instructed Jason to set down about 100 yards away from a waiting car. It was a good-sized car, but this one wasn't a limo. Bill grabbed one of the cases and trotted over to the car. A short man in his mid-sixties got out. He was alone and had a gentle face. He looked more like a grandfather than a businessman, or a crook, or whatever it was he must have been. Bill reached out with the case, but the older man put his hand on Bill's shoulder and started talking to him. He talked calmly and at length, putting his arm around Bill, who might have looked concerned; Jason couldn't tell from where he was sitting. He guided Bill into the car, and was still talking as the door closed. Jason couldn't see inside.

Jason looked over at the stadium, then at the car, then back at the stadium again.

Finally he hopped out of the helicopter and walked toward the stadium. He'd never been on the field before, and this was his chance. He found an opening in the large outer wall, which revealed a yard and then a second wall beyond that—but no doors. There were a few crates lying around, Jason grabbed two and stacked them together near the wall and stood on them, leaning on the inner wall for balance. It was the center field fence, and Jason stared out at the entire stadium in front of him. It was completely empty. The seats were folded and the tarp covered the infield.

He hadn't been there for some time. Only eleven years old, the stadium was already aging, and not gracefully. He'd read about how the Mets' ownership was cutting corners everywhere—the team sure played like it—and everything looked like it could use a touch-up—the grass, the seats, the scoreboard. But even all beaten up, it was still Shea Stadium, and the memories overwhelmed him, more vividly than he would have thought possible. He saw the Beatles there, August 23, 1966, and still had the ticket stub. Six days later in San Francisco they played live in concert for the last time. Then his mind drifted back to the year before that—he must have walked to Shea once a week, when he'd dated this girl who loved baseball. And to the old days when he went with his father whenever the Dodgers were in town. Jason never met a friend of his father's who wasn't a Dodgers fan, and even though leaving the City in 'fifty-seven was an unspeakable infidelity, they couldn't stop rooting for the team. Jason and his friends took more quickly to the hand-me-down Mets.

"Hey. What the fuck?" It was Bill.

"Can you believe these guys played in the World Series two years ago?" Jason said amiably. "Now it's like some Roman ruins." He pointed at the tarp. "Looks like they expect more rain. Better than losing, I guess."

Bill wasn't interested. "I told you never to leave the helicopter."

"You told me to leave it running. It's running." Jason didn't much like being told what to do, anyway. "Hey, you look like shit. What's the matter?"

"Nothing. Just don't screw around like that. You know what's in those cases. You shouldn't, but you do."

"Come on, we've got a stadium full of empty on our hands, nobody around for miles—"

"You never know what can happen," Bill said, with a fresh urgency in his voice.

Jason wasn't buying it. "I never know anything."

They walked back through the empty parking lot. Bill was holding another sealed, oversized manila envelope. They got back in the helicopter.

"Back to the City?" Jason ask rhetorically, looking at Bill for confirmation.

"No. Gotta make an extra stop today. Staten Island."

"Staten Island? It's gonna take every drop of gas."

"Gotta go," Bill said, looking forward.

"All right, but that's it. We may have to glide back."

17

DOWN ON THE STREETS BELOW, Adam was making his way to the Waldorf Astoria hotel, hoping, as always, to kill two birds with one stone. It was taking him a while to get there because he had become convinced that someone was following him. Not that he'd seen anybody in particular, but the feeling was overwhelming. So when he got off the train at 51st Street, instead of heading to Park Avenue he overshot and walked down Fifth, ducking in and out of St. Patrick's Cathedral in a way that would cause problems for anyone who might be trying to shadow him inconspicuously. Then, in an inspired move, he hopped aboard a bus that was idling with its doors open, waiting for the traffic to clear. He dropped a token in the box and wandered about halfway back, working his way to the center pole. Three more people got on after him, but one was a little old lady, and she was probably okay. Adam watched the driver closely until he sensed that he was getting ready to close up, and popped out the side door just in time. No one else got out of the bus as it came to life and fought its way into the street. Probably nothing, but fifty cents wasn't much of an investment for a little peace of mind.

Two avenue blocks later he was at the Waldorf, where there were scores of teenagers milling around. Some were camped out, and most were looking up, shading their eyes with their hands in a group salute—they could have been a scout troop led by Timothy Leary. Word must have leaked out, probably by the band's press agent, that The Impossible were staying there. They had rented out the entire forty-second floor and invited the press to come by for a couple of hours. A pretty good police presence was half-watching the crowd, and they had set up a few blue sawhorse barriers to keep things contained. But the cops weren't looking for trouble, and left it to hotel security to stop anyone who looked like they didn't have a room. Adam had to show his press pass to get in.

The Impossible were being hyped as the next big thing, and they were kicking off their first arena tour as headliners, with three sold-out dates at the Garden. They weren't that bad, but, even though they didn't know it, they were staring at some pretty big hurdles. They'd made it big too fast, so their first huge tour was going to support their second album, which would probably have been a hurried and disappointing slice of vinyl under the best of circumstances. Worse, they desperately wanted to be the Rolling Stones, which not only suggested a serious lack of self-awareness, since musically speaking they were much closer to the Allman Brothers, but it also required expending tremendous energy to play the part, and begged for unflattering comparisons.

Adam stepped out of the elevator and found everything exactly as it would have been described in the hard rock handbook. Music from multiple sources, drinks everywhere, a disproportionate number of very beautiful, very young women, and long tables of food visited only by reporters and the most distant hangers-on. A few uniformed cops stood around doing nothing much—they were probably there at the hotel's insistence. They were mostly scarecrows posted to make sure things didn't get really out of hand, as well as some in plain clothes mixed in unobtrusively, who were probably involved with security while the band was in town.

Adam knew he had to talk to the lead singer and the guitarist, especially if he planned to do a TV spot on the concert—the camera would accept no substitute for something along the lines of "Mik Jett told me before the show that this was the album they always wanted to make." But he also knew that if he wanted to learn more about the band, he'd have to talk to the bass player.

That was a trick he learned from Jason, who said he got it from Sammy.

He made the rounds with the band members, elbowing his way into the middle of the crowd around Mik—"We're not the second coming of anything, we're the first coming of us"; and then the smaller one surrounding Stu—"Mik's into the whole rock star thing, I'm just the guitar player," which would have had more credibility if he wasn't wearing designer sunglasses and alligator boots.

With those chores behind him, Adam was able to track down Drew Baker, who had successfully warded off those few members of the media who sought him out with monosyllabic responses. Drew had a long Beatle haircut, and the bangs went all the way down to his eyebrows, so if he tilted his head slightly downwards a curtain of hair fell over his eyes—and that was good enough to discourage conversation. But when Adam introduced himself Drew actually said, "Hey, man, I loved your book," and pushed his hair back from his face in a V. He agreed with Adam's position on the Allman Brothers. There was a guy who knew how to guarantee great press coverage. Bright fellow, that bass player. He was going to make it, whatever happened to The Impossible.

Adam caught the eye of one of the plainclothes cops, and then headed down the hallway into one of the quieter suites, and from there into an empty bedroom. He turned on the TV and flipped it to a soap opera, and as it droned on he studied the room and the bathroom. This was actually his first time at the Waldorf, though he knew a hundred people who claimed to be there in '68 the night that Keith Moon got The Who banned for life. Jason was keen to hear about the place—legend had it that FDR used a secret passage and elevator that would take him from Grand Central Station to the Waldorf's Presidential Suite without going outside.

The door opened quietly and the plainclothes cop walked into the room. He was in his late thirties, with a thick moustache, and deep lines cut into his gaunt face.

"How did you get stuck baby-sitting these guys?" Adam asked, shaking his hand.

"They got death threats."

"The Impossible? Somebody wants to kill them? I don't think so. Twenty says the manager made it up."

"It's a pretty easy gig. Fifty thousand assaults this year, I'll take the working vacation." He looked incredulously at the soap opera on the TV.

"So," Adam asked cautiously, "what do you got?"

"A whole lot of nothing."

"Then why did you signal for a meeting?"

"It's too big a change—there's been a lot of cash around the station for a couple of months. Now, all of a sudden, its dry, very dry."

"That's it?" Adam said, unable to hide his disappointment.

"Look, I'm a cop, not a reporter. If I was undercover, and the cash flow changed, I'd watch my back. If it stopped coming, I'd know I was made, and get the hell out of there."

"Okay, okay," Adam said apologetically, "but what do I do with it?"

"I don't know. You want something concrete, I've still got that guy who wants to talk about evidence tampering in the Bronx. He says it goes all the way to the District Attorney. Says what he's got is gold."

"Ah, evidence tampering—half the time they're guilty anyway. Unless that DA is covering for the Mayor...?"

The cop shook his head. "Whatever. Give me a call if you want it, I think its solid." He glanced at his watch. "I should get back. Wait a couple of minutes before you go, some of those uniforms might not be as dumb as they look."

"Sure. Hey, thanks, man, I really appreciate you reaching out to me. I know it isn't—"

"No problem."

TWO miles downtown, Alison was starting to get comfortable in her new office. She'd gotten all her books on the shelves, hundreds of big, dusty, obscure history tracts that she'd accumulated over the years, traveling the Midwest scouring used bookstores, library sales, and even picking through the bones of a few estates. She liked having them, even though it was pathetically materialistic, but a saving grace was that they weren't worth much and would be of interest only to other seriously geeky historians. And as a bonus, having all those books floor to ceiling also made the office look like it belonged to a pipe-smoking full professor, and that foundation gave her the confidence not to hold back with the plants.

Progress was visible on all fronts. Her nameplate was affixed, mailbox properly alphabetized, and there was even a guy on a ladder taking a stab at the overhead light, but that had the makings of a long-term project. Maybe she was better off without it; something about the way he turned his screwdriver was interfering with her train of thought, and she was trying to put the finishing touches on a lecture.

There was a knock at the door, and two men entered the office and purposefully walked right up to the desk, reminding Alison of the benefits of chair-desk-chair. They wore cheap suits, and one was tall and one was fat—they could have passed for body doubles in a movie called *Abbot and Costello Join the IRS*. But there wasn't a hint of comedy about them—if anything, in place of the dead stare of civil servants, Alison thought she could see a flicker of malice behind their eyes.

"We're with the Office of Public Integrity," the taller one mumbled, flashing an ID.

"Office of what? Could I get a closer look at that?"

"Sure."

"And yours?" Alison asked the second man, who was holding his hat in one hand and studying her books.

She looked at both IDs carefully, more carefully than she needed to, but she wanted to make a point. "Thank you, Mr. Yeager, Mr. Ackerman," she said, returning them.

Yeager looked at the ceiling. "Would you excuse us for a moment," he instructed the handyman.

Ackerman escorted him to the door, and closed it. Fitting his hat back on, he adjusted his jacket as well.

"As I said," Yeager continued, "we're with the Office of Public Integrity, and we'd like to know what you were looking for in the government depository on—"

"Why do you ask?" she interrupted.

"Frankly, there are some very sensitive documents held there, and we keep careful track of them. Fact is, there's a major corruption case we're working on right now, and the walls have ears. If the wrong people thought that we were looking at them, or anybody was, well, let's just say we like to keep an eye on these things." He looked at her, waiting for an answer.

"I wasn't looking for anything in particular."

"Look, Miss Monroe—"

"Professor Monroe."

"Professor of what, botany?" Ackerman chimed in. He had left the books and been touring the plants.

"History," she said evenly.

"We also understand," Yeager added, "that there were a couple of other people with you. Some associates perhaps?"

"That's why I was there. I was training graduate students in how to work with primary source material. That's what we historians do. As for the documents, they were chosen at random."

"And the students? Also chosen at random?"

"No. They were chosen by me."

"Do they have names?"

"They were there under my supervision, and my authority." Alison felt her heart pounding in her chest, but she knew that as far as anyone could tell, she was a rock. "If you're looking for anyone, you're looking for me. I won't have my teaching interfered with."

"It's just procedure," Yeager said casually, his eyes making a quick survey of the items on Alison's desk.

"It doesn't matter," Alison said definitively, "I won't make a list of my students, for any reason." She wondered if they understood the meaning behind the phrase "won't make a list," but it reinforced her courage in any event. "If there was a court order," she added, raising her eyebrows, "I might consider it." By which she meant to say she wouldn't. She shuffled some papers on her desk, removing them from Yeager's gaze and inviting them to wrap up.

"Thank you for your cooperation, *Professor*," Yeager said, and turned to leave. "One more thing. I don't suppose you need to be reminded that even though you can use those records for your research, it would be against the law to share that information with anybody else, say like your sister, or a reporter."

Alison met his stare and watched them while they left. "Leave it open, please," she called out as Ackerman grabbed the doorknob on his way out. He pulled it closed.

Alison counted to twenty before grabbing the phone book and scanning it for the Office of Public Integrity under the City of New York listing. As she suspected, there was no such listing. But closing the book back up, she noticed that it was from 1973. Tracing her finger under the date, she tapped the last digit twice, shaking loose a half-formed thought. She picked up the phone and dialed for information. Turned out there was such an office, but it was just a couple of years old. She gave them a call, and it took only two transfers to reach someone helpful.

"Yes," she asked, "I'm looking for two of your inspectors, Yeager and Ackerman. I do have the correct agency, do I not?"

"Oh yes," said the voice on the other end of the line. "But they're out on a call just now. Would you like to leave a message?"

Alison stared at the phone.

"Would you like to leave a message?"

"No, thank you," she said, and hung up.

18

JASON AND BILL CONTINUED on their flight to Staten Island. Jason was still thinking about Shea Stadium and counting how many specific memories he could associate with it. There could easily have been more, but he didn't really get out much during the 'sixty-nine season, when men walked on the moon and the miracle Mets won the World Series. He'd seen a few games in 'seventy-three, the year they came out of nowhere and won the pennant. But 'seventy-three wasn't 'sixty-nine, and there was no sense in pretending that it was. He looked over at Bill, whose face was tight.

"You get out to Shea much? I mean, you know, when it's open for business?" Jason added with a little smile.

"No, I was never much for baseball."

"Huh. I kind of had you pegged as a die-hard Dodgers fan."

"My father."

"Mine too."

That was about as much sharing as Bill seemed to be in the mood for. He shifted his weight a bit and switched hands with the attaché case he was holding, looking down at it as if it was unfamiliar. His grip seemed very tight, but Jason couldn't remember how much white he'd seen on his knuckles in the past. They sat silently.

"That old man looked familiar," Jason finally said.

Bill looked at Jason, his eyes hinting at something, but it was only a hint, and Jason wasn't getting it.

"Didn't you say you lived around here?"

"Couple of miles."

"He's from around here, too. You've probably seen him. He takes an interest in local affairs."

"He looked pretty concerned," Jason offered.

"Yeah, well, you're not the only one from Queens. Sometimes he worries about me."

"How long have you lived in Queens?" Jason asked, half for sport and half because he was still sticking with his Brooklyn theory.

Bill again turned his head and looked out the side window, ending the conversation. He looked at his watch.

"How much longer you figure?"

"Seven minutes. Unless we run out of gas, then it's probably five. You a good swimmer?"

No response. Bill was like a closed fist, and it was getting tighter. But Jason had some things to talk about, and besides, part of him was enjoying the challenge.

"You see the papers?" Jason asked. "Those four dead guys? I think one of them attacked that woman the other day. Maybe it was all four of 'em. Shot in the head."

"Yeah, I saw."

"Some people attract trouble, I guess."

"Fuck 'em," Bill said defiantly. "Sometimes the system works, you know?" He looked at his watch again.

"You sure nothing's wrong?"

"Something's always wrong."

Jason wasn't about to argue with that. He studied Bill, trying to get a fix on him. Was he pissed about being ordered to take an extra trip? Still mad at him for getting out of the helicopter at Shea? Late for a hot date? Scared by what that old man had told him? It could have been any of them. Hell, it could have been all of them, though Bill didn't look like the hot date type.

"I went to Morgan's office yesterday," Jason finally offered. "I told 'im that I wasn't going to do this anymore, after today."

"I know."

He knew? That pissed Jason off, since Bill hadn't let on until now. It was one thing for Bill to keep his own—or whoever's—secrets to himself, but this was between the two of them.

"I don't know what you guys are up to, but it's more than just city code violations."

"You figure?" Bill said. It was meant as a put-down.

"I don't mind breaking a few rules, but bending the law, that's not my style," Jason said, getting slightly more aggressive in his tone.

"If the City can't take care of itself, people got to take care of the City," Bill replied matter-of-factly.

"What's that supposed to mean?"

"Nothing. Just in the real world, sometimes you have to make choices. Not all of 'em are good."

Jason had been in this fight a million times before, with a lot of different people, not all of them bad. But they were wrong. Living in the real world didn't give you a get-out-of-jail-free card from having to do the right thing.

"Maybe you have to make tough choices," Jason explained, "but not all of 'em are bad. And if you're rich, you got more options to choose from."

"At least Morgan is staying," Bill countered. "City Hall's driving a lot of people out of this town."

Jason wanted to keep talking. He had a longer rap on this issue—what kind of compromises you can make before you become something you're not, or you weren't, or you shouldn't be. But they had arrived back in that industrial park, and Jason set the helicopter down in the same place as before. On the descent the flickering of a gas flare stack caught his eye, suggesting there was an active refinery nearby, but other than that everything looked just as it had then. Maybe it was even quieter this time, but it was the same set-up, with the big black limo idling near the warehouse.

Bill took the attaché case and hopped out of the helicopter. He looked up at Jason.

"Don't worry," Jason pre-empted, "I'm not going anywhere."

Jason watched as Bill walked toward the limo. As he approached it the back door opened again, but neither "Heavy-Set Man" nor the driver got out of the car. Instead, Bill leaned in and handed someone the case. Jason arched his back but couldn't see anything that was going on. He looked down at his watch for a second, and that's when he heard what had to be gunshots, but he hoped he was wrong. He screwed his eyes shut for a split second, flinching as the unmistakable sound passed though his body. Looking up, he saw Bill lying on the ground—the limo was already driving away. Without thinking Jason pulled the helicopter up and flew directly at the car, which drove beneath him and continued in the opposite direction. Jason looked to set down near where Bill was lying, but as he hovered over the body it was bitterly clear that Bill was already dead. Deftly maneuvering the helicopter and tilting it at an odd angle, he took a long look at the body through the passenger-side window and studied Bill's now lifeless face.

Then he pulled back up and chased after the car. He caught up with it in seconds and moved in as close as he could, trying to get a look at the license plate. Swinging around wildly, he got a good angle on the rear of the car through the passenger window— something-something-something, two-two-four. He and the limo were both swerving, and he couldn't make out the letters, but he repeated the numbers over and over in his head. He then swung around again, whipsawing so violently that he nearly lost control of the helicopter, but managed to position it in front of the fleeing car. The car stopped, and Jason hovered directly in front of it. He figured the driver would throw it in reverse, but instead, one of the doors flew open, and a man with a gun ducked behind it.

Without hesitating Jason flew forward and directly at the limo, which caught his adversaries by surprise and probably saved his life. Pouring right over the car—he almost scraped the roof—he sent the gunman tumbling to the ground. Only then did Jason pull up sharply, as fast as he could. The gunman recovered and wildly squeezed off a few rounds, but before he could get a clean shot Jason had reached a safe altitude. It was an odd standoff, more of a stalemate—the gunman kept his weapon pointed at the helicopter, but did not fire. Jason couldn't get in much closer without exposing himself to renewed gunfire, but the killers were boxed in as well, realizing that he could follow them from the air.

Jason was sorting through his options when he was interrupted by a loud beeping sound and a flashing light from his control panel. He was running out of gas, and had just enough, probably, to get back to the City. He thought about crashing into the car, but quickly rejected the idea as overly dramatic. He had a piece of the license plate. Looking at the floor on the passenger side, he also realized that he had one of Bill's big manila envelopes as well. It was time to go. Jason looked down for one last time. He saw Bill's body, the car, the warehouse, the industrial park—three gas flares were now visible, burning indifferently. In the distance, he could see the Verrazano Narrows Bridge. It was the longest suspension bridge in the world, stretching impossibly from Staten Island to Brooklyn. Over two miles long, there was something about it that was reassuring, as if it was calling him back to the City. He pulled away and headed back to town.

JASON made it back to the roof. It was abandoned, and Sammy wasn't there, which was a relief, since Jason didn't know what he would say if Sammy—or anyone for that matter—saw him. The minute he stepped out of the helicopter he felt dizzy; he'd never noticed the fumes from the helicopter before, but they were making him nauseous. He walked uneasily to the ledge, looked down at the street, and then laughed out loud at the thought of throwing up and killing someone on the ground below.

He sat himself down, mostly by choice, and looked to the west. Concentrating on the Empire State Building, he gave himself a little lecture. People died. They died violent deaths. This was not a new thing. It would happen again—there would be six murders in New York tomorrow. Once when he was a ten years old they did a duck-and-cover drill in his classroom, to help the children prepare for a nuclear attack. A few nights later there was an explosion in New Jersey—so loud you could hear it in Queens. Jason crept out of bed and snuck into his parents' bedroom to peek out the window. It probably wasn't an atom bomb, he reasoned—the Empire State Building was still there. It was still there now.

"That's enough," he said out loud. He always did well in a crisis and then fell apart afterwards, and he hated that about himself. Bill was dead. That had happened. And it wasn't going to be on the news. He wondered if anyone would ever hear about it, or if there were people who would miss him. Probably that old man from Shea Stadium.

Jason walked back to the helicopter and retrieved Bill's envelope. Then he went over to Sammy's booth and sat down, which he'd never done before, but he needed to use the phone.

"Yeah?" Adam never said his name or even hello when he answered the phone at work.

"Hey."

"Who is this?"

"Jason."

"No shit. I didn't recognize your voice. What are you using, two Dixie cups and a string?"

"Meet me in The Cone," Jason said, and hung up.

"The Cone" was a reference to the "cone of silence," also known as the unused staircase at the far end of the building. It wasn't easy being Adam. He was convinced that anything said in his office or on the phone would immediately be known by his enemies, whoever they were, or at least his adversaries. But sometimes he needed to talk but was too busy to leave the building, so he used the staircase. There were two of them, one near the elevators, which was almost never used, and a second, tucked away near the decommissioned manual service elevator, that few even knew existed—it was a vestige from when the building had been a hotel of some repute in the 1920s.

Jason wasn't afraid of talking in Adam's office; he just couldn't bear the thought of seeing anybody and didn't want to be interrupted. He slipped down the main stairs, nervous only during the short flight that led from the roof to the top floor. After that it was smooth sailing, but Jason went down a couple of extra flights before cutting across to the second staircase. Adam was already waiting when he got to the seventeenth floor.

"What's up?" he asked cautiously. Adam was used to calling for meetings in The Cone; he couldn't recall ever being summoned there himself.

They stood in the staircase and Jason brought Adam up to date. As always, the poor lighting exaggerated the intensely isolated atmosphere. The walls were painted that distinct industrial green-gray that someone long ago had decided was perfect for urban staircases. Only one naked bulb illuminated each landing, and the inadequate light bounced off the surroundings in a way that threw either exaggerated shadows or an otherworldly glare. The walls offered only the bare essentials: the floor number was stenciled in red, and two signs—one of those black and yellow "fallout shelter" symbols, showing some rust, and, affixed next to an elaborately spooled fire hose, another that read IN CASE OF FIRE, USE STAIRS.

After Jason finished, Adam just stood there, running over it in his own mind.

"You sure you're all right?" he asked again.

"Yeah. Not a scratch," Jason said, studying the backs of his hands for confirmation. "I've seen worse," he added in a quiet voice.

Adam shot him a quick glance, but Jason wasn't looking his way. "You want to look in the envelope?"

"I guess," Jason responded, holding it up to the light. Then he handed it to Adam and sat on the steps, looking at the platform halfway down to sixteen. "You do it."

He heard Adam rip open the envelope and ruffle through some papers, then sift through them slowly, one after the other.

"Well?" Jason finally asked, not turning around.

"Nothing."

"Nothing, like in a bunch of blank pages?" Jason didn't think that's what Adam meant, but he was rooting that way. It would be fitting. One more thing about nothing.

"No, nothing, as in just a bunch of numbers."

"What do you mean, numbers?"

"Maybe twenty pages, mostly columns with numbers. Looks like bookkeeper's records."

That sounded to Jason like it could be important, but Adam's voice was full of disappointment.

"What were you hoping for, a map to the place they dumped Hoffa?" Jason stood up. "Let me see them."

He took the papers and started pouring over them, turning the pages and reading parts out loud. "One-twelve, two thousand; One-fourteen, three thousand. Three-fifty-six, five thousand. What a load of crap."

"What do you think?" Adam asked.

"I think it's a coded record of where all that money has been going. But that's just what it looks like. Could be anything you want it to be—unless you know the code. But from where I sit, I'd say Morgan looks to have half the City on his payroll.

"Most of that under that table," Adam chimed in, starting to smell blood. "Might not look like much, but I bet it could send someone to jail. Maybe it's a tax scam. I told you Cohen was sticking it to Morgan with those licensing fees. Maybe Morgan is fighting back; I don't see him as a guy who backs down from a fight. Maybe this is how he's able to keep operating in the City."

"They don't kill you over tax evasion," Jason said quietly. "It's the other way around. They get killers for not paying their taxes." He walked back to the stairs and held onto the railing.

"You didn't see who shot him?"

"I told you. No."

"But it was the same car as the other day."

"Yes."

"So it was probably the same people."

"I guess." Jason closed his eyes and tried to summon an image of the people from the first Staten Island drop, but it wasn't coming to him.

"Some well-dressed guy and his driver," Adam added, thinking if they kept talking about it something would click in Jason's mind.

"That's who it was the time before. I told you, this time I only saw the driver, and I couldn't even tell if he was the same one. Could have been anybody—at least, anybody who knew enough to be there."

"What do you mean?" Adam could tell Jason was thinking something he wasn't saying.

"Well, the old guy at Shea Stadium—he must have been the one who sent Bill to Staten Island. I don't think Bill was originally planning to go there." Jason regretted bringing it up. He replayed the meeting in his mind. "No. Couldn't have been him."

"Why not?"

"I saw him and I saw them. It was like he was talking to his father."

"You saw a guy once, a hundred yards away," Adam countered. He wasn't attached to the Shea Stadium guy, and liked him as a suspect. "Don't get sentimental on me."

"Sentimental?" Jason vivisected the word.

"Yeah, sentimental. I know you. You are one sentimental mother. Don't even think about arguing with me on this. You don't want to know how sentimental you are."

"Nevertheless," Jason said, shifting back to the topic at hand, "I know what I know. And I know this: that guy in Queens was no killer. Or he's a better actor than Brando. Bill trusted him. But the one in Staten Island, he was pretty pissed off the other day. I could hear him shouting over the blades."

"Fine by me. Just so long as you're taking a stand."

"I'm taking a stand about the old man in Queens, not the bum on Staten Island. Just cause he was mad, that doesn't make him a killer."

"It does make him a suspect," Adam insisted.

"Suspect?" Jason repeated, this time prepared to go to the mat over Adam's choice of words.

"Sorry. He's a key piece of the puzzle. I mean, he's furious one day, and it was his car, or one that was supposed to look just like it. If we want the story, we've got to figure out who he is."

"Good luck finding him. Probably only a few thousand cars with two-four-four in the license plate."

"We'll find him. You never know. Things turn up. Like just this morning, I'm in my office working on my riddle of the sphinx."

"Huh?"

"You know, how the City is providing the same services with less money."

"Oh, right, the sugar and coffee thing." Jason turned away. He didn't have much energy for that at the moment. He peered down at the rectangular gap formed by the descending stairs. He could see all the way to the bottom. Leaning over, he tried to see how many flights down he could still see the actual steps, before the angle became too steep. Jason loved staircases and bridges. They had a stately beauty. And they took you from one place to another.

"So I'm working on my riddle, and, you know, it is actually like ancient Egypt in there, too. It's worse than you've ever seen—I've got papers stacked so high they look like the pyramids."

"The ruins of tombs," Jason said into the gap, just loud enough for it to echo.

"Gimme a minute, will you? I'm listening to *Highway 61 Revisited*—a little 'Tom Thumb's Blues'—and old Bob sings out, 'the cops don't need you, and man they expect the same.'"

Jason pulled back up but didn't turn around. "No argument here."

"And it dawns on me. Just out of the blue. Maybe there's more than one way to fix the books. So I call over to public information. I don't say who I am, but it doesn't matter, they can't turn me down the way Records can. You know those bastards—"

"You going somewhere with this, or just out for a spin?"

"Okay. Turns out there are just as many cops on the street, but arrests are down, way down."

"It's probably seasonal."

"It's summertime!"

"So?" Jason said, finally turning to face Adam.

"So if I'm right, you've got one more reason to be a white man.

The city has decided to use the same number of cops, but in a more concentrated area. Get mugged in the wrong neighborhood, good luck…unless someone happens by with a spare helicopter."

"You really think—"

"What did you say? No cops 'as far as the eye could see' three blocks from the police station?"

The silence was broken by a loud ringing, and the sound of footsteps. They looked at each other uncertainly. It was probably a fire alarm, but they'd never heard it before. Then the stairwell door swung open, and a man in a blue pinstriped three-piece suit rushed past them. He was taken by surprise by their presence, and lost his footing momentarily navigating around them, but he continued at breakneck speed, without saying a word or looking back.

"Hey man, what's up?" Jason shouted.

"Fire!" he shouted back, filling the staircase with the sound of his footsteps.

Adam leaned over the rail. "Where?"

The footsteps got more distant and the door opened again. The bells got louder when the door was opened, and a few more people entered and headed down the staircase like school kids let out of class, chatting and watching their steps. Smoke started to drift in.

"Where's the fire?" Adam asked the crowd collectively.

"One of the offices," a woman responded, fixing her hair as she descended the stairs.

Adam pushed past the people entering the stairway, forcing his way towards whatever it was everyone else was running away from. Jason looked toward the stairs, but reluctantly followed him. Adam walked briskly down the hallway, with Jason trotting to keep up. As they progressed, there was more smoke and confusion and it got harder to push upstream against the flow of people heading for the exits with somewhat more urgency than the first wave. Harry was standing on a desk directing traffic. Jason could tell that if his ship had gone down during the war, he would have been the last man to leave.

"Head directly for the stairs in an orderly fashion!" Harry was calling out. "Remain calm. Do not use the elevators!" He annunciated loudly and carefully.

Jason pushed more aggressively past people and almost caught
up with Adam. "Adam! Adam! Where are you going?"

"I have to save the papers in my office!"

As they got closer it became clear that Adam's office was where
the fire was at its worst. For the first time flames were visible, just
reaching out the door. Adam hesitated, and Jason saw that he was
about to charge into the room. He grabbed Adam and pushed him
against the wall, hard, holding him there.

"What the hell are you doing?" Jason screamed in his face.

"My whole life is in there!"

"Forget about it—there's nothing you can do! Let's get the hell
out of here!"

"No, let's get the hose!"

"What?"

Adam broke loose from Jason and ran back the way they came,
this time pushing past people heading in the same direction. Jason
followed as best he could and found Adam back at the staircase,
unspooling the fire hose.

"Does that thing even work?"

"Try turning that wheel!"

Jason struggled at first but managed to turn the small red wheel
attached to an oversized pipe that could have been a water source,
while Adam continued to free the hose. He looked down at and saw
that water was dripping from the nozzle. "Let's go!"

Adam dragged the hose back down the hallway, again struggling against people trying to leave the building. The hose was
leaking water, and they moved awkwardly, slipping twice. Back at
Adam's office, the fire hadn't advanced much beyond where it had
been, but you could feel the heat more intensely than before. They
crept slowly towards the doorway, now more alert to the danger of
the situation, with the hose dripping at their feet. Adam held the
nozzle and Jason was right behind him with a couple of feet of the
hose in his hands.

"I don't think you can put out a fire with a dripping hose," Jason shouted with half a smile at the absurdity of the situation. "Now what?"

Adam looked backed at the gray canvas length of hose. It was firm and full of water. Looking down at the nozzle, he noticed a small lever. Pressing his arms against his sides and squinting through scrunched eyes he took a tentative step into his office, pointed the nozzle of the hose at the fire, and shifted the lever. Water exploded from the hose with such force that it knocked both of them down. Adam didn't lose his grip, but the water sprayed everywhere. It blasted a stack of burning papers and sent them flying. Some landed on Adam, setting the cuff of his pants leg on fire. He didn't notice and Jason took off his coat and dove to the floor, smothering the fire at Adam's feet and getting a kick in the face for his efforts.

Adam moved farther in, still struggling to gain control of the nozzle. Lurching backwards, he misfired and blew a series of framed album covers and photos from the wall one by one like ducks in a shooting gallery, and they fell to the ground, each one a witness to the disorder—*There's a Riot Going On* by Sly and the Family Stone went first, followed by a picture from the Kent State shootings. But in relatively short order and despite Adam's inefficiency, the sheer force of the water brought the fire under control, even if it did trash the place in the process.

19

ADAM'S OFFICE WAS BADLY DAMAGED in the fire, and what wasn't burned had been knocked around pretty good by the water. But they had contained the fire; there were some smoke stains on the walls but nothing else outside the office was damaged, and in retrospect everybody was pretty pleased with Adam and Jason's performance. Adam hadn't made a lot of friends at the station, so most of them were patting Jason on the back, which was a pretty big laugh because if Adam hadn't been there, whoosh, Mr. Helicopter Hero would have been the first one down those stairs. Adam was avoiding people in any event—he was devastated, splashing around his office trying to assess the damage, which was extensive. The firefighters that eventually arrived—not too late by city standards but long after the show was over—only added to the carnage. Their job was to put out fires, not to worry about anything that got in their way. A few firemen were still milling around the station, checking rooms, inspecting electrical panels, and leaving wet footprints everywhere.

Adam opened a few file cabinets, slamming the last one shut. "Nothing! Nothing! Maybe half the stuff in the file cabinets survived. Everything else is gone."

"Well, that's something," Jason said, trying to be reassuring without sounding like he was faking it. "At least you still have—"

"I've got nothing," he said, correcting Jason, something he was still fully capable of. "Remember the pyramids? Well, they're gone.

The ashes of history. All the stuff I was working on." He slumped down on a box. It was solid, and reaching one hand hopefully inside, he fished something out. It was a copy of his second book, and his face on the cover stared up at him with an expression Jason had, back in the day, incisively labeled as "über-poser." He looked over to see if Jason was smirking, but he looked dead serious, which was a bad sign.

"Somebody out there is laughing at me right now."

"Look," Jason told him, "this just happened. Right now you can't face the thought of pushing that rock all the way back up the hill. But you can get past this." Adam pretended not to listen, and flipped through his book. "You know what you know. And there's still some stuff here, stuff that can be replaced, the library—"

"I've got nothing. Just theories. Theories! From staring at those papers for so long that I felt I could levitate them. Nothing really solid—I could only half convince you, and you *have* to listen to me."

"Come on, just a few hours ago you solved the riddle of the Sphinx."

"Yeah, I started out in Egypt and ended up in Pompeii. In a few thousand years somebody will dig this all up and prove I was right."

"Or maybe tomorrow." Jason jumped on the optimism that lingered at the end of Adam's last thought. "You know what you know. Even if it's gone now, you've seen it. Nothing can change that."

"Maybe it was a mirage. Look at something long enough you start to see what you want to see."

Lou ducked his head in the room. "Jason, Harry wants to see you in his office."

"See me?" Jason asked, hoping Lou would realize he'd made a mistake.

"Yeah."

"Did he say what he wanted?"

"Probably another interview with our resident hero," Adam chimed in.

"Lou, there is no way on this planet—"

"Save the Greta Garbo routine," Lou said, cutting him off sharply. It wasn't his style, but there were people marching all over the place, and he still had a show to put on. "We're not in the business of airing our own dirty laundry. You want to see that, you'll have to turn the dial."

"Then what does he want?" Jason asked.

"How the hell should I know? He just barked out that he wanted to see you—probably wants to thank you. You lunatics don't play fireman and we're off the air." That was enough time in one place for Lou, and he was gone.

Jason looked over at Adam. "Go ahead," Adam instructed. "If I jump I'll leave my final instructions on the windowsill."

"All right. I'll be right back. But type 'em. You know I can't read your writing."

Jason walked down the corridor and approached Harry's office, which was in the corner of the newsroom. The office had large windows with Venetian blinds, so Harry could see the whole newsroom but still have privacy when he needed it. At the moment they were drawn but not shuttered, and through the blinds Jason could see Harry and a police detective, who looked so much like a detective he might as well have been walking around under a neon sign, but just in case anybody wasn't sure he wore his badge on his belt. The cop was talking and waving his arms, and finally he pointed dramatically to the floor with both hands. The whole thing played like an old film noir, and Jason panicked, convinced he was being cast as the fall guy. They probably knew everything about Bill, he thought, and he was being set up. There was probably one of those suitcases full of money planted in his apartment right now. Faye Dunaway would double-cross him in the movie version.

Jason started to back off slowly, planning to ease down the corridor. Were those two firemen walking toward him, or just walking? They stopped at the coffee machine. That seemed innocent enough, but Jason felt pinned between the cop that was waiting for him and the firemen clogging the hallway. After seven seconds of just standing there he leaned back against the wall, took a breath, and reassessed. On second thought, he probably wasn't being set up to be the fall guy. Whatever it was, he decided, making his way slowly back to Harry's office, better to confront it head on.

"You wanted to see me, Harry?" he said in his most innocent voice as he entered the room.

"Yeah, and hey, thanks again. Tell Shaker, too. Oh, sorry, let me introduce you. This here is Detective Stanton."

"What's he want?" Jason said directly to Harry, not making eye contact with the Stanton. "I mean, I don't know anything, I just fly helicopters. I don't see why I have to—"

"Jesus, kid, he's just here about the fire," Harry interrupted, holding up both hands.

"What does a cop know about fire?" Jason asked, still looking only at Harry.

"We know something about arson," Stanton replied.

"Arson?" Jason finally made eye contact with the detective, who was half-sitting on the edge Harry's desk.

"Maybe," Harry interjected. "They have to check. It's procedure. We're getting a little ahead of ourselves here."

"So why am I here?"

"I need you to fly Carol out to Brooklyn for Maynes's funeral." Harry looked over at the corner of the room as he said it. Carol had been sitting there the whole time, but Jason was so charged up he hadn't noticed. "What with the fire and everything, we lost track of the road crew, and now they're stuck in Brooklyn. I sent them straight to the cemetery; you'll fly her there."

"So that's it? I mean…sure, whatever." Jason looked over at Carol. "You ready?"

"I need five minutes." She turned to Harry. "You want one-on-ones, or just background?"

Jason headed for the door. "I'll pick you up at your office," he said, barely looking over in Carol's direction. He couldn't get out of that room fast enough.

"Hey." Stanton stopped him.

"What?" Jason responded at the edge of rudeness.

"Where were you during the fire?"

"Around," Jason said, making a twirling motion with his fingers.

"You were in the air?"

"No. Here at the station."

"Where?"

Jason was sick of this cop and he knew his answer wasn't going to go over well, nor did he feel like explaining to Harry and Carol the intricacies of The Cone of Silence. "In the stairwell," he said casually, trying to make it sound like it was a perfectly normal place to be.

"What were you doing there?" Stanton asked predictably.

"Ask my lawyer." Jason stared as hard as he could.

"Easy, kid," Harry chimed in. "He's a little sensitive about that sort of thing," Harry explained to Stanton.

"You see anything?" Stanton continued.

"I told you. I don't know anything."

"Yeah, that figures," he said, looking Jason up and down like a Chicago cop would have at the '68 convention.

"Actually, right after the alarm went off, some guy in a suit went down the stairs. At almost exactly the same time, now that I think about it. Well ahead of anybody else. Impeccably well dressed, kind of guy you'd see at a PBA function."

"Really," Stanton said skeptically, slipping off the desk. He put his hands in his pockets and his shoulders rolled forward. "What did he look like?"

Jason squared off, confrontationally. "I don't know. All guys in suits look alike, don't they, Detective?"

Stanton leaned in even closer, and Jason figured it was a good thing that Harry was there. "No," he said in a loud, hoarse whisper that suggested he'd seen both Dirty Harry movies more than once. "It's niggers and wise-ass hippies that all look alike."

"Depends on what you mean by wise-ass."

"Let me see your shoes."

"Got a warrant?"

"Jason, show him your fucking shoes," Harry ordered. He'd had enough of the whole act. He didn't like the cop and he didn't like Jason's attitude.

Jason lifted his leg and propped the heel on Harry's desk. Stanton dragged his index finger theatrically across the sole of Jason sneaker, and sniffed it.

"You can take your foot off my desk now," Harry said, trying to keep in the mix.

"You got a little kerosene on your shoes, fella."

"How long you been a detective?" It was a good shot, and Jason was close enough to see Stanton's jaw tighten.

Harry stepped forward, not quite getting between them. "Hey Stanton, he's one of the guys put out the fire. Saved our asses. He was standing in the middle of it. Anything on his feet must have come from there. I saw him come from the stairway."

"Before or after the fire? Half the time the torch puts it out himself. Gives them a chance to play hero." Stanton smirked when he said it, but he turned his back on Jason and walked a few paces away.

"You finished?" Jason asked. He toned it down just a notch and hoped it would get him out of the room.

"For now."

"Five minutes," Jason said to Carol. "Don't be late." He left the room without closing the door, having rejected the alternatives of slamming it and shutting it quietly.

Jason walked back to Adam's office. Adam was sitting with his head resting on his desk. He could have been sleeping. Adam had this philosophy that you should sleep when you were tired. He probably slept about five or six hours in any twenty-four hour period, though once a month or so he'd crash. He also only ate when he was hungry, which worked well for him, but the combination sometimes made it hard for him to connect with regular people, since they worked their lives around sleeping and eating, rather than vice-versa.

"Hey," Jason said quietly.

"Hey back," Adam said without moving. He wasn't sleeping.

"Feel like taking a free copter ride? It's been a while. Just the thing to clear your head."

"Fuck you," Adam mumbled.

"Suit yourself. But I'm heading out to Sid Maynes's funeral. I hear it's gonna be a hell of a show."

"I hate funerals."

"No, that's me," Jason reminded him. "I hate funerals. You love them—it's birthday parties you hate."

"Whatever."

"Five minutes. Meet me on the roof."

Adam didn't move and Jason knew if he left now the part of Adam that wanted to go would be much more persuasive than anything else Jason had to say. He headed back in the opposite direction—it would be quicker to cut through the studio than to pass by Harry's office again, and besides, the company would probably be better. As he neared the studio he noticed that the stage lights were on and he could hear the rhythm of Nate's voice, but before he got any closer someone stuck a hand right in his face. It was Lou, keeping him off the set. They were shooting an editorial.

"Mock Live?" Jason mouthed the words at Lou, with a little twinkle in his eye. It was much more fun to ridicule TV than to be on it. Lou didn't respond, he just quietly walked over and stood behind the camera. Nate was standing at full attention, turned ever so slightly to his left, against a light blue backdrop with a map of the City (not to mention the station's logo and call letters) painted on it.

"…We at Channel Six appreciate the deep financial difficulties that the City finds itself in, and we applaud Mayor Cohen's skillful stewardship during these difficult times. Indeed, we are proud to have endorsed his candidacy in the last two elections. But we would argue that trying to close the fiscal gap with unprecedented increases in regulatory fees is misguided, disproportionate, and, perhaps worst of all, almost certain to backfire. Fees so high that they force stations off the air will not increase revenue; the end result will be nothing more than fewer stations paying higher taxes, amid the wreckage of job losses and reduced viewing options for the public. We urge the Mayor to reconsider this short-sighted measure. And we hope you, the viewing public will join us. Please write the Mayor at the address printed on your screen, and let him know that you're opposed to raising taxes that will cost jobs and force your favorite stations off the air. For all of us at Channel Six...I'm Nathan Johnson."

That's taking a bold stand, Jason thought, walking though the studio after Lou had waved him on. Turns out the TV station is against higher TV licensing fees. Must have been up all night debating that one. Now that this hot potato is out of the way they're probably ready to take a stand on school busing.

"Do we have time for one more?" he heard Nate say as he walked though. "I think it would be stronger if we added that sentence about our support for the parking fee surcharge."

Nate was the James Brown of the broadcasting business—nobody worked harder. Jason swallowed a smile as he pictured James Brown's version of the same editorial. "Forget about crime, traffic, and sanitation, everybody write the Mayor about those sky-high TV licensing fees! Papa needs a higher profit margin. *Yeow!*" Now that might just push that letter-writing campaign into the double digits.

20

JASON, CAROL, AND ADAM were crowded together in the helicopter. It would have been awkward enough for the three of them just to share an elevator, even on a good day. In fact, almost any twosome would have set off some unpredictable sparks: Jason–Carol, or Adam–Carol, or even Jason–Adam with Carol nearby. And it wasn't a good day. Carol had never been in a helicopter before, and she had that hollow look people get when they try to figure out why the thing actually flies. But she was more ambitious than scared, and nothing was going to stop her from doing a remote this big. Adam was a fatalist, so he wasn't afraid of much, but he hated flying under any circumstances because he couldn't stand being put in someone else's hands. He was also still reeling from the fire. If anything, Jason was the most put together of the three of them, which was not an inspiring thought. He needed to keep an eye on how Adam was doing, and that helped distance him from Bill's murder, but only so much and not all the time. He was grateful he'd been looking away at the moment of the shooting. As it was he still saw the body whenever he closed his eyes.

"Are you sure he's allowed to sit back there?" Carol asked Jason.

Carol was sitting in the passenger seat, and Adam was cramped awkwardly in the space behind them. Jason was quite certain Adam wasn't allowed back there. He hadn't mentioned to Harry that he was bringing him and made Adam kind of sneak on, though Sammy couldn't have missed him.

"He's probably in violation of some code," Jason said, amusing himself at Morgan's expense.

Carol looked out the window but quickly decided that looking in was a better bet. "How are you doing back there?" She called out. Adam didn't answer, so she twisted her body in the confines of her seat and arched back towards where he was sitting. "I said, how are you doing back there?"

"I heard you. I thought you were just making conversation."

"I was."

"That's more of an elevator thing," Adam said cooly.

Carol's gymnastics had caused her skirt to slip up past her knees to her mid-thighs. Jason noticed this and glanced over briefly, several times, making mental notes. Adam never said anything about not looking at her legs.

"Really," she responded, with no intention of letting anybody shut her down. "Is that from Emily Post?"

"You know what the problem is with television?" Adam asked, more aggressively. "You've got to talk at a certain time, for a certain time, even if there's nothing to say. Before you know it you're walking around like that, even when the camera's off."

Carol twisted back to her seat, causing Jason to turn his head suddenly, but at least he managed to refrain from one of his brilliant camouflaging sneezes. Fortunately, Carol was more concerned about him as her pilot.

"Everything okay?" She looked uneasily at his face, searching for hints of some unstated mechanical problem.

"Sure. Just a lot of things to keep my eyes on," Jason explained, gesturing at the instrument panel.

Adam snorted. It was directed at Jason, but Carol took it personally.

Carol looked out the window again, ignoring him.

"How much longer?" she asked Jason.

"Still a while. We have to take a wide circle around Kennedy airport."

She turned back again toward Adam, apparently choosing him over the window as the lesser of two evils.

"Why are you here?" she asked him pointedly, almost existentially.

"Covering the funeral."

"Last time I checked, you were in entertainment. Have you been promoted?" She lingered on the last word and arched her eyebrows, pulling rank.

"What do you expect out there — news or theater?" Adam asked sharply, even for him. "You gonna interview the brave widow? Get some shots of the kids holding their teddy bears? 'How do you feel, kids, how does it feel now that Daddy's gone? How does it feeel?'" He gave her the full Dylan treatment, extending the *e* and glaring at her with an accumulated contempt for her entire profession.

"Are you always this much of an asshole, or just on days that your office burns down?"

"How would you like —"

"Hey, take it easy guys," Jason intervened, trying to cool Adam off and maybe scoring a few chivalry points in the process. "No fighting in the copter. It's one of the few rules I believe in. Relax. Enjoy the ride. You guys could be down there in a van." He pointed at a long line of traffic below.

Carol took his word for it. She was through looking out the window.

"Nice to see you can play the peacemaker," she said to Jason.

"What do you mean by that?"

"That cop today." She turned back to Adam. "He picked a fight with a cop."

"I did not."

"Bull," she said directly at Jason. She turned back to Adam, her voice rising. "In Harry's office. I thought he was going to hit him!"

"He's done it before," Adam said casually.

"Hit a cop?"

"You know that isn't true," Jason insisted.

Adam maneuvered in his space, getting a little closer so he could talk to Carol and torment Jason at the same time. "Let me tell you a little something about our friend here. Jason, see, he doesn't like cops much. Why, back in nineteen sixty-seven—"

Jason turned around and looked squarely at Adam. "You tell this story like it's supposed to be some defining moment. Let me tell you something, there's no such thing as a defining moment. People are a little more complex than that. This is an overrated story. You need new material, that's your problem. One of your problems."

"Aren't you supposed to look forward when you drive this thing?" Adam asked.

Jason glanced forward for an instant, and then looked back again at Adam. "I happen to have very well-formed opinions, and I got them on my own. Maybe some of them have been reconfirmed more or less at one particular moment, but which they would have been the same regardless." Jason was talking so fast the words were falling over each other. They didn't quite add up, but he'd made his point. "I don't like anchovies, you know, but it's not like I was ever attacked by one."

"Hey, I'm not the one who brought it up." At least Adam was enjoying himself. "Besides, if it's not such a profound story, why should it matter if I tell it?

"Well, you can't not tell it now," Carol added.

Jason turned and faced forward, and made a slight course correction designed to serve as a subtle reminder that their lives were in his hands. Carol took a small quick breath.

"Now then," Adam began, like he was narrating a documentary, "back in nineteen sixty-seven, old Jason here had just finished his first year of Harvard Law School—"

"Harvard?" Carol seemed more surprised than impressed, though a little bit of impressed hung in the air.

"Oh yeah, Jason was quite a tiger back then. You know what they used to say about him? He didn't see much coming but he reacted really well."

Jason grunted.

"Anyway, as I was saying, he chose to intern at the San Francisco office of the ACLU. That was Jason all over: idealistic and practical at the same time. I mean, with all due respect to Mark Twain, nothing's nicer than summer by the Bay. 'Up and down the San Fran-cis-co Bay'," he added, in a brief homage to Van Morrison.

"You gonna tell the story or play tourist guide?" Jason asked without turning.

"You ever hear of the Sunset Strip riot?" Adam asked Carol. He was back to his normal voice.

"No."

"You know, from that song 'For What it's Worth,' by Buffalo Springfield?"

She shook her head. "No."

This was unacceptable to Adam. "Sure you do," he insisted, and started singing "there's something happening here, what it is ain't exactly—"

Jason cut him off. "She said no." If there was one thing Adam couldn't do, it was sing.

"Well, that one was in LA anyway," Adam continued. "But it was the same story all over. The Summer of Love," he said with a cynical smile. "Hippies flocked to California, started to fill up the streets. They were everywhere."

"War protesters?" Carol asked

"Not really. Just kids looking for something, I guess. In 'sixty-seven the whole thing was still more about business than politics. But either way the local storeowners asked the cops to clear the streets. They thought the hippies were scaring away customers. But things got a little out of hand. You know, kind of a dress rehearsal for Chicago 'sixty-eight." He swung his arms to illustrate the point. "It was complete anarchy. The cops kind of waded in, ordered everybody to 'disperse,' and most of them did, but they really had nowhere to go. Everybody's just milling around, one thing leads to another, maybe some names thrown back and forth. Some of the cops get a little excited, then a few more."

His voice trailed off, and he held them both in suspense for a moment. "One thing you may not have experienced, Carol, given your lifestyle choices, is that when a cop comes running at you, you get this overwhelming urge to run. Even if you haven't done anything wrong. It's just something about the uniform. So before you know it, cops are chasing kids all over the street. Everybody's scrambling around like one of those fast-speed silent movies. Finally, one of them pulls his nightstick out, and just hits this kid right in the head. Boom! Down to the ground."

Carol turned to Jason. "Was that you?"

"No," Jason said flatly.

"That's actually what makes this story so interesting," Adam continued. "Jason wasn't with them. It was kind of a younger, more-unemployed type crowd, whereas our hero was a very purposeful fellow at this point in time. But we're not quite there yet. Once the first nightstick comes out, then all hell really breaks lose. Somebody throws a bottle—at least that's what the papers said—and we're looking at something that's known in the trade as a 'police riot.' Now here comes Jason, who, as I said, wasn't involved in this at all, just walking back to work from lunch. Minding his own business, he sees a cop catch up with some kid and start to beat the hell out of him with his nightstick. I mean, he's just whaling on him, and he's not stopping."

"So what did you do?" she asked Jason.

"Nothing. What anyone would have done."

Adam smiled. "What anyone over here did was run over and put a flying tackle on the cop. And I mean flying tackle—running, diving, tackling—peeled him right off the kid. The cop screams for help, and before you know it the nightsticks are everywhere. Jason and this other kid are hauled off to jail, bashed-in and bleeding—the kid got sixteen stitches down the side of his face—charged with assaulting an officer."

"Wow!" Carol exclaimed.

"Yeah, Jason's got a lot of wows in his past."

The helicopter veered downward, sharply and without warning. As designed, it sent Adam tumbling.

"Hey!"

"We're here," Jason reported.

"So what happened?"

"Nothing," Jason said. "Turns out the kid was the son of some state senator. His lawyer shows up a couple of hours later, and we're kicked. But I never played the piano again."

21

～

THEY SET DOWN GENTLY on a concrete square in the middle of a large grassy field adjacent to the cemetery. A WNYS-TV6 news van idled in a small, otherwise empty parking lot in the near distance, beyond which were a smattering of stone benches, a large flagpole, and a path that led to what must have been an administrative or sales office that looked closed. You couldn't see any tombstones from where they had landed; a gently sloping but formidable hill obscured the view. Jason had overshot the cemetery by about half a mile before swinging around and descending to the helipad; nobody wanted any aircraft buzzing the service.

Carol got out first and was greeted by two crewmen who had hopped out of the van as they arrived. Jason caught up with her just as she was opening the passenger side door.

"Hey, you going to need a ride back?"

"No," she said quickly, looking over at the helicopter like it was a German shepherd threatening to break off its leash. "I'll go with them." She got in and closed the door, and talked through the window. "It should be okay, we'll be going in the opposite direction of the rush."

"Your funeral," he said, walking away, two steps later hoping she found the unintended joke clever.

"You guys want a ride over?" She called out when he was already about fifteen feet away.

Jason checked over at the helicopter; Adam hadn't gotten out yet. "No thanks, we'll hoof it."

By the time he got back Adam still hadn't stirred, nor did he give the impression he planned to.

"Don't make me go to this thing alone," Jason said. "Besides, if anything happens to the copter when you're in it, insurance won't cover it."

Adam didn't respond, but he dragged himself out and they walked slowly toward the cemetery. The hill was bigger than it looked when you were walking it, and it started to rain lightly.

"Go ahead, rain on me, it won't make any difference," Adam said in disgust, looking up at the sky.

They continued walking, and the rain got a little harder. "She didn't even offer us a ride, did she, the soulless whore."

"That she did," Jason answered. It might have been an afterthought, but he let her get full credit.

"Huh, I must have been wrong about her."

"Really?"

"Yeah, maybe she's got a soul."

"You're just bitter 'cause you never made it with her."

"How would you know that?" Adam asked in a worldly voice. It touched Jason for a second, but only just.

"Because there is no way you wouldn't have told me."

"You think I tell you about all of them?"

"I don't think you tell me about half of them. But you would have told me about her."

They finally reached the top of the hill and started down the other side. They could see the Maynes service in the distance.

"Yeah, I guess I would have, eventually," Adam conceded. "But just for the record, I never tried."

"I see."

"Really. I wouldn't want any part of it."

"I don't know," Jason said. "Most guys look at her, I figure they're saying, 'That's an amusement park I'd like to visit.' Not to mention the sheer curiosity factor."

"I thought you found her fascinating, you know, in an intellectual sense."

"I wasn't talking about me, I was talking about most guys."

"What, you're not most guys, but I am?" Adam said, lowering his voice as they approached the funeral.

"I'm not saying you're most guys," Jason said, steadily lowering his voice to a whisper. "I'm just saying that's what most guys would think, and it wouldn't be surprising if you shared that particular thought."

They slowed as they approached the crowd. Jason didn't know how popular Maynes was when he was alive, but he managed to draw a very large gathering to his graveside. The rain had tapered off again and was somewhere between a light rain and a heavy mist. Most of the spectators were in raincoats but didn't use umbrellas, giving Adam and Jason a clear view as they approached, since they were still on slightly higher ground. The casket was suspended above the grave in the center, attached by red straps to a brass-colored frame. The mourners formed a U-shape around it, set back by about twenty feet on each side. At the top of the U there was a dais crowded with dignitaries, and a podium with a microphone set in the front.

Adam and Jason stopped near the back of the crowd, leaving a small space so that they would be able to see everything, but not so far back that they obviously stood out. A contingent of reporters stood behind the dais at a discreet distance, but a lone unmanned camera was set up in front to film the speakers. It must have been going on for a while, because the Mayor was already giving his speech. An aide was standing next to him, holding a large umbrella. Adam and Jason listened, but they also scanned the crowd as the Mayor spoke.

"…I met Sid in 'fifty-three. Too young to fight in the big one, he'd volunteered for Korea and had just come back." Cohen was in good form. There was a warmth in his recollections, but he wrapped his words with just the right weight for the occasion. "He worked full time and put himself through law school at night, supporting three generations of his family. In nineteen seventy-one he became the youngest borough president in the City's history."

"Yeah," Adam whispered, "he was a real prince." He pointed out someone on the dais to Jason. "There's his good friend, Dominick Labetta. I've got a picture of him and the Mayor meeting at a...."

"What?" Jason asked.

"I don't have that picture anymore. I don't have any pictures. I don't have anything. What's the point. The whole thing is a joke."

Jason leaned over without moving his feet and nudged Adam's shoulder with his. Then he leaned in a little more, and Adam had to take a small step to keep his balance.

"It's a bump in the road. Looks big now, but the farther you get from it, the smaller it'll seem. Nothing's ever slowed you down before."

Adam looked Jason in the eye. "You're not exactly a poster boy for 'It'll work out,' you know?" It was more pessimistic than aggressive, and Jason sensed Adam was letting the conversation continue.

"Shake a tree and crooked politicians will come falling out faster than light-hitting shortstops. You just gotta keep shaking."

Adam looked at the ground, unconvinced, and Jason returned his attention to the Mayor, who was still going on.

"...This city never sleeps and neither did Sid. If he stumbled toward the end of his journey, it was due to the unforeseeable twists in the fate of the path, not the price of his remarkable pace. He packed two lifetimes into forty-five years, and our City was better for it, and those of us who knew him well...." He paused for a moment, and looked past the crowd, as if to gather his emotions, though he betrayed none too obviously. "Those of us who knew him well... all I can say is, we were thankful for the privilege. Farewell, my friend."

Cohen stepped back, and his aide slipped off to the side, lowering the oversized umbrella as he left the dais, revealing a group of four men. He exchanged a few short handshakes as he worked his way back towards the center of the platform, and the empty chair waiting just to the left of where the four men stood quietly in a row.

After the Mayor was settled, a rabbi appeared at the podium. He was old but not frail, and carried himself with an assured, gentle confidence. Speaking with a hint of rabbinical vibrato, he brought some spirituality to an occasion that many in attendance were performing as a professional obligation.

"And now the time has come for the beloved family and cherished friends of Sidney Maynes to return his body to the earth," he concluded.

There were no formal prayers as the casket was lowered mechanically into the ground. Everyone stood silently, watching it descend, and when it reached the bottom four workmen quickly and quietly removed the frame and more roughly pulled the red straps from the grave. Then one by one, in an order that had to have been determined in advance, officials from the dais joined family members and selected friends as they walked over to a large stack of dirt. Two more cameras were set up in the distance and they captured the procession of people as they ritually pulled a shovel from the pile, scooped up some dirt, and tossed it into the grave.

Jason elbowed Adam to attention and pointed toward the line. "Who are those two guys?" He whispered, with a little urgency in his voice that didn't register with Adam.

"Which ones?"

"In line behind Cohen. Not the old black guy right behind him, but the old man right after him, and that big, heavy-set guy two farther back."

Adam found the line, scanned it quickly and smirked. "Sometimes your ignorance blows me away."

"Just tell me who they are."

"Let me ask you something, Encyclopedia Brown, who's the head of the CIA?"

"George Bush," Jason folded his arms and glared at Adam as he responded.

"And what's the capital of Laos?"

"Vientiane. That's two for two, okay, so why don't you tell me who the fuck those guys are," Jason snapped.

"The tall guy at the end is George Gekin, Staten Island Borough President. As for the old man you're so curious about, let me first alert you to the fact that he's standing between Ben Frankel of the Bronx, and that person you described as "that old black guy" but who is known to millions as Arthur Harrison, the Manhattan BP. Anyway, his name is Abe Saperstein — he's been your borough president since the Stone Age. Oh, and I should probably mention, the guy in the casket — that's Sid Maynes. He was from Brooklyn."

Jason took a deep breath, and steadied himself by shifting his feet. "Huh. What do you know about Gekin?"

"Nothing much," Adam said dismissively. "Now Harrison, he's an institution — did time in Congress years ago — probably the most respected black leader in the City. And Saperstein, he's supposed to be a man of the people. Both of them are big figures in the City since the Depression, like Cohen. You know, up-from-the-tenements types. Gekin and Frankel are next-generation guys — post-war professionals. Career politicians like Maynes. Why do you care?"

Jason felt a little light-headed and leaned into Adam. "'Cause Gekin is the guy who owns the car from Staten Island," he whispered into Adams ear, then took a step back to gather himself.

"What? The shooter?" Adam whispered so loudly that a woman nearby shot them a silencing glance. Jason stood motionless, staring at the funeral, and Adam had to grab him by the elbow to tug him back a few feet.

"Are you kidding me?" Adam asked.

"And Saperstein is the guy from Shea Stadium," Jason added. "I never saw the other two."

Adam looked like he might explode. He pulled himself together and looked at Jason for confirmation. "You're not kidding me."

"I'm dead serious."

Adam turned on his heel and briskly walked anyway from the crowd, heading deeper into the cemetery. He moved fast, weaving through rows of headstones as if he'd suddenly remembered where he'd buried treasure. He disappeared over a small hill, and when Jason caught up with him he was pacing between two rows of headstones.

"Gekin?" he asked Jason. "Are you sure?"

"Him and Saperstein I saw, for sure," Jason said. He was feeling stronger from both the walk and the distance it created. "Saperstein was the one who seemed like a nice guy."

"Gekin shot Bill?" It was phrased as a question, but sounded more like a declaration.

"I did not see who shot Bill," Jason said emphatically. "Say it with me. I did not see who shot Bill."

"Okay, okay, it doesn't matter." Adam stopped pacing for a moment, eager to make some sort of declaration, but it wasn't quite there.

"Do you have any idea what this means?" he asked grandly, as if he was talking not only to Jason but to the vast silent audience of tombstones arrayed symmetrically around them.

"No." Jason was the only one who answered. "Do you?"

"Yes," Adam said slowly, even though he was still working it out as he spoke. "Morgan was…funneling money…to the borough presidents!"

"Well, at least to Gekin and Saperstein." Adam was back in business, so Jason had to return to his post, the sheepdog that kept Adam's brain from wandering too far off.

"And Maynes, too!" Adam said loudly, and then checked to see if anyone heard them, but it was just them and the tombstones. He lowered his voice again. "Remember that report about money found in Maynes's car? It must have been one of those briefcases Bill was always carrying around."

"Could have been," Jason corrected. "But why? I don't get it."

"I told you Morgan and the Mayor were at war! I knew it the minute I saw those licensing fees go through the roof. That was no accident. Cohen was sticking it to him good."

"I still don't see what Morgan could do with the borough presidents," Jason protested. "And it doesn't tell us anything about why Maynes was murdered."

"Oh, so he was murdered?" Adam said triumphantly. "One question at a time. Morgan must have been trying to get around the Mayor. But exactly how, we don't know. Do you still have those papers from Bill?"

Bill. For a moment Jason had almost forgotten. "Yeah."

"We've got to take a closer look at them. And the city charter—maybe this has to do with the way the City was incorporated. It happened in eighteen ninety-eight." He was pulling ideas out of the air. "You should call Alison. She would know that." He was pacing again.

"She's a *medieval* historian."

"Well, she would know where to look. Maybe it's something else." Adam was stoked, and when he was this excited he had a tendency to fire off questions like Adam West's Batman bouncing ideas off Robin in the Batcave. "Question: how do you get around the Mayor? And not just any Mayor, but this Mayor. I don't know. How much time do you have before you have to get back?"

Jason looked at his watch. "About forty minutes."

"Give me half an hour," Adam said, already on his way. "I'll meet you back at the copter."

"Where are you going?"

"I want to look around. See who else is at the show."

Jason watched Adam disappear over the small hill and was left to his own thoughts, and he slowly turned his head, taking in a panoramic view. There sure were a lot of dead people. He decided to make his way back toward the helicopter, choosing a circuitous route that avoided the funeral. He would have made an effort to avoid it in any event, but now he was nervous about being recognized. Both Gekin and Saperstein had looked over at the copter.

It was a long walk, and it gave him some time to settle down. Even the Six Million Dollar Man would have had trouble making out his face a hundred yards away through the glass of the helicopter, and those guys didn't look like they had bionic eyes. And it really didn't matter who shot Bill, he was still dead. Maybe at least he died for something. Jason's mind drifted off the subject as he made his way among the headstones, and he started to play games with the dates. Which was the most ancient? Which was the most recent? Who had the longest life? Elsie Fienberg, 1842 to 1929—eighty-seven, not bad. Who had the shortest? Was it better to live a long, uneventful life or a short, purposeful one?

Reaching the grassy field, he walked over to one of the stone benches and tested it with his hand—it was dry. He sat down, then lay on his back, looking up at the empty flagpole and the clouds beyond it. Letting his eyes close, his mind filled with a rush of images. Funerals remind you of other funerals, which is odd, because baseball games don't make you think of other baseball games. But now he could see Martin Luther King's funeral, plain as day, and he realized that he actually had seen Harrison before. When MLK came out against the war in 'sixty-seven at the Riverside Church in Harlem, the speech set off a firestorm of negative reaction. Harrison took him out to dinner.

The sound of wheels driving across gravel brought Jason back to the present, and lifting his head he saw a limo slowing on the road on the other side of the field. The driver got out and started walking in Jason's direction. He sat up and watched him. It was a long walk, and Jason stole glances here and there to see if there was anyone else around. There wasn't. The driver got closer, and Jason fixed his gaze directly at him, as hard as he could. He got himself ready to move quickly if he needed to.

"Something I can help you with?" Jason asked when he was still several feet away.

"Would you come with me please." It wasn't a question.

"Why should I do that?"

"Man in the car would like a word with you."

"If he wants to talk to me, he can do it right here."

"He says you guys used to hang out on rooftops together."

Jason exhaled. He nodded and walked back to the limo with the driver, who opened the door and then closed it behind him.

Morgan was alone, and motioned for Jason to sit across from him. Jason sat with his back to the front of the car—the partition was drawn and the front was not visible.

"Nice day for a funeral," Morgan finally offered. "I don't know about you, but I wouldn't want to be buried on a sunny day. People would rather be elsewhere."

"I don't think much about it."

"No, I imagine not at your age."

"I wouldn't want to die in the rain, though."

"Agh." Morgan waved his hand. "Doesn't matter where you die, you do that on your own time."

"Sometimes there are other people around."

Morgan let that sit for a moment. Then he moved forward in his seat. "How you doing?" he asked. It seemed sincere. "You all right?"

"More or less."

"The, uh, cops talk to you?"

"Not yet," Jason said, purposefully leaving some uncertainty to see what would happen.

"I doubt they will. Come to you, I mean. They may not find a body, and they'd still have to place you at the scene. So I don't think they'll come to you."

"Are you saying you want me to go to them? Because that's not—"

"Heavens no!" Morgan's voice jumped a bit, and it took Jason by surprise. "Just the opposite."

"You don't care about what happened?" There was a hint of contempt in Jason's voice.

"Let me tell you something I've learned over the years," Morgan responded, raising his finger and speaking in earnest. "Life is for the living, and vengeance is bad for business. Any personal feelings I have, they're personal; I don't need to put them on display for anyone." He locked his eyes on Jason for a moment before getting back to his point. "And above all, I never lose sight of the right move." He sat back. "And right now the right move is to let this go."

"If that's how you want it."

"Just one thing," Morgan said, too casually. "You talk to him?"

"What do you mean? Ever?"

"Before he died."

"No," Jason said quietly, once again seeing the body from above. "There wasn't any chance."

"Did he leave anything behind?

"Huh?"

"Did he leave anything behind? You know, lots of green stuff in those cases."

"You ought to know by now I don't want what isn't mine," Jason said softly, looking out the windows. They were tinted, and you could see out but not in.

"Of course, of course. I meant anything else, like papers? Or any sort of documents or envelopes?"

"None that I noticed. I was kind of busy, getting shot at and all."

"You know, the business I'm in, that sort of thing can be quite sensitive."

"I guess."

"You know what it is I'm doing?" For a man who talked around things he said it point blank, and it caught Jason off guard.

"You seem to do a lot of business with borough presidents. And you don't seem to like the Mayor much." Jason stopped himself before he said any more. Maybe he'd already said too much.

"And how do you add all that up?"

"I don't. I'm just a pilot."

"Wise words, Mr. Sims. Words to live by."

22

T HE MUSIC WAS LOW. Jason had thought for hours about what to play. He would have killed himself over the music in any event, but the pressure was really on since he only had two tasks for the evening, and only one, "get candles," actually required any effort—the other chore being "pre-heat the oven to 350 degrees." Alison was taking care of everything else. She'd cooked dinner for them at her place and brought it over.

He'd considered and rejected the Band's *Music From Big Pink* (too dark), Van Morrison's *Astral Weeks* (too ambitious, save for later), and an Etta Baker tape he'd made (played female blues last time), before settling on one of his newest bootlegs, *Bruce Springsteen Live at the Bottom Line*, August 8, 1975. Adam had been at the show last month and managed to score a copy of the soundboard tape. Jason didn't play it for a couple of weeks, thinking that Adam was trying to deliver some message—the date was written in big letters on the front of the blank box, and Adam surely meant to call attention to the fact that it was one year to the day after Nixon resigned. But after the new album came out and he heard some of it on the radio Jason found the box and compared it with others that Adam had given him. It turned out the writing was pretty much the same from box to box.

The evening was going very well—the food was great, and the conversation flowed easily. Alison started them off with a salad, which was a little too busy and had vegetables in it that Jason didn't recognize, but he kept that to himself. The second course was a simple shrimp thing that was very good, and the beef that followed was outstanding. It went really well with the wine, which Jason rarely drank, because for some reason it went right to his head, and he never felt comfortable with a glass of wine in his hand, either. He thought about getting himself a beer but didn't have the guts to find out how rude that would be. They had just about finished eating.

"That was fantastic," he said.

"You sound surprised."

"Well, I am, a little, I mean, I thought—"

"That I couldn't cook?" There was a slight edge in her voice. Ugh. He was just trying to compliment her cooking.

"No, no, I just thought that, uh, maybe you would have avoided it…you know, to make a point…?"

"I don't make points. I like to cook, so I cook." She got up from the table, taking the bottle of wine with her. Jason grabbed his glass and followed her to the living room, where she plopped down on the floor near the couch and poured herself a little more wine. He sat down as well, not too close, and weighed an apology. It was the first missed note of the entire evening and he wanted to get back to where they'd been.

"What are you doing Sunday?" she asked brightly.

"Sunday?" A voice inside Jason's head wondered if she was still mad, but it was drowned out by another voice that screamed "Shut up and move on, you idiot!"

"I'm free all day," he said with a smile.

"My department is having a picnic in Central Park. I thought you might like to come and watch my back."

That had dental appointment written all over it. "The park is pretty safe during the day," he offered. It seemed like a good cautious noncommittal maybe-not.

"No, silly, I mean from my colleagues. There'll be maybe three women there."

"What time?" he asked, still searching for an out.

"It starts at eleven and goes till two. It's a barbecue. They didn't ask me to cook anything," she said slyly.

"Sounds great. I will be there," he added awkwardly. "I'll come by your place about ten-thirty?"

"Make it eleven."

"Eleven it is."

Alison turned and watched the wheels of the tape rotate slowly. In the evening after a few drinks those turning wheels could be mesmerizing, and you could almost see the music rising from the tape. Jason gave her major points for listening at that particular moment. It was a quiet version of the song "Thunder Road," the best track from the show. There was an aching in Springsteen's voice when he sang "So you're scared and you're thinking that maybe we ain't that young anymore," which wasn't bad for a twenty-five-year-old.

"What is this?" she asked.

"Bruce Springsteen. Hear it now, cause it's never going to be the same again."

"Why not?"

"He has this new album out, just out, and Adam says he's going to be huge. At least it's really good."

"At least?"

"Yeah. It's hard to be really good and really popular, so it's nice that it's a good album."

"Why?" She asked it sincerely, and Jason felt like he was about to tell her that there was no Santa Claus.

"Because it's hard not to be affected by fame and money. By not being able to walk down the street, or eat in a restaurant, or even know who your friends are. Or to be able to write without thinking about your reputation."

"Wow," she said slowly. "I never really thought about it." Then she gave her head a quick shake. "Wait. Is this just one of those tricks you've made up so you have to be unhappy no matter what happens?"

"No, that's Adam. He thinks it's impossible to be good and

popular, at least nowadays. I didn't say it was impossible, I said it was really hard. It takes an uncommon discipline—the power not to care."

"Are you sure you're not just switching one trick for another?" she asked, probing further. "And 'the power not to care' is an excuse to champion apathy?"

"No. You're not going to pin that rap on me with this one." He said it good-naturedly, but he meant it. "It's selective—you have to care about the music but not care about the audience."

Alison scrunched her nose. "Then why have an audience?"

"Because…this sounds like a small thing, but it's not. It's great to have an audience. And it's great when they applaud. But once you're playing *for* the applause, it's over. And it's hard not to."

Alison took a long sip of her wine without taking her eyes off Jason. "So do you think he can do it?"

"Who, Springsteen? I don't know. Maybe he can, maybe he can't. It helps that he's not too young. But no matter what, we're listening to one of the last things he ever recorded when he was just some guy with a band. And that's precious. Like seeing Dylan in 'sixty-three."

Alison thought about all these things for a while. When she saw Dylan in 'sixty-five, he was already Dylan. But he wasn't afraid of being booed off the stage—she saw it happen. While he was playing some of the greatest music that would ever be. Who was he playing it for? She tried to come up with a definitive answer, but couldn't. There probably wasn't one. But the question seemed important. Jason poured out the rest of the wine between them.

"Oh, I can't go Sunday," he remembered, trying to sound a little disappointed. "I have to fly a maintenance run of the copter, do some tests that I can't do with a passenger. We have to do it every three months to make sure everything's in order."

"What if it's not?"

"It's nothing. We just have to do it to be able to say that we've done it, in case anything ever does go wrong. TV union. Got to make sure the talent is safe." He smiled. "Doesn't matter what happens to me. Very strict safety rules for the talent. What would the City do without Dave Edwards telling them they're stuck in traffic?"

Alison drank the last of her wine and set the glass down. "Do you like it?" she asked, tilting her head slightly.

"The wine?"

"Your job."

The question took Jason by surprise, and he hesitated before answering. "I like flying. I like the feeling. And I like not having some boss looking over my shoulder."

"How long do you think you'll do it for?"

Jason finished his wine, stood up, and walked his glass over to the table. "What do you mean?"

"Nothing, nothing," Alison said quickly, but she didn't let it go. "It's just that, I guess, I mean, you know, flying other people around, did you think that this is what you would end up...."

Jason walked back over to the living room and sat down at the edge of the sofa, taking the higher ground, but it didn't help. "It doesn't matter, anyway. Chances are I'll get fired. I think Morgan has had enough of me. I don't know if he bought anything I said in the limo."

They hadn't talked much about everything, and Alison's voice softened. "Listen, I'm sorry. It's been some stretch, huh?"

Jason leaned back and rubbed his eyes. He felt warm, and the breeze from the window didn't cool him off, it just gave him the chills. Alison got up and sat on the couch.

"I mean, I can't imagine what it must have been like. I've never seen anybody, you know.... Just thinking about it, it seems so impossible...."

Jason massaged his forehead with his fingers. "Yeah, well," he said, somewhere between a whisper and a sigh, "he's not the first guy I've seen shot."

"Didn't you have a college deferral?"

"No...I mean, yeah." He folded his hands and rested his chin on them. "This was here. I mean in the States." He took a deep breath and let it out, then gently rubbed the sides of his nose and closed his eyes. "Bobby Kennedy," he said, his eyes still closed. Then he opened them. "I was in the room when Bobby Kennedy was shot."

Alison watched him as he sat there. He looked forward without focusing, as if he was seeing it all happen again. She waited for him to say more, but he didn't, and he avoided her gaze. Sliding in closer she put her arm around him, and setting her other hand on his shoulder she gently steered him around and drew him in from behind. Leaning back against the arm of the couch, she folded her hands across his chest, and he tipped his head back and rested it against her body. They sat like that for a minute, somewhere between sitting and lying down, both staring off into space, lost in their own thoughts. Jason finally spoke.

"I don't think I've ever said that out loud before. Strange. Must be three or four years now."

"Seven."

"Seven?"

"Uh-huh."

"Seven years." Jason repeated it quietly, with a hint of wonder, like he'd never done the math before.

"And three months," she added.

They thought about it separately again. Alison massaged Jason's chest absent-mindedly. The tape had ended, and the silence was broken by the sound of a distant siren, so far away it sounded like whale song. It took a while to fade.

"An ambulance can only go so fast," Jason mumbled.

"What?"

"An ambulance can only go so fast."

"No, I heard you," she said gently. "I just didn't know what you meant."

"It's this line from the new Neil Young album. Adam gave it to me."

"Is it good?"

"It's tough, really tough. And it sure won't sell. But I haven't been able to get that line out of my head."

"That's tough, too."

"It captures a certain type of desperation. Or despair. Or something.... I mean, think about it," his voice dropping to nearly a whisper, "you're in the ambulance—there's hope, you know, that you can make it. You just have to get there. But then you realize that maybe you won't. Can you imagine being in that ambulance? It's not fair. It's devastating. To me at least," he added, still quietly but with his voice coming a little bit back into the room. "That's not the way he sings it. He sings it with more, I don't know…resignation. Or maybe acceptance."

"That's worse, I think. Don't you?" she asked.

He didn't answer, but tipped his head back as far as he could, meeting her eyes. Then he came back down again, took another deep breath, and started talking.

"After my first year of law school, things started to get really interesting. Up in Cambridge and back in New York, there was this real buzz about him. Years before I hadn't been a big fan—I thought he was kind of a nasty punk when he was Attorney General. Not at the time, I was too young, but I held it against him at first when he became Senator. But I knew he was for real in 'sixty-six, after the South Africa trip, then when he went down to the Delta—to Mississippi. He grew into the person he was becoming. You could really see it in 'sixty-seven, and it was cool because even though he was older, it was like we were growing up with him. When he started to run, for real, some of us took off from school, started to travel with the campaign.

"It was incredible. We traveled across the country, everywhere. He gave about four speeches a day, and at least one would be in a black neighborhood. A couple of times I'd skip some dinner thing and slip back to catch a few gigs in the local juke joints. Once, only once, I actually sat in with one of the bands.... Anyway, we were pretty low down on the totem pole, but after a while, he really liked young people, he ate with us a couple of times, knew us a little.

Then, when he started winning, man, it was like…anything was possible."

Jason stopped talking and closed his eyes. Alison waited for him to resume, but he didn't.

"Then what?"

"That night in California, it was a big win. We'd just lost in Oregon, and even though the pros shrugged it off, we were a little thrown by it. But that night—we knew that he'd get the nomination. I hate LA. I hated it the entire time we were there. You can't walk anywhere. Couldn't move in the ballroom either. Everyone was there. It was packed. Alive. When Bobby came out, the place exploded. It was a moment when you could imagine—when you could know for sure—that everything would fall into place. That he *would* win the nomination, that he *would* kick Nixon's ass in the general election, that he would…." Jason's voice trailed off.

"Anyway, it was a great speech—no one remembers that. All they remember is 'Now on to Chicago and let's win there.' The way those words hung in the air—hang in the air—forever. I was looking right at him. Right at him. I guess everybody was. I can't describe to you that feeling, of being right in the middle of something and knowing there was nothing you could do. Pandemonium. Madness. Rushing, rushing to get help. Didn't matter."

Jason stopped talking again and sat up. He turned around to face Alison.

"Seven years." He still couldn't believe it.

"I'll never forget it either," she said. "We watched the news on TV. They kept talking about how it was only two months after the King assassination. Remember, that night? Bobby was at a rally in Indianapolis, and told the crowd himself from the back of a flatbed truck. I don't remember what he said, just the beginning: 'My favorite poet was Aeschylus.' But it was the first thing I thought about that night, because it suddenly brought home the loss—I didn't think Humphrey or any of the others had a favorite Greek poet. But Bobby did. And Indianapolis was the only city that didn't have riots the night King died."

"I know," he said with quiet confirmation. "I was there."

"Do you remember the line?"

"'In our sleep, pain which cannot forget falls drop by drop upon the heart until, in our own despair, against our will, comes wisdom.'"

"You believe that?"

"I never met a blues man who didn't."

Alison put her hands on Jason's shoulders and kissed him, softly at first, but then passionately, squeezing his left shoulder so hard he thought she might have broken the skin with one of her fingernails. She pushed him back on the couch and climbed on top of him. Jason caught up more quickly this time and tried to move faster, hoping to establish some point of no return that he had failed to reach last time, though Alison was not giving the impression she had any intention of turning back.

This time they made it to the bedroom. Alison continued to dictate their pace, and Jason was content to let her. She seemed committed to being on top, and Jason almost laughed out loud when he had the fleeting thought of asking her if she was trying to prove a point, but that thought was quickly overtaken by others.

He was quite pleased with himself afterwards, and Alison seemed happy. The sheets were tangled around their waists, but she made no attempt to pull them up further, which Jason appreciated, for a number of reasons. She had a self-confidence that didn't come across as arrogant. And he liked looking at her.

"What are you doing tomorrow?" he asked, gently tracing a line from her neck to just above her belly button.

"Big day locked in my apartment. I have this paper I absolutely must finish."

"Maybe I'll stop by," he said innocently, letting his finger drift to where the sheet met her hip.

"Oh, you don't want to see me when I'm trying to finish a paper."

"Really? I like everything I've seen so far." He decided to push his luck a bit, curious how she would react, but she didn't make even a subtle move to cover herself. He thought more about it. She always looked good, but dressed pretty conservatively, even outside of work, and when he imagined them together he had figured her for a coverer.

"Trust me," she said, propping herself up on her elbow. "How about tomorrow night? Are you playing?"

"Nope."

"I could go for a late dinner."

"Sounds great."

She leaned in a little closer and kissed him gently on the shoulder. "When are you playing again?"

"Tuesday. Always Tuesday. Some Fridays. We used to get a few more gigs on the outside, but it's been a little quiet. Of course Oz pretty much has work all the time."

"How come you never play lead?" She asked it casually, but Jason could tell it was important to her.

"Not everybody can play lead."

"Shouldn't everybody want to?" she asked.

Jason pulled the sheet completely off her, and looked at her naked body.

"Shouldn't everybody want to?" she repeated, without moving a muscle.

There were many circumstances under which he would have gotten angry about being cross-examined, but this was not one of them. He was tired. He really liked her. And the arch of her hip had a certain perfection that he hadn't fully appreciated until now.

"You never let up, do you?" he said with a good-natured smile. "What is it that you want me to do?"

"What do you want to do?" she asked.

"What's that supposed to mean?"

"It means that I want you to do whatever it is you really want to do."

"I know exactly what I want to do," he said, and leaned over and kissed her. As he maneuvered across the bed she deftly slid past him, switching sides, and put her palm on his chest to push him on his back.

"Don't you want to live in a society where women have the confidence to let a man be on top every now and then?" he asked, laying his arms out in surrender and looking up at the ceiling with a broad smile, as if appealing to a higher authority. He knew she'd never get out of that one.

"If you think you can handle the responsibility," she said wickedly, grabbing him and pulling him on top of her.

23

JASON WOKE UP WITH THE SUN hitting him in the face, which meant he'd slept for a long time. The clock showed 11:30, and he was so disoriented with sleep that it took him a second to realize that if the sun was out, it must be 11:30 in the morning. Rolling over, he found that he was alone in the bed, and he got up to see if Alison had left. He pulled on a pair of underwear in case she was still there, but didn't put on his pants, for the same reason. It didn't matter; a quick tour of the grounds proved that he was alone.

She'd taken all her stuff with her and straightened up those things she had been directly responsible for putting out of place, but the apartment was looking even messier than usual. In the dining area he found a note written in surprisingly girlish handwriting.

"I thought you should sleep—I had to get to work. I had some coffee—don't you get the *Times* delivered? Don't come by before 9! Pizza? See you then!"

He read it a few times to figure out what it meant. She hadn't mentioned the sex, but women probably didn't do that. Still, she might have alluded to it with an "I had a wonderful time" or something. On the other hand, there were two exclamation points, and she still wanted to see him late this evening. These were positives. And she wouldn't have had that cup of coffee if she was trying to slip out as quickly as possible. It wasn't an easy note to decipher. He eventually decided, after considerable deliberation, that she was trying to say that she had to get back home early to work on her paper and that she'd see him later.

Opening the front door, he saw the *Times* at his feet, which meant that she must have left before seven. A confirming glance at his watch suggested that she'd probably been working for more than four hours already, while he was just waking up. He tossed the paper on the table and decided it was time to take another crack at Bill's manila envelope. He put up some coffee, and while he was waiting cleared the rest of the dining table and tidied up the living room a bit, just enough to reestablish its baseline messiness.

A dedicated half-hour studying Bill's documents proved utterly fruitless, and Jason abandoned the effort. Even factoring in the borough presidents, he still couldn't figure out exactly what they meant. They were definitely records for some sort of payments scheme, but nothing that would prove anything—for all anyone knew they were bowling scores and league dues. He switched to the *Times* and caught himself stealing a quick look at the first section—scanning the headlines, flipping the pages, and noting the op-eds. Usually it was the part of the paper he discarded immediately. But it was just a glance, and he was happy to get to the sports page. The Mets would still be in last place, but he liked to check and see if they had a better record than the last place team in the western division.

The phone rang, which was a relatively rare event. If he had any small pets they might have been alarmed.

"Hey." It was Adam.

"Hey."

"What's up?" Suddenly Adam had discovered the art of small talk.

"Nothin'."

"Listen, did you find that stuff, you know, from the other day?"

"You mean the secret documents from the dead guy?" Jason felt like screaming out, just to freak Adam out. He didn't think his phone was tapped.

"Yeah, I've just been looking at them," he said instead.

"Really?" Adam sounded genuinely surprised.

It was Jason's turn to talk. It's hard to shake people off with your eyes on the phone, which was one reason Jason found it to be a singularly inefficient form of communication. He let the silence hang in the air.

"So, uh, anyway," Adam eventually continued, "I want to see them again. I have some new ideas."

"Sure. What's good for you?"

"I got to meet some people today," he said with appropriate vagueness. "How about tonight?"

"No, I'm seeing Alison tonight," Jason said, letting her name slip into the conversation to see if Adam would take a nibble at it. "How about tomorrow?"

"Yeah, great. At the diner?"

"Yeah, noon."

"All right."

"All right."

Jason hung up the phone and looked around. It was a good day to try and get something done. Maybe really reorganize his stuff. He had an elaborate system for classifying his music collection—categorized by genre, with intricately nested sub-genres, organized first by recording date and only then alphabetically by principal artist, but for a while he'd just been dumping in the newly acquired stuff with the old and not putting things back in the right places. There were also more instruments lying around than he really needed. He never played bass, but had somehow managed to acquire two, which largely served as landing spots for discarded shirts. This could take a while. Not the kind of project that you could embark on without a good shower first.

He took a long hot shower, at least twice as long as usual. He remembered two more things that were great about New York, both water-related. First, the tap water was outstanding; best tap water in the world they said—in its purest form, sampled from an open fire hydrant. This was one of the reasons, appreciated by very few, why the City's bagels and pizza were so good, and so impossible to reproduce elsewhere. Second, even pretty lame apartment buildings had great water pressure. It was hard to imagine they had better water pressure in the White House. He stuck his face right into the blast and shook his head back and forth. Seventy-five years ago most people didn't even have running water, and now most guys off the street could shower like the President. Maybe better.

Jason got out and was drying off, still riffing on the whole New York water thing, when he thought he heard the doorbell. Phone calls, doorbells, could a telegram be far behind? Dropping his towel to the floor he reached for his robe—a ridiculous garment, thin, faded, and fraying, it didn't even make it all the way down to his knees. But he lived alone, and didn't really need a robe. He couldn't remember where it was from or the last time he'd put it on; it just kind of lived there on the back of his bathroom door. But it turned out the doorbell was in fact ringing, and the robe was better than wrapping a towel around his waist, especially because he didn't have the greatest towels, either.

He came out of the bathroom and made a spot check in the bedroom mirror off to his left to assure that some minimum level of presentability had been achieved. "I think it's open," he called out towards the door.

The door swung open, and Carol Chase walked in. Jason once had a dream that started like this, and he was a little light-headed from the steam, so he did a quick test to make sure he was awake. It probably wasn't necessary, since he wouldn't be caught dead or dreaming in that robe; it would have been a fine, precariously-knotted towel. But it was reassuring just to know for sure anyway. Carol was wearing a white button-down shirt, with a couple of buttons open, and a short, tight light-blue skirt that wasn't inappropriately short, but still got your attention.

"Jason? Sorry to barge in. Nice robe. You know the downstairs buzzer is broken?"

"Yeah. I don't know if it's ever worked."

"You always leave your front door open?"

"Yeah, no, I mean, if you unlock it to leave you have to lock it from the outside with the key. Or you can lock it from the inside, but if you.... Anyway, point is it won't lock on its own."

"I see." She assessed the robe a second time, then looked over Jason's shoulder.

"So, uh, what brings you here?"

"I had to be in Queens today, so I decided to look you up."

It was plausible, but unlikely. "Yeah, almost everyone has an Aunt who lives around here," he said, inviting her to elaborate on her story.

She didn't respond, but sort of drifted towards the kitchen, checking out the apartment. It occurred to Jason that the appliances were probably as old as the building. A more pressing concern was his acute awareness of the fact that while she was fully dressed, he could feel the thinness of the robe against his body. He thought about excusing himself to get dressed, but decided that it was his apartment and she was going to have to take him the way she found him.

"You once asked me what I did with my free time," Carol said, walking toward him. She was striking, and Jason reconsidered getting dressed. She walked right past him and went into the living room, and with her back to him he took the opportunity to adjust and refasten his belt, trying to at least get a little double-breasted action in the front.

"Yeah," he responded. "You didn't seem to have any."

Carol wandered around the living room and traced her fingers across a stack of books before bending over, as if to look through one of the milk cartons filled with records. It was a brilliant performance. Her shirt opened a bit, and she made no effort to catch it with her hand as she flipped through the albums to sample the collection. He'd noticed that the shirt was just thick enough to conceal whether or not she had anything on underneath it, and it took a tremendous amount of will power not to take advantage of the occasion to confirm the situation one way or the other.

"I didn't," she answered, standing back up. "But I might, you know?"

"How do you figure?"

"Are you going to take the traffic job?"

"Probably not." Definitely not, but he wanted to see where she was going.

"You should. It would change a lot of things."

"Like what?"

"Like your whole life. You wouldn't believe what they pay on-air talent."

"Probably not." He was in full rope-a-dope mode.

"And you're a natural," she added. It sounded sincere, and he kicked himself for caring. "Did you see our interview?"

"No."

"It came out great." Her eyes were always a little brighter when she talked about TV. "You looked really good. And I thought we had a real connection. Most of the time I don't get that much eye contact."

For some reason Jason felt a wave of guilt about the whole eye contact thing. "Yeah, well, eye contact isn't—"

"It's everything," she interrupted forcefully. "Your education, your instincts—all the things you've ever done. What people are… it comes across on TV."

"You must have a really good set." He said it with a straight face, and when the words left his mouth he was pretty sure he was talking about her TV.

Carol smiled, and resumed her survey of the living room. "Just think about it." Her back was to him, and now it was time to be impressed with the skirt. No elaborate bending this time, which now felt like a privilege withheld, but impressive nevertheless. "You have no idea what it's like."

"Being on TV?" He asked pointedly

She turned on her heel. "Being a star."

Man, she was good. She nailed that line, and she moved around his apartment like she'd choreographed it in advance.

"I've met a couple. Singers mostly."

"You could be one too," she said provocatively.

He was taking too many hits, and it was time to find out where she was trying to lead him. "Why the sudden interest?" he asked. "I've been around for a while."

"Yeah, like every other loser in the station."

He shot her a look, and she took a few steps in his direction.

"But now it seems you're not quite what you appear to be. First the helicopter hero thing, then that interview, which, I already told you, was terrific—and those stories Adam told—not that many of my drivers have been to Harvard, even for a visit." She gestured at some of the instruments littering the room. "And you really are a musician."

"You doubted me?"

"You wouldn't believe the stories I get. When a man is talking to me, he's usually lying. Or staring at my chest. Or both." Jason shifted his gaze upwards as subtly as he could. "I've been hit on by at least half the men at the station. The married guys even more than the single ones."

"Huh. I would have guessed the other way around."

"Married men think they don't have anything to lose," she said with a casual dismissiveness, the way you sweep a cat off the furniture to sit down.

"What do you mean?"

"Men aren't that complicated, Jason, most men anyway." She added the qualifier late, and it wasn't convincing. "They're all sex and ego—the only variation from one to the other is the relative portions of each. You shoot down a single guy, he's naked, nowhere to hide. Humiliated. Married guys, they can tell themselves that they were just flirting. Or even that if they weren't married, it would have been different. They have no fear of failure holding them back."

She turned again and flipped through more albums. Jason knew that she was toying with him, and he was dancing around the mousetrap. But it was entertaining, and he wanted to see how far she'd take it. And there was a small part of him that wanted to buy her story. She didn't know anything about him till a few days ago, really. And what she found out didn't look so bad on paper.

"Who are these guys?"

"Old bluesmen mostly. That's Skip James, the original recordings from nineteen thirty-one. He didn't record again till nineteen sixty-four, three weeks after they found him in a Mississippi hospital bed." She didn't seem to get it, so Jason steered her towards more familiar territory. They were standing pretty close together. "The newer stuff is over here."

"Oh, hey. Bruce Springsteen, *Born to Run*. I've heard of this. I think Shaker did a story on him. I don't usually pay attention when he's on," she said giving Jason a knowing look, "but he said this guy is gonna be big." She stepped back and studied a collection of framed pictures and posters mounted on the wall. A few gaps, like missing teeth, suggested that some had been removed over the years. "Who's that?" she asked, pointing at one of the photos.

"That's Willie Dixon. He did time for refusing to serve in the Army."

"Who didn't?"

"No, this was different," Jason explained. "World War II—it was a much bigger deal not to serve. He was arrested on stage in nineteen forty-one. On stage—can you imagine? He said he and his people were treated like subjects, not citizens, and he would not serve. He was in jail for a year."

"Prison, huh. You think he could have cut a deal." Leaning back on a table covered with stacks of tapes, she scanned the wall a little skeptically. She seemed not to recognize Walt Frazier.

"Yeah, well, that doesn't come easily to some people." He decided they would be better off not talking about music. "Listen, would you like anything?"

"Coffee would be great." She picked up Jason's cup, which was still half full. "Yours?"

He nodded, and she walked toward him with it. The gentle disturbance of her separation from the table sent a few of the precariously perched tapes tumbling, and the noise momentarily directed their attention. Turning back around, Carol bumped against a chair, which caused some coffee to spill on her shirt.

"Shit!" The exclamation was jarring, and it didn't sound quite like her, but it made sense that soiled clothing was a major crisis given her lifestyle.

"You okay?" He was a little rattled. "Can I...." Actually, Jason had no idea what he might offer.

"It's all right," she said, calming down. "Why don't you get the coffee and I'll put some water on it. The bathroom is this way?" She walked down the hallway.

"No, that's the bedroom." But she was already gone, and didn't come immediately back. "Carol? Carol?"

She finally came out, seeming distracted, looking down and pulling at her shirt. "That's the bedroom," he explained, pointing. "That's the bathroom."

Jason went into the kitchen and started working on the coffee. The action messed up his robe again, and he abandoned any efforts at style to focus on getting the belt good and tight. He even thought about double-knotting it.

Filling two cups of coffee, he headed back out to the living room. With one cup in each hand, he noticed the hot liquid swaying dangerously as he walked. Eager to avoid another incident, he held them away from his body and walked with care.

"Jason?" It sounded like she had been calling him, but he hadn't heard her in the kitchen. She leaned out of the bathroom. She was topless, and held her forearms bunched up in front of her chest, but the sides of her breasts and the cleavage between them were abundant and very visible, and she looked for all the world like an Angie Dickinson poster. "Jason, this shirt is a total loss." Her arms moved ever so slightly when she talked. It was a great effect and he wondered if she'd ever practiced in front of a mirror, or whether it just came naturally. He couldn't decide which would have been more dangerous. "Do you have a shirt I can wear?" She asked sweetly.

"Uh, well…sure." He let the answer drag out, and didn't make an immediate move toward the bedroom to get her one. He had abandoned his no-staring policy.

Suddenly the front door swung open. It was Alison, carrying a big brown basket.

"Jason?" she called out, "are you up? I decided to treat myself to a little lunch break. We can have our picnic today instead of…."

She looked up and saw them. Everybody was motionless for a moment—if Carol's arms moved slightly, they went down, not up.

After three seconds that felt like thirty, Alison set down the basket, turned on her heel, and pushed the front door a bit wider out of her way. It swung shut with a decisive thud. Jason looked at Carol, then down at the hot cups of coffee that were still steaming in his hands. He set them down on the table, scalding his left index finger in the process, and headed for the door.

She'd already made it to the elevator. The outer door was slowly closing, and he raced over to try and catch it. "Alison? Alison? Wait a minute!"

He got to the elevator just as the little white ball of light from the window of the car disappeared on its way down. He turned and ran back and spun around to the stairs, but his robe had come completely undone and running down the stairs didn't seem like a viable option. He grabbed enough material in front to bunch it closed with his fist and reentered the apartment. He took Carol by surprise—she had dropped her arms, and he saw the muscles in her shoulders tighten for a split second, as if she had thought about pulling her hands back up but then decided there was more dignity in staying the way she was.

He rushed past her down the hallway toward his bedroom without breaking stride, but he did manage to commit everything he could to memory. He threw off the robe. He couldn't find his underwear. Where were they? Probably the bathroom, from the shower. No time for that, he spun around and grabbed his pants from the floor. He could see Carol down the hallway, hands half on her hips, watching him. There they were, naked and alone in his apartment. Mission accomplished, he said to himself sarcastically, pulling on his pants and grabbing a shirt. In two more seconds he had committed forty-eight more frames to memory.

He ran back down the hallway, yanking on his shirt. "I'll be right back!" he said over his shoulder to Carol, and for some reason he could hear Dylan singing "We watched with one last look," from *Chimes of Freedom*.

He bounded barefoot down the stairs, taking them four at a time, and then charged out into the street. She was already almost a block away, and he ran after her. She was walking at an even pace, and betrayed no emotions when he caught up. But she didn't stop walking, and he got in front of her and walked backwards.

"Just wait a second, will you? Can't you just wait one second?"

"Why?" she said calmly.

"We have to talk. I mean, it's not what you think—"

"How do you know what I think?"

"Well, it's just…I know what I would…you know, it's just not what it looks like." He wished he had better material than that, but he was walking backwards, winded from running, and the hard, uneven concrete of the sidewalk was starting to really hurt his feet.

"Does that matter?"

"Of course it matters!" Jason said desperately.

"I've been in a lot of apartments, Jason. I know what happens in them."

"But this wasn't—"

"Listen," she interrupted, her pace slowing slightly, "you don't owe me anything."

"How can you say that?"

She stopped walking, and met his eyes with a look that betrayed nothing. "What would you have me say?"

What would he have her say? Jason reached out toward her, but she stepped back and left his arm hanging.

"Look," she said, her voice finally breaking from a mechanical monotone, "why don't you go back to your apartment. You've got some things to take care of; I have a paper to write."

"What about tonight?"

"I've got two classes on Monday, and a conference on Tuesday. I'm way too busy to—"

"But…you can't just—"

"I'll call you," she said, making it clear that he was not to call her. "Later in the week, after I've taken care of the things I need to do for work. We'll talk."

24

THAT NIGHT, ADAM AND JASON went to the Irish Cottage to commiserate. Things were even worse than they seemed. When Jason had returned to his apartment after chasing down Alison, not only was Carol gone, but Bill's envelope was gone as well. It couldn't have been picked up by accident either, since he was sure that he'd left it underneath the *Times*. Adam was also in pretty bad shape. He thought he'd been onto something with his police theory, but his sources had run dry. It was killing him, since even though he'd never admitted it to anyone, he'd been on too many stories where he was just following a hunch but was never sure for certain that it was for real. Now he knew something huge was right there in front of him, but he couldn't quite make it out, and every time he got closer it just slipped farther out of reach.

They put away a lot of beer while Jason brought Adam up to speed. He gave an abridged version of the Alison story—she cooked, they did it, he was great—but gave him the whole Carol caper blow-by-blow.

"And that was it. The only thing missing was Alan Funt with Candid Camera. Standing on the street in my bare feet and no underwear, and being told *she'd* call *me*. It's like I'm in some holding cell, waiting for the jury to come back."

Adam took another big sip of beer. "Man, that's the least of your problems. I can't believe you lost that envelope."

"I didn't lose it," Jason said impatiently. "Do you listen to anything I say?"

"You sure you looked everywhere?"

"I thought you looked for it."

"Oh, that's clever."

"I told you. It was definitely on the table. When I got back, it was gone. Carol was gone. There's some inescapable math here. She must have taken it." Jason downed the rest of his beer.

"Jeez." Adam turned to the bar. "Pat? Pat! Two more."

"You were right about her all along," Jason admitted.

"Now let's not be too hard on her," Adam said jovially. "After all, you're a hero, a great interview, and she just loves the way you got beat up by cops in your youth." He laughed before he got to the end, and slapped the table repeatedly with his hand.

Jason turned his head toward the stage so Adam wouldn't see his smile. He saw the young singer who was there the first night he'd spoken to Alison, and the grin felt heavy on his face. Watching him tune his guitar a bit more elaborately than necessary to the adoring eyes of the assembled college girls, he felt the compression of time. He'd been in those shoes, and wished the kid better luck.

Pat brought over two more tall beers. "You guys keep this up, it might actually be worth having you around."

"You'd think the bartender would toss in a free round every now and then," Adam said without missing a beat.

Jason studied his beer. The bubbles were floating to the top in a distinct pattern. He wondered whether they always did that, and he'd just never noticed, or whether it was the beer, or the shape of the glass. He looked at Adam's beer, and then at Adam. He was glad he was there. How many beers had they shared? Five thousand?

"You take all the times I've screwed up with women, every single one, and stack them one on top of the other, they don't come close to this."

"You talking about Carol, or Alison?"

"Alison, you asshole."

"Oh, I don't know about that. You've fucked up pretty bad in the past." Adam knew it was a funny line, but it was a clinical diagnosis.

"Maybe. But this is different."

"I keep trying to tell you, they're all different."

"Well, this was different different." He shot a quick glance toward Adam. He'd kept his Alison stories short, and he wasn't sure Adam would get it. "Special different."

"Yeah, I know," he said quietly, and pressing his feet against the long brass rail that ran along the bottom of the bar, tipped his stool back and looked down at the floor. But within seconds he snapped his head back up. "Now if you really want to talk different, did I ever tell you about this gymnast I dated? She could put her head between her legs...." He made a big counter-clockwise circle with his hand. "...by going *backwards*. Can you even begin to imagine the implications of that maneuver?" His voice rose with glee.

"You are so full of shit."

Adam raised his hand. "My hand to God. True story."

"I didn't say it wasn't a true story." Jason took another long drink, and smiled wistfully. "And I'm telling you, I could hear 'Chimes of Freedom.' Plain as day. I even thought maybe a neighbor was playing it, but it couldn't have been."

"So what are you saying, that your subconscious has decided you're among the 'confused, accused, misused, strung-out ones and worse'?"

"I figured it meant I was a 'gentle soul misplaced inside a jail.'"

"You see yourself as gentle?"

"Well, if I have to choose between gentle and strung out, I'll take gentle. But that's not the part of the line I was thinking of."

"And just what do you think you were getting a last look at?" Adam asked devilishly, "Alison leaving or Carol's tits?"

Jason didn't answer, on purpose. He swiveled in his chair and played with the pretzels he'd lined up in front of him. He stood two of them up by balancing one against the other, noting their perfect symmetry and admiring his handiwork. "They're the same size, by the way."

"What?" Adam asked like he thought he missed something.

"Her tits. Left and right," he said, poking the air in two spots with his index finger. "They're the same size."

"No shit?"

"Yeah. I'd say exactly."

"Well, you're one up on me," Adam said wistfully. "I just thought it would help."

"Yeah, it did." Jason was sinking back into I-fucked-it-up-with-Alison-land, and he turned his eyes back to the stage again. Mr. Young-and-Impossibly-Cool-Without-Caring had started to play Richard Thompson's "Meet on the Ledge"—Jason recognized it from the first few notes. The girls all looked up at him as he started to sing. Not an easy song to pull off, but the kid chose the right songs for his voice, which was something that most people only came around to later on.

We used to say/there'd come the day

We'd all be making songs

Or finding better words

These ideas never lasted long

It occurred to Jason that somebody up there had decided to punish him by having this guy narrate his life like a one-man Greek chorus. He contemplated this possibility while intently studying the performance, swiveling back to the bar when the song went into its first instrumental bridge. He had survived *"Too many friends who tried/blown off this mountain with the wind,"* but had no intention of enduring *"Now I see I'm all alone/but that's the only way to be."* Grabbing the last handful of pretzels from the bowl, he began work on a new project, making a circle with them on the bar.

"No playing with the food," Pat said sternly. He was holding two more beers. "Two on the house," he said, looking at Adam. "Gotta keep the big spenders happy." He set the beers down, but gave them a hard look and dragged them back towards his side of the bar. "You guys aren't driving, are you?"

"You know I don't have a car," Jason said, as if the very suggestion was offensive.

Pat pointed at Adam. "I meant him."

"Yeah, I'm parked out front," Adam said, straightening up.

Pat looked at him, and drew the glasses back another inch.

"But I can leave it there overnight, if you want, Mom," Adam added.

Pat slid the beers back toward them, but didn't let them go. "Hey, I don't care if you crash it, it's just that a bunch of uniforms from the 112th have been setting up checkpoints. A little old lady got hit on Queens Boulevard the other day. The guy wasn't drunk or anything, but they have this new rule—you get busted, we could get fined."

"Argh," Adam didn't want to hear another word about cops, or rules, for that matter. "Can't drive anywhere, anyway, the whole city's a fucking roadblock. They can get me for STWI—sitting in traffic while intoxicated."

Jason and Adam found this terribly amusing. "Just walk the fuck home, okay?" Pat said, letting go of the beers and heading back down to the other side of the bar.

They sat with their thoughts for a moment, and Jason could hear the end of "Meet on the Ledge" in the background.

"Why do we even live in this city, anyway?" Adam asked, trying to reassess his life from scratch.

"Where you gonna live?"

"You mean there's nowhere else in the country to live?"

"Where you gonna live," Jason repeated flatly. "It's not even a question. There's no place else to live—it's not a choice thing. Being on TV, that's a choice."

"Again with the TV?"

"You wanted to talk about changing things, not me."

"Well, something's gotta give," Adam said, his voice trailing off a bit as he looked at the big mirror behind the bar. Two potentially lovely women had taken up seats about six stools down from them, and he was trying to catch the right angle to check them out. "You know Cohen has them doing roadwork at night now? Those are union guys. Night work is double scale."

"So?"

"The Sphinx, you asshole. The pyramids are gone, but the riddle remains."

Adam tried to alert Jason with his eyes toward the reflection in the mirror, but Jason was diverted by his attention to two men who had just entered the bar, whom he viewed with enormous suspicion, although he realized that he might just be projecting the angry part of his current frustrations. In any event he didn't like them. They looked out of place, like they had just stepped out of the 1940s and were trying to adjust to unfamiliar wardrobe. The shorter of the two had a round face and a serious gut that was squeezed into a thin leather jacket. He reminded Jason of William Conrad—and not the affable private-eye from the popular TV show "Cannon," but the tough guy who iced Burt Lancaster thirty years ago in *The Killers*. The second man was big—Jack Palance big—and he was measuring the room with his eyes. Jason thought they stood out by trying to fit in, and he didn't like the way their shirts were buttoned all the way to the neck. They were too well dressed to be narcs, but checked out the crowd the way cops would, and even though they approached the bar, they didn't get quite close enough to order.

"There's no way the City can afford all that construction," Adam continued. He picked up the empty pretzel bowl and shook it at Jason. "You're supposed to share these with everyone," he said a little too loudly, and slipped off his stool. He took the bowl with him and walked down the bar. There was a full bowl of pretzels near the reflections that called for additional assessment. One of them, a redhead with what looked to be a cynical smile and attentive eyes had piqued his interest.

"Whaddya mean?" Jason called after him. "Highway money comes from the feds. The sphinx thing doesn't apply here."

Adam turned just shy of his destination. "What are you, taking accounting classes at night?" He forgot about the women momentarily and furrowed his brow, looking like a guy who expected to find his bagel ready but discovered someone had unplugged the toaster. Then he shrugged his shoulders and refocused on the pretzel bowl in his hand. "Whatever…there's still way too much construction to make any kind of sense. And that still doesn't explain...." He stopped talking, trying to process why his voice had gotten so much louder. It hadn't—the redhead was staring at him with penetrating green eyes. Actually, a small cluster of people had abandoned their conversations and were all looking right at him. And not in a good way. Wait—they weren't looking at him—they were staring right through him.

"Nobody move. This is a holdup." It was the Palance-like fellow, and with his size, not to mention his message, he commanded the room. Everybody stopped talking, and the contrast between the din of the bar noise and the silence that replaced it was more jarring than anything else. A collection of people in a bar, not drinking, made for an unnatural group—and they looked like they were caught in a game of musical chairs they didn't know they were playing.

His heavy-set companion, living up to the image of the noir doppelganger that Jason had assigned him, had drawn a gun and was pointing it at Pat. But it was Palance who did the talking, and he looked to be calling the shots. He did not brandish a weapon, which somehow added to his menace, and to the impression that he was in charge.

"Everybody stay calm and no one's going to get hurt," he said, with a resolute but measured voice that suggested he had done this sort of thing before. "Heads down, eyes front. Down on the bar. Down on the tables."

Nobody panicked and everybody did as they were told. Jason put his head down but kept his eyes on the gun.

"Get the money from the register," he ordered Pat. He pulled out a sack and approached the bar, while his partner kept the gun on Pat. But as Pat turned toward the register, Jason saw the gunman shift and point his gun directly at Adam. Jason grabbed the empty barstool next to him and swung it wildly, hitting the guy hard and knocking him down. The gun discharged and fell out of his hand as he crumpled to the floor, dazed but still conscious. At the sound of the shot people started screaming and diving to the floor, but nobody was hit.

Jason jumped up and kicked the gun farther across the room. The gunman was gathering himself, rolling over onto his stomach to gain momentum, and Jason kicked him in the head and sent him tumbling further. It was the first time in his life he wished he wasn't wearing sneakers. "Run!" he screamed at Adam, and they scrambled out the door.

The other man—with his well-groomed, jet-back hair he *could* have been Jack Palance—dropped the sack he was holding and started to reach into his jacket, but before the sack hit the floor Pat hit him hard with a stickball bat, right across the chest, catching both his arms with such force that he staggered backward and crashed into a table, knocking it over and sending its occupants fleeing. Glass shattered and the commotion elicited more screams near the front. The other side of the bar was much farther from the unfolding action, and in the increasing confusion a few guys made a dash for the back door, which set off an alarm when it opened. Whatever the plan was, it was unraveling fast.

Palance righted himself and managed to pull his gun from his jacket. He scanned the room quickly to make sure nobody was coming at him. Everything was still again, but when he looked up he saw that Pat had his own gun pointed at him. They stared at each other for a minute. The alarm was still ringing, and Pat had a look in his eye—some mixture of confidence, excitement, and curiosity—that suggested he wouldn't mind rolling the dice.

"Let's go," the big man called to his partner, without taking his eyes off Pat. After retrieving the errant gun and casting a few menacing glares to deter any further free-lance heroics, the two men walked slowly to the door, putting their weapons back in their jackets as they exited.

Adam and Jason had stumbled out of the bar, and made it to Adam's car—a large green convertible with the top down. They dove in without opening the doors. Adam fumbled for the keys and got it started just as they heard the sound of the alarm coming from the bar. Adam looked over.

"Move, move, move!" Jason shouted at him.

Adam started the car and pulled out wildly, swerving into the street. Jason looked back and saw the men from the bar run to their own car—a light blue two-door Lincoln. Adam's car swerved again, causing Jason to fall forward into the dashboard.

"Are you okay to drive?"

"No!" Adam shouted back, but at least he had regained control of the car. He turned at every opportunity, and at one point went the wrong way down a side street.

"Just drive the fucking car!" Jason screamed, catching Adam dividing his attention between executing wild maneuvers and peeking in the rearview mirror. Jason sat on his knees and looked out the back. He couldn't see the Lincoln, but it couldn't have been too far away.

"What the hell happened?" Adam asked.

"He was going to shoot you!"

"Me?"

"You!"

"Shit!"

Adam took another sharp turn onto a bigger street, and Jason had to hug the headrest for balance. But they only made it about half a block before Adam had to slam on the brakes. The light was red and there were cars in front of them in both lanes. They stared impatiently at the light.

"You know what this means?" Adam asked.

"No."

"I must be on to something."

Jason looked back again and could now see their pursuers gaining ground. There were two cars between them, so it was possible they hadn't seen them yet, and Jason ducked his head.

"Yeah," he responded from his crouch. "Or vice versa!"

"Come on," Adam said anxiously. "Let's go…let's go…green, green, green."

The light changed but nothing moved. Adam reached for the horn but stopped himself. "Do they see us?"

Jason looked back. One of the Lincoln's big doors was swinging open. "They're coming!"

Adam leaned on the horn.

"Forget it," Jason shouted, "it's gridlocked!"

Adam pulled the car out into the opposing lanes. No cars were coming at them, and Adam floored it as he headed for the intersection. But it wasn't gridlock—the street had been closed off for construction—and he had to pound the brakes again, this time so hard the car skidded out sideways and they crashed through some wooden barriers. They plowed through orange cones, blinking yellow warning signs, and several huge mounds of dirt, one of which finally stopped the progress of the car—which was a good thing since it was either the dirt or the huge ditch next to it. The site was abandoned, with no workmen around.

"You okay?" Adam asked Jason, who had been thrown to the floor.

"Yeah. Let's go."

They climbed out of the car and ran through the construction zone. Jason fell once and scraped his leg, but got up and kept running. He followed Adam, who turned and ran down the block toward an elevated train station. Jason took a quick look back— Palance and Conrad were in pursuit, their distinct silhouettes visible in the darkness about one block behind. Adam bounded up the stairs and into the station, with Jason still a few steps behind him.

There was a train waiting on the tracks, brand new, one of the cars painted with red, white, and blue stripes for next year's bicentennial. Adam hurdled the turnstile and Jason followed, while the token booth clerk watched passively. The two-note "dingdong" sounded, meaning that the doors were about to close. Adam stumbled for a second, but caught himself with his right hand and pushed off the ground, diving between the closing doors. He crashed to the floor of the car and then bounced to his feet to catch the doors, but it was too late, they had already shut. They stared at each other through the glass as the train started to pull away. Adam tapped on the glass and mouthed the name "Mon-i-ca" in exaggerated fashion.

Jason looked up and down the now abandoned station. Only one guy had gotten off the train, and he was doing everything he could to avoid eye contact. Jason could hear the sound of footsteps, shoes running on concrete, and he felt fenced in by the train tracks. Those guys might have been after Adam, but they couldn't have been too pleased with him, especially the one he kicked in the head.

Jason jumped down onto the tracks, and gave the third rail a long hard look before running off in the direction of the train, which pulled ahead of him until it disappeared completely from sight. He ran as hard as he could. Even drunk and dazed he could feel a surge of adrenaline, and he ran past the end of the station, continuing on the elevated tracks and into the darkness.

Jason heard the footsteps again. He couldn't see anything when he looked over his shoulder, but they must have followed him onto the tracks, and it sounded like they were making good time. That fat guy was in better shape than he looked—William Conrad had gone his whole career without so much as breaking into a trot. Maybe he could outrun them—maybe he would trip in the darkness. Maybe they would get close enough to try their luck with their guns.

Jason kept running, and looking up he saw headlights—a train was approaching from the opposite direction on the parallel track. Without hesitation he leaped over the third rail—though in mid-air he heard nothing but the sound of his beating heart—landed safely, and ran forward in the small space between the tracks, his eyes on the headlights. At the last moment he danced over the other third rail and dashed across the parallel tracks just as the other train rushed by. For a moment the train separated Jason from his pursuers, but the back of the train was fast approaching, and the victory was fleeting. He quickly looked around. Whatever he did, he only had a few seconds more to do it with no chance of being seen. He climbed to the far edge of the track and looked out. There was no way to get down, but not far away was a rooftop, about ten feet below. If he stood on the retaining wall, the height would probably make the distance reachable. He couldn't run much farther, and with little time and no other options he pulled himself up, held his breath, and threw himself across the abyss.

25

JASON REACHED THE ROOFTOP, but hit it on one foot, awkwardly and hard, and tumbled out of control. Two skylights were coming up fast, one open and one closed, and he managed to aim for the open one. He fell through it and dropped another good seven feet, landing on the floor with a thud. He was starting to feel like a cartoon character, except that the lumps were adding up, and he didn't see the humor in it.

Letting his eyes close for a moment, he took a deep breath, and then another, before looking around. The room was poorly lit, but between the skylight, a small lamp, and the partially open door, you could see pretty much everything, if not well. He was at the foot of what must have been a large circular bed—and then suddenly was face-to-face with Richard Nixon, who peered at him from over its edge.

"Pardon me!" Nixon said loudly.

A second Nixon appeared. "Pardon me!" he said in exactly the same way.

Jason scrambled backwards in terror until a wall stopped his progress. Half-sitting and staring wildly ahead as if he'd seen two rattlesnakes, he took two quick breaths through his nose, eyes riveted on the apparitions in front of him. If this wasn't a nightmare, he thought, he'd never be afraid to go to sleep again. It took him longer than it should have to realize that they were wearing masks. However unlikely it was that the first one was really Nixon, two Nixons were almost certainly impossible. But the masks were thin rubber, and very realistic, and he was having a rough day.

From his new vantage point against the wall, he could make out that there were a total of four people on the bed. Two Nixons, each wearing dark jackets, white shirts and skinny black ties on top but only boxer shorts on the bottom, were sharing the company of two women who were wearing evening gowns. They weren't actually having sex, but they seemed to be well on their way. He heard giggles and figured they were all high on something, or at least very drunk, not that he cared much what people did with their free time. One of the women leaned forward. It turned out to be Pat Nixon, though it only took him a split second this time to realize that it was a mask.

"Come on over!" she called out.

A second Pat emerged from the shadows. "Always room for one more Dick!"

All the Nixons found this hilarious, and let out screams of laughter. One pair of Nixons got into a more heated embrace, and quickly they were all rolling around the bed, their apparently limited attention spans exhausted. Jason looked toward the bedroom door, and, unwilling to turn his back on any Nixon, real or fake, he felt his way toward it. Circumnavigating the room, he kept his distance from the bed like he was backing away from a Mexican standoff. He was just a few feet away from freedom when one of the Pats rolled over and called out to him.

"Where you going?" she asked cheerfully.

The second Pat popped up on her knees, losing what was left of her gown in the process.

"Don't be shy, now!" she said, leaning forward and tilting her head invitingly.

Jason looked her up and down in horror, going back and forth between her ebullient figure and Pat Nixon's tight, frozen smile. He figured it would take a year of primal scream therapy to get the image out of his mind.

"Uh…maybe later," he managed to squeeze out, taking one more step back and reaching for the door.

"Let me make one thing perfectly clear," one of the Nixons called out from the darkness.

"I am not a crook!" finished the other, coming into view as he playfully tackled one of the women and climbed on top of her.

Laughter erupted again as the foursome returned their full attention to each other. Jason backed quietly out the door, only to bump into someone in the next room. It was yet another Nixon, holding a drink. He also wore a dark suit, white shirt, thin black tie, and boxer shorts. This one still had his black shoes and socks on.

"Pardon Me!" he said loudly.

Jason staggered backwards and leaned against a large column. He was in a vast open living room with a very high ceiling—the apartment must have been something between a duplex and a loft. Hanging over a raised platform at one end of the room was a giant banner that read: "PARDON ME! SEPT 8, 1974–SEPT 8, 1975." The din of the party contrasted with the relative quiet of the bedroom where the Nixons were enjoying their orgy. It was very bright, and the loud, inevitably awful disco music pounded so relentlessly that you could feel the bass competing with your heartbeat. The party was a crowded, catered affair, with most of the guests dancing euphorically under flashing lights. As he studied them, Jason realized that they were all made up to look like figures from the Nixon administration. Some wore masks; the Nixon outfit, in particular, was very standardized: mask, black suit and tie, no pants. There must have been twenty of them. Others were more creatively made up, probably because it was hard to find an Ehrlichman or Haldeman mask, even at the finest costume store.

A woman with a long flowing gray wig danced over to him, tall mixed drink in hand. "C'mon, baby, let's dance!" she said in a very thick southern accent.

Before Jason could respond, the music came to a halt, and the crowd let out a big cheer. A man who had a big "PRESS SECRETARY" button pinned to his lapel walked up to the podium on the stage.

He made a reasonably plausible Ron Nessen, and he pulled the mikes forward and tapped on them before he spoke, the amplified thuds calling the room to some semblance of order.

"Ladies and gentlemen, your attention please! Let's hear it for my boss, without whom none of us would be here, the President of the United States!"

Accompanied by a fresh round of cheers from the crowd, and "Hail to the Chief" blasting over the speakers, a man in a convincing Gerald Ford mask trotted up the three stairs on the side of the stage, stumbling on the last one. It wasn't obvious that he did it on purpose, but the crowd roared in laughter, and as he righted himself, he pointed to the large Band-Aid he had placed on the forehead of his mask, to more laughter. He stumbled again at the podium.

"Thank you all for coming," he said, pretending to struggle with the microphones. "Rest assured that if any of you misbehave tonight, especially you ladies, you can stop by the Oval Office for a little something I like to call the full Presidential pardon!"

There was still more laughter from the crowd, and Ford hammed it up, pointing at people in the audience.

"Before things get any more out of hand," he continued, "my advisors have informed me—Ron, is this true? That it's time to give out the awards."

Nesson leaned over and spoke into the microphone. "Yes sir, Mr. President."

Ford leaned back in. "So here with the inside info on the awards—he may have been disbarred, but still knows where all the bodies are buried—first fink John Dean!"

There was enthusiastic applause as a small man approached from the wings.

"Thank you. I'd first like to say a few words about the process by which—"

"No!" the crowd shouted him down almost collectively, as if they had rehearsed.

"Very well, but it would be unwise not to heed my counsel." The Dean character hadn't worked much on his costume, primarily an oversized set of glasses with the left lens much larger than the right, but he nailed the voice and monotone modulation so well it was spooky.

"The award for most realistic Watergate figure goes to…." He pulled an envelope out of his jacket. "…Gordon Liddy, for holding his hand over a candle until we could all smell the flesh burn!"

A man who looked way too much like Gordon Liddy leaped up onto the center of the stage in one bound. His hand was wrapped in a towel, and he waved it to the crowd, eliciting cheers. He stiffened as he approached the podium.

"Thank you," he said coldly. He turned to Dean but leaned into the microphone as he whispered, "You know, I urged the President to have you killed. But he wouldn't listen to me."

Jason lost his ability to focus and saw the ground coming up at him. He instinctively reached out and grabbed the shoulder of the woman next to him, which was just enough to keep his balance.

"Hey there!" she said, "Y'all okay?"

"Yeah," he said unsteadily, taking his hand back.

"You sure, honey? You don't look so good."

He studied her face, and found it more reassuring than the awards ceremony that continued on stage.

"Who are you?"

"Why, I'm none other than Martha Mitchell."

That wasn't what he meant, but he'd always had a soft spot for Martha. She was the only one of the lot of them who told the truth, or at least said what she was thinking.

"I thought they had you sedated and locked in a hotel room to keep you quiet."

"Now don't you make fun of me, boy," she said sharply, but seemed pleased he knew her story.

"Where's John?"

"Still in jail, I'm afraid. Couldn't make it."

"I always knew he'd end up there," Jason said wearily.

"Me too. He was a no good…." She stopped and touched his face. "Hey, you're bleeding. Let's get you cleaned up."

She took him by the hand and led him across the room, weaving their way through the crowd, most of whom were still watching the stage and bursting out in occasional whoops of glee and applause. They reached the bathroom door, which was closed, and Martha knocked repeatedly, to no response. She shrugged her shoulders and opened the door.

They entered to find a man on his knees sniffing a line of cocaine off the closed toilet seat. He looked up—it was a very convincing Henry Kissinger.

"Excuse me," he said with a thick German accent, "these are very delicate negotiations. My work here cannot be interrupted. It may take years before success is achieved."

"But the President needs you," Martha said sincerely.

"Very well," Kissinger said, adjusting his glasses. "As you know, I serve at the pleasure of the President." He turned and snorted one more line, shook his head like a bridled racehorse, then stood up, drew himself into an impossibly dignified pose, regarded them both, and left.

Jason sat down while Martha wet a washcloth. It was a relief to be in the bathroom with less noise and no crowd. She knelt down next to him and wiped some of the scrapes on his face. When she switched sides he grimaced.

"Hey," she said. She pulled back, her eyes widening. "You really are hurt."

She adjusted her wig and studied his face more closely, evaluating the bruises.

"What did you think?"

"You can't see anything in there." She still had a southern accent, but it was much softer. "I thought you came as a war protester or something."

Jason smirked. "No, I just dropped in by accident."

"Really?" Her eyes traveled from his beat-up jeans to his bruised face. "Do I know you? You look kind of familiar."

"No. I'm just—"

"Haven't I seen you on TV?"

The door burst open, and a man in a Spiro Agnew mask took

one step into the room. "Have you seen Secretary Kissinger? He was holding something for me."

"He just left, honey," Martha said, picking up her accent, "I think he had his own plans."

"Everyone in this administration has abandoned me!" Agnew shouted, slamming the door as he left.

Jason took a deep breath. He had seen enough of these people, and his head was clearing up just enough for him to feel more of his injuries.

"You want to go somewhere else?" Martha asked.

"I just need to find a quiet place to crash."

"Come with me. My apartment's on the fourth floor."

She took him by the hand and led him out of the bathroom and back again through the pounding music. The dancing had resumed. A pale, thin woman with very short jet-black hair wearing a dark man's suit walked right around Martha and leaned against Jason.

"I'm Deep Throat," she whispered in his ear. "I can prove it."

He tried to make eye contact with her, but there was nothing there, just the vacuum of her dilated pupils. "Sorry," he mumbled.

She was gone in an instant.

"What'd she want?" Martha asked.

"I'm not sure…nothing really," he said, leaning more heavily on her arm.

It was only two flights down to Martha's apartment, but they took the elevator. Her place was blissfully quiet and cozy, with a very homey feel. It wasn't small but there was a little too much furniture, with two sofas and big ornate wooden pieces that made Jason wonder if she'd inherited the stuff from an old relative.

"Wait here, I want to get out of this dress," she said, leaving him on one of the couches.

She was gone for longer than he expected, and after a while he kicked off his sneakers and lay back on the couch. It was really a nice place—she lived like a grown-up, with real art on the walls, nice rugs on a well-maintained floor—and everything where it was supposed to be. A big gray cat walked toward him and hopped up on the couch, resting on his stomach. He pet it absent-mindedly, but felt a little trapped by its girth.

What was taking her so long? Some of those women at the party were scary, and she was pretty quick to bring him home. But the couch felt good, and he shook those thoughts off and rested his eyes. Anybody who dressed up as Martha Mitchell couldn't be that bad.

Something cold landed softly on his head. He reached up—it was a wet washcloth. Pushing it up slightly, he opened his eyes and saw her sitting in a big easy chair across from him, with her legs tucked up under her arms. She was wearing sweats and sipping tea from a ceramic cup.

"You want some?" she asked, raising the cup. "Or something else? A beer?"

"No thanks. I've had my share and then some." He rubbed his eyes. "Jeez, what the hell was that?"

"David Goldstein's first annual pardon party. It was a year ago today, you know. The pardon."

"No," he lied.

"Well, it's a huge deal with this crowd. Dave and his friends are second-generation Nixon haters. Their parents hated him in the 'fifties, then their kids picked up the torch."

"Some life, hating for a living." Jason shifted his position slightly, dislodging the cat, of whom he had enough.

"How'd you know?" she asked.

"How did I know what?"

"That they did it for a living?"

"I didn't—it was just a figure of speech."

"Well, they do, or at least they did," she explained. "They're mostly lawyers who work for a public interest firm that challenged his policies in court."

"The good fight," Jason said passively.

"They were hoping to prepare a brief for his trial, but when the pardon came...." She didn't seem sure how to describe what they must have felt.

"There was nothing left for them to do," Jason said, finishing the thought for her.

"Right. You know, we were probably the only two people there who weren't lawyers—you're not a lawyer, are you?"

"No."

"I didn't think so. I'm just a neighbor. I mean, I hate Nixon and all—don't get me wrong," she said with a disarming smile. "But I was never much of a radical. I was 'Clean for Gene' in 'sixty-eight, and even with that my parents almost disowned me—but I'm in publishing."

She looked at him like it was his turn to talk. "What do you do?" she asked.

It wasn't an easy question to answer. He studied her face, and wondered what she was thinking about.

She put her tea down on the table and leaned toward him a bit. "You're that guy with the helicopter, aren't you?" she asked. "I saw you on TV."

"No...yeah." He was tired of lying. "But I'd just as soon not—"

"What did it feel like?" She wrapped her arms around her knees and pulled them closer. "I mean that moment, right before. Right before you decided what to do. It must have been terrifying. I know I would have been just paralyzed."

"No, it's not like that. Really, it's...it's the opposite of that. I mean, when I saw that girl...it was a chance. A chance." He repeated it firmly, as if understanding it himself for the first time.

"A chance for what?" she said softly.

"A chance to do something. Something that mattered, even if it was just for one person. Most people go through their whole lives... they never get a chance like that."

"You think most people want a chance like that?"

"I don't know what most people want. Hell, I don't even know what I want." He closed his eyes. The cat had made its way back onto his lap, nestled in determinedly, and, meeting no resistance, was generating a contented, tranquilizing purr. "Listen," Jason mumbled, "I don't mean to impose or anything, but I don't think I'm going to be able to get off this couch anytime soon."

26

JASON WOKE UP EARLY the next morning, more sore than hung over, and in better shape than he anticipated. Tiptoeing around Martha's apartment, he cautiously peeked into her bedroom, half-guilty—who knew how she slept—but she was still wearing the sweats, probably because he was there. He didn't want to wake her, at least not until he had some time to think. The cat was following him around from room to room, keeping an eye on him, or looking for attention, or both, and watched from just outside the bathroom as Jason tried to put himself back into some presentable form without making a mess of the place. It soon got impatient, and the meows grew alarmingly loud. Jason found some dry food in the kitchen and gave him some to quiet him down.

He found the phone and called Adam's apartment. There was no answer, which he expected, but it couldn't hurt to check. Adam always assumed that people were going to come after him, and he had escape routes and contingency plans, as he called them, for almost every possible scenario. Finally, his paranoia was paying off—no one had ever bothered to chase him before, not even a jealous husband.

Most of Adam's safe houses involved old girlfriends, who were surprisingly tolerant of him. What was the name he had mouthed through the glass last night before the train pulled away? *Monica.* Now Jason remembered her name. Which one was she? He could probably find the number back at his apartment, but Adam's paranoia had rubbed off on him, and he wasn't ready to go home yet.

It was probably safe; if they had been after him, they would have taken him out first, since he was closer—or at the very least they would have been paying enough attention to avoid letting him level one of them with a swinging barstool. Chances are they had no idea who he was, he told himself again. Still, he wasn't quite ready to go home.

Jason decided to fix himself some coffee, and rummaging around he also found some Cap'n Crunch cereal. Good woman, that Martha. The kitchen was very well stocked; she must have cooked most of her own meals. He was settling in when there was a soft thud at the door, and he was filled with dread at the prospect that one of her friends from the party was stopping by. Sidling over to the peephole, the cat one step behind, he was able to make out the back of the paperboy, walking away—the Sunday *Times* had some good weight to it. After he was gone Jason quietly opened the door a bit, using one foot to block the cat if necessary, and pulled the paper into the apartment.

Returning to the kitchen table, by force of habit he rearranged the sections while scanning the headlines. Sunday, September 9. That meant something. Shit. The maintenance flight. He looked at his watch—if he left immediately, he'd only be a half-hour late. There was a pad by the phone, and he decided to leave Martha a note.

"Martha: thanks for everything, you really saved me. If you hadn't been there, the Nixons would have gotten me for sure. I always knew you were too good for John." He walked back to her bedroom and watched her again, even though he knew it was probably wrong to do it. But he was overwhelmed by the memory of the only time he ever toured as a musician, the summer in between college and law school. No matter how far you drove into the night, the next day you'd reach another city, with thousands of people living their lives. And then the next day you were gone, on to the next one. Here she was—only about a mile away from his apartment, actually—living her life, stuffed with its own hopes, dreams, disappointments, vet bills, and so on. It seemed pretty well put together.

A nice woman who drifted by with a life preserver just when he needed one.

He left the note on the kitchen table. He didn't sign it, but he added a PS: "You were probably right about my costume." And then he was gone.

HE made really good time into the City. It was a quiet Sunday but he got lucky with the trains, and he even had a little spring in his step when he got to the roof. It was a nice day to fly, and being up in the air would give him a chance to think.

Sammy was waiting. He rose from his chair with a serious look on his face, and Jason could tell he was going to give him the business for keeping him waiting. Maybe he'd cut him some slack when he got a look at his sorry state.

"Hey, man, sorry I'm late," Jason said with a sheepish grin.

"No problem, Mr. Sims," Sammy said stiffly.

"Hey, I'm not that late. Especially considering. You wouldn't believe—"

"No problem at all, sir," Sammy interrupted, which was noticeable, since he usually liked a little elbow room before he spoke.

"Hey, I'm going to need that—"

"Right this way!" Sammy interrupted again, and guided him toward the helicopter.

Jason followed him, confused. "Anything I need to know about?" he asked, offering Sammy an opening.

"Nothing more than usual," Sammy almost mumbled, and continued to avoid any sort of eye contact.

Jason climbed into the helicopter and started the engine. As always, Sammy handed up the clipboard for him to sign out and gave him the maintenance log book as well. As the noise from the rotors got louder, Sammy leaned into the cockpit.

"Which route you gonna take?"

"You know I like to fly out to tar beach," Jason said, referring to a neighborhood out in Brooklyn known for its rooftop sunbathers.

"Nice day like today, you're better off heading to Staten Island."

"No way—just a few weeks left of summer. Not going to see any women out by the Verrazano Bridge. Just Lady Liberty. And she's old and wearing a robe."

"Sounds like Robert Johnson talking, to me."

"What's that mean?" Jason said sharply.

Sammy stepped away and put his ear protectors on.

"Nothin'!" he shouted out. "Don't mean nothin'!"

Sammy stepped farther back. Jason looked down at the console and started to pump his fist as he turned his head back. Sammy's fist was raised but motionless, and he didn't meet Jason's gaze; he was staring down at the clipboard cradled in his arm. With the brim of his Mets cap turned up, he looked as much like the Statue of Liberty as a black man possibly could. Jason hesitated, waiting for him to look up, but he didn't, so he pulled the helicopter into the air.

Jason headed out towards the East River, thinking about everything, wondering if Martha had woken up yet; where, and with whom, Adam was hiding out; and what, if anything, Alison was thinking at that moment. He should have asked Sammy about Alison. Sammy always had the right answer, even if he'd only tell it to you in the form of a long story.

He was already across the river when he circled around and headed toward the Statue of Liberty. Now that he thought about it, put a Mets cap over that spiked crown of hers and it would be she who looked like Sammy, not the other way around. Besides, it was safer to do these tests over water, anyway.

Halfway between Lady Liberty and the bridge he hovered, putting the copter through its paces. Staring at the panels, checking out the instruments; looking at his watch, seeing how long it took to descend 200 feet. He brought it down fast, trying to break an old personal record, which, of course, was not the point of the exercise, but it helped pass the time and keep things interesting. It took a bit of effort to level off, and he must have come within a hundred feet of the water, a little close for comfort. Regaining control and then holding the copter steady, he leaned over to consult the maintenance log, but as he turned his head the oil pressure gauge caught his eye. Boy, that's low, he thought, and before the thought had finished forming the red warning light went on.

He tried to pull up quickly but couldn't. The copter started to shake, and the rotors above started to hum the mechanical equivalent of an irregular heartbeat. Four other warning lights erupted simultaneously, and if his life wasn't in danger it would have been pretty funny, something out of a Woody Allen movie—*Bananas* or *Sleeper*, he'd have to decide later—but it was either the executive desk exerciser or the kitchen-of-the-future. In any event, right then he had to give all of his attention to holding the sputtering craft together for as long as possible. He figured that down was better than up, and the closer he got to Liberty Island, the more likely it was he'd be rescued by a Port Authority boat, assuming he survived the crash. Especially on a late summer Sunday, a busy tourist day would draw more cops.

Struggling to maintain control, he successfully pointed the copter in the direction he wanted to go, and also headed down, though there really wasn't much choice about that part. The key question was whether he was flying or falling. The engine cut completely, answering that question definitively about halfway to the water. At that point there was nothing left to do but pray—there was a very real chance that this was the kind of crash one would not survive, and even those odds might have been shaded by wishful thinking. But after taking a nanosecond to weigh the pros and cons, he decided that wasn't the last thing he wanted to do on this earth. Better to face this with a clear head, as the person he was. Looking down, he noticed that he'd never buckled in properly—attending to that seemed like a good use of the limited time remaining. That quickly turned out to be easier said than done, as the helicopter slipped into a dizzying spin, disrupting his coordination while enhancing the beat-the-clock quality to the belt-fastening enterprise. Finally he clasped it shut, and looking up, saw water in every direction. Grabbing the sides of his seat, he closed his eyes. Not a single scene from his life flashed before his eyes—he thought of nothing but the moment, concentrating in the darkness on the inevitability of what was coming next.

He hit the water, hard. Very hard—the impact exceeded even the dire expectations that he had steeled himself against. Still, the evidence suggested he had survived the initial impact, so that was something. Water rushed into the cockpit from all sides with disorienting force, and as Jason reached down to undo his belts he felt a searing pain in his chest that limited his breathing to quick little pants. The craft pitched backward, leaving him looking up at the bright blue sky, regretting that he couldn't see the Statue of Liberty, which might have made for a fitting end. Still, despite the desperate little gasps and searing pain, it might not be the end— and either way, better to go down fighting. He calculated that the helicopter would probably float for a while, but if he was going to lose consciousness—a mortal danger that had to be accounted for—it was probably better to try to get out than to risk going down with it. As the helicopter continued to tip backwards on its tail, trying to kick out through the front seemed like the best hope. Jason looked through the windshield, strategizing about how this might be accomplished, and the last thing he remembered was seeing the rotor, bent over the front and rotating awkwardly.

JASON OPENED HIS EYES. The rotor was still spinning, and his chest still hurt. A momentary surge of panic accompanied the thought of getting out of the helicopter before it was too late, and he tried to push his arms out to the sides and behind to gauge the water level, but nothing met his hands. Something was limiting his reach, and his body mobilized a wave of adrenalin should emergency measures be necessary. Instead, Jason took a calm, shallow breath, felt around again, and, shifting his eyes from the spinning rotor, re-assessed his environment. Turned out he was in a hospital room, not the helicopter. A ceiling fan was spinning lazily overhead. It was a private room — not a half-vacant semi-private — with touches of wood and a general ambiance one step up from standard dreary-hospital pewter. He was on his back in a light blue hospital gown, left arm bandaged and left ankle aching, and it was hard to move. Sometimes it hurt to breathe, but he was reassured by the fact that he wasn't attached to any machines, or even an IV.

Despite his limited mobility, a TV remote and a call button were within reach, and he chose the remote first, deciding to gather as much information as he could on his own. His watch was still working; it was almost seven, and Carol's smiling face slowly emerged on Channel Six as the TV warmed up. That meant it was morning, probably Monday.

He watched Carol and Nate trade some happy talk and waited for the headlines at the top of the hour. He was able to confirm that it was Monday, but seven o'clock came and went with no mention of him or the helicopter—or traffic at all, for that matter. At 7:15, Carol announced, "And now here's Dave Edwards with the traffic," and a picture of Dave beside a map of the City came up on the screen. The voice of Dave described how bad the traffic was everywhere, and little red lights popped up on the map to illustrate which delays he was talking about. It occurred to Jason that there was no reason not to do it that way all the time.

Then it was back to Carol in the studio. Her familiar good looks were so reliable that Jason forgot for a moment that he had reclassified her as a force for evil. "Thanks, Dave," she said with a winning smile. "For those of you just tuning in, we've been having some problems with our remote camera, but it should be up and running tomorrow."

Jason turned off the TV and thought about ringing for the nurse, but he decided to rest for a few minutes. Morning light was creeping in through the windows. He would rest, and then think, and then plan.

These prospects were disrupted by a knock at the door, which Jason decided to ignore. After a second set of knocks, the door opened slowly.

"Jason? You awake, son?"

"Who's there?" Jason asked. The voice was familiar.

"It's me," Mayor Cohen answered, stepping out of the shadows. "They told me you'd probably be able to talk."

Jason's heart sank, imagining the media hordes that followed the Mayor wherever he went, and which he was unable to fathom confronting at the moment. "I'm not ready to see—"

"It's just me, son," Cohen interrupted, in a quiet, level tone. "I'm alone. It's just you and me. Nobody knows you're here." He dragged a chair toward the bed and sat down, as Jason replayed the Mayor's words in his mind. The accent had been on the word *nobody*, which gave the sentence an ominous quality. "Nobody knows I'm here," Cohen continued. "And they never will." He retained the hushed tone to his voice, but in fact it wasn't sinister—it was more like he was sharing a secret than keeping one.

"What do you want?"

Cohen gave a knowing look, and a weary smile. "Just want to talk a little. Some things we have to go over. You're in a little over your head, and I'm here to help pull you out."

"Then you know everything that's been going on?"

"Nothing happens in this city I don't know about," Cohen said with a hint of pride, but mostly stating a fact. "We just need to get on the same page, get a few things squared away."

Jason tried to sit up, but it was too much of an effort. "I don't know what I can tell you. I know Morgan has been working against you, but I can't see—"

"Jeb Morgan? Dear friend of mine. He financed my first campaign—right out of his pocket, never asked a question about a penny of it."

Jason felt a knot tighten in the pit of his stomach, and had a quick flashback to the helicopter, spiraling out of control. He subtly clenched his fists under the sheets, and wiggled his toes. He could probably move if he had to. "I don't understand. Didn't you raise the licensing fees?"

"Sure did. And ol' Jeb just got a special waiver from the FCC. We pushed it in Congress. Next time this year, he's going to own three stations in this town. Law says you can only own one. But they decided, what with the fiscal crisis and all, that if he was willing to keep those stations running, probably better for the people than just having them shut down. Now I would imagine in a few years, those fees might slip back down a bit."

"So…you're in this together?" Jason asked, making an effort to minimize the astonishment in his voice. He still didn't know for sure what exactly he meant by "this," and he was trying to gauge, in the light of this new development, whether he was in immediate danger.

"In this together?" Cohen repeated, with more than a hint of mockery in his voice. "If you mean taking care of business—of course," the Mayor said, as if he were stating the obvious. "Just how do you think this city is run?"

"I don't know. I guess—"

"Don't even try. This city can't be governed, at least not by the book." He got a stern look in his eyes. "You know what they call it? Us? 'The Ungovernable City.' *Ungovernable.* Everybody says it. Well, that's an easy thing to say, but somebody's still got to govern the damn thing! And right now that somebody is me." Cohen got out of his chair, circled around, and gripped the back of it like it was a podium. He leaned forward to lecture at Jason. "Half the tax base—the people who make their fortunes in this town—they've slipped away. Outside the city limits."

Cohen stood straight up, as if newly outraged by the very thought, and walked a few steps across the room towards the window. "Now that makes it very hard for me to do my job. And you know what my job is?"

"You mean that stuff about making life matter?"

Cohen spun around quickly for a man his age. "I'm not talking about that shit now. I'm talking about looking out for the people of the City of New York." He pointed at Jason with his finger. "The working people. The people who walk the streets and ride the subway. One billion passengers rode those trains last year. One billion." The light was glowing through the shuttered, translucent blinds behind him as he spoke, casting his face in darkness, and giving the impression that it wasn't so much Cohen that was speaking, but the Mayor, and every mayor that had come before him.

"What about the poor?" Jason said, probing the breadth of Cohen's confidence.

"What about 'em?" Cohen said defiantly. "You have a plan in *your* hip pocket to win the war on poverty? Let me tell you something about the world: the poor will always be poor, and the rich will always be rich. And there's nothing that any mayor—*any* mayor—can do about that. The mayor's job—my job—is to make the City work for the millions of people whose lives I can make a difference in. That's what I do. And I do it well."

"Even if that means working with the mob?" Jason said, testing a theory he hadn't even shared with Adam.

"Mobs, unions, cops, I got deals with every one of 'em. The racket boys are the easiest of the three. They're predictable. And when you tell them to shut the fuck up, they usually do. Usually," he repeated, with a slight edge in his voice, and shifting his eyes at Jason.

"But they're criminals, common criminals. And you look the other way. Even let them do jobs for the City."

Cohen wouldn't back down an inch. Whatever he was up to, he believed in it; it wasn't a series of random decisions that had caught up with him. "I govern," he said, enunciating the word. "And that involves making choices and choosing priorities. Hooking and gambling are victimless crimes—it's not my job to tell people what to do with their spare time." He looked derisively at Jason. "You kids should appreciate that more than most. So if I spare the over-stretched cops and overcrowded courts a lot of nonsense by looking the other way, as you call it, well, maybe those criminals you're so worked up about owe me something in return. Hell, they run protection rackets in those neighborhoods anyway, so why can't they do a little free-lance law enforcement for us?"

"Because that's not justice," Jason responded just as firmly. Cohen's cynicism was so deep that it outflanked him, and unexpectedly left him as the idealist in the argument, which was old and now only vaguely familiar territory. "Those four guys—what did they do to draw a death sentence? What you're doing isn't right." They were having an argument, and part of Jason was loving it. He had drawn a line, and he was going to defend it. What was right was right.

Cohen took a deep breath. "I do, I will do…whatever is necessary."

"Including murder?"

"It hasn't ever come to that."

"A lot of bodies lying around," Jason observed.

"I know," Cohen said more gently. He took a few steps back towards Jason, and his features came into view. "That's why I'm here. Things got a little out of hand. I've put a stop to it. You and your buddy are safe, for now. But you boys are gonna have to leave town."

"Leave town?" Jason shot back. What was this, the Old West?

Cohen didn't respond, but made his way to the other side of the room and cast his eyes at a large reclining chair, as if addressing its invisible occupant. "It was all coming together so nicely," he said wistfully. "All that highway money our boys in Congress delivered...." He turned and looked at Jason with new life in his eyes. "You got any idea what the composition of the current Congress is?" he asked. It wasn't a rhetorical question.

"No idea," Jason said flatly.

"Two hundred and ninety-one Democrats—more than twice as many Democrats as Republicans! Watergate was the best thing that ever happened to this city. That putz Nixon—fuck him—I met him in 'forty-eight, the little red-baiting prick." He turned back to his invisible confessor in the lounge chair. "Overspend like crazy on construction—those are good union jobs, especially nowadays with the economy. And the traffic jams, a little poetic justice to boot. On top of that, it gave the excuse to raise those tolls and parking fees. You know what I call that?"

He looked over triumphantly, but Jason just stared blankly, waiting for him to finish the show.

"Reclaiming our tax base," he said, a phrase he was obviously pleased with. "And almost all of it in cash! General-purpose revenues." He waved his arm with a magician's flourish. "You helped us move it around."

"I always wanted to work for the City," Jason said quietly. He felt used, but didn't blame them for it. He had made choices, too, and could have asked more questions—or a question—and didn't.

Cohen shook his head. "After Maynes, though, things just fell apart. Gekin and Frankel, goddamn punks, they panicked, and the mob covers its tracks on instinct. Bad break. Bad, bad break."

"I don't know," Jason said, finding his own voice. "Bad breaks, they don't come from nowhere."

"How you figure?"

"You sleep with someone, they rub off on you a little."

Cohen didn't snort, but he might as well have. "Bullshit beat poetry," he said, answering with a little rhythm of his own. "Maynes just got greedy."

"Not like you," Jason said deadpan. He wanted to find a way under Cohen's skin and finally found one.

"You college boys don't understand much, do you?" Cohen said, angry for the first time. Coming closer to the bed, he stared at Jason so hard his left cheek gave a little flutter. "You listen good," he growled through tight lips, underlining each clause with a jabbing index finger, "I've never taken one penny, not one, that the people of this city didn't vote me."

"And your dear, dear friend Sid Maynes?" Jason asked, calling Cohen on his funeral speech.

"Far as I'm concerned, he got what he deserved."

"You sound more like an accountant than a mayor."

"When were you born, 'forty-five, 'forty-six?" Cohen asked. He wasn't angry anymore. "What do you know? Kids like you, spoiled rotten. You don't understand just how thin the line is."

"The line?"

"Between then and now. You take it for granted. People from my day, lot of times we didn't know where the next meal was coming from—or who was going to serve it. You think just because it isn't like that now, it can never be again. But people like me... people like your father...we were hungry. That's not a figure of speech, kid. You know any history, or you just read about it?"

"Maybe you can draw on that," Jason conceded for the sake of the argument, "but it's not a blank check."

"Times make the man, you know." Cohen was speaking expansively again, as if there were others in the room. "During the war, that was a good time to be a hero. These are more...pragmatic times."

"Times for knowing the right move," Jason offered, reciting a phrase he'd picked up from Morgan.

"Exactly. And the right move now is for you kids to take off."

"No chance," Jason responded coolly, and it was clear he meant it. "And even if I did, Shaker would never go."

Cohen sat back down and dragged his chair closer.

"Look, you've got nothing. That body—I doubt it will ever be found. You've lost whatever thin scraps of paper you had. We own the tabloids. And the *Times* won't touch a story without hard evidence. Real hard evidence. You boys are in serious trouble. Serious trouble. These people—how can I put this—they don't care for loose ends. I'm offering you a chance. You don't take this deal...."

Cohen got up again and walked slowly to the window, letting the silence do his talking.

Jason let the silence linger. "You ever see Dave Edwards on the news?" he asked after a while.

Cohen fiddled with the blinds and didn't look back. "I don't watch the news. I make it."

"He does the traffic. We shoot him live, from a camera in the copter. It's mounted behind my seat—points right at him."

Cohen turned slightly, but still didn't make eye contact. "I'm familiar with the concept."

"Well, a while back, I got to talking to an old friend, and it occurred to me that maybe I needed to watch my back. So I decided to keep the camera rolling, you know, whether I was flying with Dave, or...with anybody."

Cohen turned the rest of the way.

"The bottom line is, I've got shots of the murder, the money, the shooter, and a nice picture of the license plate. Sure looked like Gekin's car to me. You think the *Times* would be interested in *that* sort of hard evidence?"

"Don't be stupid," Cohen said, with genuine concern in his voice. "That film sees the light of day, they'll kill you. The cops won't help you, and I won't be able to protect you."

"I don't see why anybody has to see it. But suppose, just suppose, that me and my friend stick around. Anything happens to either of us, and I mean anything, the film would show up all over. It's been copied, and the copies are safe."

"I'm glad to see you can talk like a pragmatist after all," Cohen said, quickly adjusting to the new realities he was presented with. "It's a language I appreciate."

"Then we have a deal?" Jason asked.

"In my business, we call it an understanding."

28

JASON WAS IN THE hospital for two more days, and when he was discharged they explained that it "wasn't really" a collapsed lung, which didn't seem like the most precise medical diagnosis, but it didn't sound so bad, so he decided not to push it. They also gave him a cane for his leg, which "might help if it got tired," another profound piece of doctoring. On the bright side, they seemed to think that he was in pretty good shape—nothing was broken, and when he inquired about the bill he was told that his "Uncle Al" had already taken care of it for him.

He carried the cane most of the way home but found himself using it on the walk from the subway station back to his apartment. It was good to be back in the neighborhood and to have a relationship with every storefront he passed. Even the ones he'd never set foot in—the shoemaker that must have been there since the twenties, and a small clothing boutique—offered a comforting familiarity. He rarely came home in the morning, and it was interesting to see people from the other direction, when they were just starting out instead of getting ready to close up. It was a nice day, late summer, and the slow pace of his walk forced him to think about things. He wondered if Alison had tried to call him. She'd said "later in the week," but didn't seem to mention any business after Tuesday, and it was already Wednesday.

He finally got back to his building; he'd been through a lot, but everything was exactly in its place. There wasn't a scrap of mail waiting for him, not even a bill. Choosing the elevator, he poked the button with his cane, and watched the floor count slowly march towards five—number three didn't light up, he couldn't remember when it had ever worked—but now he thought it might be a cosmic message. He had two or possibly three calls to make—did the missing three mean he should make the call, or that he shouldn't?

He half expected the apartment to have been ransacked or something, but it wasn't, not that an outsider would have noticed a huge difference. He rummaged around for his address book, which took a while because he hadn't used it in ages. It turned out not to be anywhere near the phone, but was underneath a stack of take-out menus in the back of that kitchen drawer where he kept stuff.

The first call was to Adam, who was probably still hiding out with Monica. He didn't know her last name but didn't need to; she was listed under "G," for Adam's girlfriends. 516 area code—out on the Island. Jason didn't remember Monica, but Adam must have figured it was probably wise to get out of city limits, and most likely had doubled back and grabbed the Long Island Railroad at the Jamaica station. Adam hadn't caught up with many of the fugitives he chased over the years, but he sure learned how to run, Jason thought as he dialed the number.

"Hello?" answered a woman's voice.

"Monica?" he waited for her to correct him and she didn't. "Is Adam there?"

"Who? I'm sorry, you must have the wrong number. Good—"

"Wait! Tell him it's Jason."

"Look, mister, you have the wrong number. Don't—"

"Listen, before you hang up, if you have a houseguest, tell him that 'Waterloo Sunset' is an overrated song."

She hung up. A minute later the phone rang.

"Obviously, you've never heard the Kinks do that live," Adam said without as much as a hello.

"I was standing next to you at the time, O senile one. Just trying to get your attention."

"Oh, yeah, jeez, what was that, 'sixty-seven? I forgot. Hey, you okay? What happened? They stopped doing the traffic. I didn't want to call your house. I haven't talked to *anyone*. Been at DEFCON 1, you know—total radio silence. Are you safe?"

"Yeah, fine. Just a little banged up. I can't seem to keep the damn helicopter in the air."

"Are you alone?" Adam asked suspiciously.

It took Jason twice as long to convince Adam that he was alone than it did to bring him up to speed with everything that had happened. Then it took even longer to convince him that releasing the murder film wouldn't "bring the City to its knees," as Adam proclaimed, since nobody would recognize Bill, the location, or probably even the car, not to mention the shooter. Adam finally agreed that they were better off keeping the copies along with carefully annotated notes in a safe place as an insurance policy, and immediately switched over to scheming about how and where to secure them, and "how best to ensure that they would surface in our absence should the need arise." He also said that he should probably stay out on the island for a couple of more days, but Jason figured that was for an unrelated reason.

Jason got up and tidied the apartment a little. Alison's picnic basket was still on the kitchen table where he'd left it last week. He wondered if there were any perishables in it; there was nothing he could smell from the doorway and he didn't feel like checking it out either way, so he worked around it.

The second call was to the station; Jason was handling them in increasing order of difficulty.

"Harry Ross's office," answered a chipper voice. Jason didn't even know Harry had a secretary, but it made sense that he would.

"Is Harry in?"

"No, he's unavailable. May I take message?"

"Just tell him that Jason Sims called, and he can reach me at—"

"Could you hold a moment?" she interrupted.

Jason held the phone for more than a minute, and decided to look out the window and come up with some decision rule about how long to wait before hanging up.

"Jesus, kid, how are you?" Harry's voice boomed over the line. Didn't anybody say "hello" anymore?

"I'm fine."

"The copter was a total loss," Harry explained, filling in his side of the story. "A couple of cops came by the station, gave some half-assed story about a crash, and told us you were alive, nothing more. They wouldn't tell us where you were taken—are you in some sort of trouble?"

"Almost," Jason smiled at the phone. "But no, I'm not in any trouble. It was all about Adam, and I kind of got caught in the cross…caught in the middle."

"Shaker? No shit. His music reviews are okay. But I never thought he'd dig up enough dirt for anyone to go after him."

"Yeah, me neither."

"Is he with you? We haven't seen him, either, not that we're not used to…is he…uh…"

"Yeah, he's fine too."

"Oh, that's good."

There was a long silence.

"Listen, Jason, why don't you take the rest of the week—how does that sound?"

"It's not a problem. I could be in sooner if you want," Jason said, hoping desperately Harry would give him the week.

"Nah, don't worry about it. We still don't have a new helicopter, anyway. You should see Dave's face; he does it all off camera now—it's killing him. Anyway, come in on Monday, and we'll see what's what."

"Sounds good."

The third call, the maybe call, he wasn't quite ready to make. Technically, she could call anytime between now and Friday afternoon and still be operating within the designated window. On the other hand, she probably would want to know about all the things that had happened during the last few days. In fact, she could even be upset if he didn't call to tell her about it. Or maybe that was a stretch.

He decided to work on the living room for a while, and really get it organized. That turned out to be a much more ambitious project than anticipated. Gathering and putting away the accumulated clothes and stuff that was just left where they were dropped didn't take all that long, nor did throwing out a year's worth of read and unread magazines. Still manageable but requiring somewhat more effort was assessing and determining the fate for his stray instruments. But getting the records back in serious order, reassessing some of the genre and sub-genre classifications, attributing principal contributions, and certifying the differences between recording and release dates was taking hours. He was stuck, agonizing over whether Derek and the Dominos was blues or rock, and whether, in either case, it should be filed under "D" for Derek or "C" for Clapton, when there was a soft knock at the door. He stopped what he was doing and listened, since a knock made little sense given the doorbell, and the people who knew him would have expected to find the door unlocked anyway.

On the second set of knocks he tiptoed to the door—not an easy maneuver with a bum leg—and actually looked out the peephole, something he'd always considered undignified. It was Alison. He took a deep breath, and then another, and opened the door.

"Hi." She said. It wasn't a bad hi, but it was hard to read. He resisted the urge to hug her.

"Hi," he said back lamely. At least it was English.

They stood there staring at each other for a moment, and Alison had a slightly ghostly quality from the greenish tint of the hallway lighting.

"There are some things you have to do in person," she said— kind of sadly, he thought.

"Yeah," Jason exhaled, mentally trying to brace himself for another crash, but hoping for something better.

"So…can I come in?"

"Oh, yeah…sure," Jason said, making a space for her to duck through while holding the door open.

She walked in and sat at the table. Jason followed, subtly playing up his limp. He wished he hadn't left the cane in the kitchen.

"You wouldn't believe—"

"I know," she said. "Adam called and told me everything. It's incredible. Are you okay?"

"Yeah. Apparently it's not really a collapsed lung," he said with a weak smile.

"What about Adam? He sounded pretty bad on the phone."

"Really? He doesn't have a scratch on him." At least, none that he didn't want, Jason thought to himself.

"Oh, I know, that's not what I meant. But, you know, it's all over—no more grand conspiracy for him to chase. And I think for him it's more about the hunt than the catch. It's weird; I moped around for a week after I handed in my dissertation. I felt like an idiot till someone told me it happens to everyone. And he's got it worse—he finally reeled in the great white whale, and then he had to throw it back. What's he going to do now?"

"I hadn't thought about it," Jason said slowly, replaying his conversation with Adam in his head. Had he been selfish, or tone deaf, or did Adam talk differently to Alison than he did with him?

"Of course," she said tentatively, "I'm a little more curious about what you're going to do now." She looked right at him, but her eyes had a little less certainty than usual.

"Look, about the other day—"

"I don't want to talk about the other day," she said firmly, before he could make any progress into the Clarence Darrowesque summation of his defense that he'd rehearsed in his mind a thousand times.

"But we have to. It's important—"

"No it isn't. I don't need to hear this speech. I'm not interested in some version of events, or some retrospective interpretation of what it means or didn't mean." She stood up, looked toward the hallway the led to the bedroom, crossed her arms, and then sat back down. "Look, Jason, I'm not going to tell you that I don't care about the other day. I was pretty upset when I got home. Then I fin-

ished my paper, and then got upset all over again. But that's not…
but I won't be.…" She stopped for a moment, trying to find the
right words, and when it looked like Jason might speak, she raised
her hand to silence him. Then she clasped her hands and leaned
forward on her elbows. "The bottom line is, I, we, people like us—
some of us—aren't living the life our parents lived." Her eyes focused with purpose. "These are the rules we have chosen. And it's
naïve to think that they don't come with their own complications."

Jason didn't have anything that could compete with what she
was putting out, so he tried retreating. "But if you don't want to talk
about it, how will we be able to—"

"Who would that discussion be for, Jason, you or me?" she said,
cutting him off. She stood up again, and this time walked away
from the table. "Maybe one day, maybe even soon, we'll come to
our own understanding about what our relationship means. Assuming that we have one. But we're not at that point."

"And you don't even want to know that—"

"I don't want to talk about that day," she repeated, now definitively. "I want to talk about all the other days."

"All which other days?"

"All the days of the rest of your life."

"What do you want me to do?" Jason said, raising his voice and
stretching out his arms in an overly dramatic way.

"Something. Anything."

EPILOGUE

THE NEXT FEW MONTHS flowed rather easily. They were both fired from the station—Adam unceremoniously, Jason after a nice heart-to-heart chat with Harry, who even wanted to throw him a going-away party. They were each offered six months' severance pay, which Jason wanted to turn down; he knew it was Morgan's way of trying to keep them quiet, or of insulting him with the suggestion. But Adam offered him a better deal: if they both took the money, he promised not to find another job in TV.

Jason wasn't sure about it until he talked it over with Sammy, who had already saved his life once. Sammy had showed up too early that Sunday and bumped into a couple of thugs just as they were leaving the roof. He'd had no idea what they were up to, but they had pulled their guns and had hidden up there till Jason showed, telling Sammy if Jason didn't take off, they'd kill them both.

Sammy now told Jason to take the money, and sat him down and told him that life was a never-ending struggle between doing right and getting by, and he needed to get by if he wanted to do right, and it was okay if he had a little fun along the way. Of course he told it in the form of a story, and after several detours, explained that the Reverend Gary Davis once told Sammy that this, more than anything, was the message of his 1957 album *Pure Religion and Bad Company*.

It was almost Thanksgiving, and Adam and Jason were sitting at the Irish Cottage over a pitcher of beer, arguing about nothing.

"I never said that," Adam said, smiling. "Never."

"Yes, you did. The waitress from the coffee shop."

"Oh, her," Adam said, his voice raising an octave. He looked into the distance, thinking about it. "Possibly."

"Possibly? How can you not be sure? You said you have to turn your entire—"

"Best player ever?" Adam said loudly. "The big O. Oscar Robertson. No doubt about it. You just say Frazier cause you're from here. Now I love Clyde, but—"

Jason looked up to see that Alison had arrived.

"Shaker, the only time I hear you talk sports is when you don't want me to know that you're talking sex."

Adam looked at Jason. "Sounds like there's a reporter in our midst."

"There are," Alison said, dropping the *New York Times* on the table. "Two."

"Tomorrow's *Times?*" Jason said excitedly. "Is it in?"

Alison nodded and Adam took the paper and unfolded it on the table. The right-hand side had a large four-column headline: CO-HEN WON'T SEEK THIRD TERM. The sub-headline read "End of an Era." Adam flipped it over, searching below the fold. On the lower left side of the page there was a picture of Carol Chase, with the headline CHASE NAMED SECOND WOMAN TO ANCHOR NETWORK. He pointed at her picture. "Hey, what do you know!"

"Nice to see old friends get ahead," Alison said sweetly.

"Uh…where are we?" Jason asked, tugging the paper across the table away from Adam.

"There." She pointed to the lower right, to a smaller headline: BRONX DISTRICT ATTORNEY LINKED TO EVIDENCE TAMPERING, by Adam Shaker and Jason Sims.

"To our first win," Adam said triumphantly, lifting his beer glass.

"We'll see," Jason said. "This guy ain't gonna just fold. We've still got a ways to go."

"To your first *fight*," Alison said, revising the toast.

The sound of electric instruments coming to life began to fill the room. Pat was standing on the stage, next to Oz and the band, who were waiting for him. Pat rarely ventured on stage, but he had his hand on Oz's big shoulder and it looked like they were sharing a private joke.

"Whoops, that's me," Jason said, taking a quick drink of beer, kissing Alison, and running over to the stage.

"Ladies and gentlemen," Pat announced with gusto, "We've called the band back to play this one last song for you tonight. So once again, here's One. Mile. Short!"

There were cheers from the crowd, and the band started to play the intro to the Jimmy Reed song, "Baby What You Want Me To Do." It was a song that could not miss. After letting the instrumental go long, Oz growled into the microphone: *"You got me running, you got me hiding."* He was in rare form and built to a roar when he reached *"any way you want to let it roll,"* letting the audience fill in an exuberant *"yeah, yeah, yeah."* But when he reached the chorus, he stepped back, and with dancing eyes pointed at Jason, the way John Lee Hooker would tell you it was your time to go. But Jason looked more like a kid who didn't expect to be called on in school, and didn't move. Literally without missing a beat, the band took another trip through the first verse, which Oz ripped through, before he pointed again.

This time Jason was ready, leaned into the microphone, and looked out across the room. His voice was a little rusty, but it was on key, and it was real. *"You got me doing what you want me…baby, what you want me to do."*